Gaby's heart felt as though it were about to jump out of her chest. She wanted to break free, but the body sprawled on top of her held her down. And, she discovered, her hand was mashed against the lower part of his body. "Let me up," she choked.

"You're so—" he murmured huskily.

His head lowered. Paralyzed, not breathing, Gaby felt the warm, reluctant touch of his lips.

Then his mouth covered hers, rough, insatiable. It was like being enveloped in flames; an inferno that blazed up between them, taking them both by surprise. Was this the famous Latin passion? she wondered crazily. She was drowning in it! If something terrible was about to happen, she knew she didn't have the will to resist. . . .

Miami Midnight

Maggie Davis

BANTAM BOOKS
NEW YORK · TORONTO · LONDON · SYDNEY · AUCKLAND

MIAMI MIDNIGHT
A Bantam Book / July 1989

All rights reserved.
Copyright © 1989 by Maggie Davis.
Cover art copyright © 1989 by Pino Dangelico.
No part of this book may be reproduced or transmitted
in any form or by any means, electronic or mechanical,
including photocopying, recording, or by any information
storage and retrieval system, without permission in writing from
the publisher.
For information address: Bantam Books.

ISBN 0-553-28140-2

Published simultaneously in the United States and Canada

PRINTED IN THE UNITED STATES OF AMERICA

O   0 9 8 7 6 5 4 3 2 1

Miami
Midnight

Prologue

A full subtropical moon rose over the neon glitter of Miami Beach and the dark waters of Biscayne Bay, catching in its silver light the sleek white shape of a power cruiser anchored just offshore. The night was sweltering, the bay's surface unruffled by even the smallest breath of a sultry breeze, but on the yacht's decks noisy party-goers gyrated to earsplitting Latin salsa music. On the shore a slender woman in a glimmering white satin evening dress stood under a thick canopy of banyan and palm trees. She tried to shut out the noise as she bent over a row of guttering candles set on a stone slab.

The body under the woman's hands twitched at the touch of the point of a knife.

"Lady of lightning and thunder, come to me." Her red-painted mouth twisted cruelly. "Hear what I ask for! Give me what I desire!"

A sudden wind whistled in the sabal palms and the woman bowed low, her long dark hair falling forward. With a quick movement she moved a small statue into the ring of lighted candles. The brightly painted plaster image was that of a woman draped in medieval robes of red and white, holding a sword in one hand, the other hand resting on a miniature crenellated tower. Fingers trembling, the woman caressed the statue's expressionless face and the painted folds of its gown. "I give you this blood,

1

oh, dark lady," she whispered hoarsely. "I sacrifice for you, Chango—now give me my revenge!"

At that moment someone dove, or fell, from the anchored yacht into the bay. There was a sudden silence. The blaring music died, followed seconds later by piercing shrieks. Voices shouted confused orders in English and Spanish, mixed with drunken bursts of laughter.

The woman under the trees paused and shut her eyes, her concentration broken. Then she shook herself slightly and bent to the warm, fettered flesh under her hands.

"Come, Lady Santa Barbara!" She spoke loudly over the raucous voices drifting shoreward. "Goddess of the fire and the lightning, who is also Chango, come to me!"

The knife blade poised over the body on the stone slab.

Someone was coming down the path from the house. Under the thick cover of jungle canopy, the footsteps were muffled but determined. A man called out.

"Chango, Chango, hear me!" the woman pleaded hurriedly. "I give you this life, and blood! Now give *me* what I desire!"

A life preserver had been thrown to the people frolicking in the water. From the deck a more sober voice urged everybody to cool it or someone would call the police.

The man coming down the path shouted impatiently. At the sound of his voice the woman in the gleaming white gown shuddered. Quickly, she raised a bare arm high. The knife fell. The flesh on the stone slab quivered once, then was still.

The man burst through the trees. He was tall, wearing only swim trunks, impressively virile in his near-nakedness. An opened bottle of champagne dangled from one hand. If he was as drunk as the rest of the guests aboard the cruiser, he didn't show it. "Where the hell have you—" he began.

He took in the woman's blood-spattered dress and the knife, and he froze. The expression on his handsome face changed from disbelieving shock to slit-eyed fury as his gaze swept the stone altar, the small plaster statue within the ring of candles, and the torn, bleeding body next to it.

"Jesus!" The exclamation ripped from him. "What have you done?"

The woman turned. As if in a trance, she wiped her bloody fingers against the satin dress.

Behind them on the yacht, half hidden by the shoreline trees, the swimmers were being pulled from the water. Someone hailed the shore, yelling for the lone person in the water to hurry up, for God's sake.

The tall man took a deep breath. "Damn you." The words came out heavily. "I could kill you for this!"

The woman's gaze dropped to the bright streams of red blood trickling over the stone and into the sand at her feet, and she smiled.

"You promised me," he ground out. "You promised me no more of this damned, murderous—filth!"

For the first time she looked directly at the man. "It's too late." Her tone was indifferent. "Don't shout. You can do nothing about it."

With an abrupt movement he stepped forward, raising his hand. The woman held her ground, the curious smile still on her lips. "No matter what you do," she murmured, "I have made my gift of blood. And Chango has accepted. *Está terminado.*"

He stood frozen with anger, his black eyes glittering. "We left all this shit behind, remember? Doesn't that mean anything? Damn you! You *promised!*"

He stepped toward her again, almost menacingly, but she raised one slender hand imperiously. He stopped. "Whatever you say, whatever you do"—the note of triumph in her voice warned him—"it changes nothing."

She lifted her chin, giving him the full force of her dark luminous gaze. The tall man stepped back, unwillingly.

Her dreamy smile grew. "*Está terminado,*" she told him. "You can do nothing. The spell is finished."

He visto vivir un hombre
Con el puñal al costado.

I've seen a man who lives
With a dagger at his side.

JOSÉ MARTÍ

Chapter 1

*T*he annual champagne brunch and charity fashion show of the Coral Gables Hispanic Cultural Society was going smoothly until the redheaded model lost her balance. She teetered wildly on the makeshift runway that spanned the lily pond, then fell into the water with a resounding splash.

For a long moment, no one moved or made a sound. Then a concerted gasp rose from the fashionable crowd at the lunch tables.

Gabrielle Collier was still struggling with the lead for her story, and had just written: "Dark colors definitely usher in the fall season for fashion-conscious Floridians." As she bent over her yellow legal pad and scratched out the word "usher" and substituted "bring," the model in the lily pond got to her knees, slipped on the algae-covered bottom, and sat back down again.

The crowd suddenly came alive. A loud, dismayed scream reverberated in all four corners of the vast blue-and-white striped tent that covered the back garden of one of Miami's most elegant estates.

Gaby looked up, confused. She was aware, as the new fashion reporter for the *Miami Times-Journal*, that her writing was "inept," a description her boss, the features editor, used almost daily. But shrieks of horror? she thought. When she'd hardly gotten the words down on the page?

The *Times-Journal* photographer had shot out of her

chair at the first splash. Now Crissette Washington waded into the lily pond in her French jeans and strappy gold sandals, the *szznick-szznick* of the black woman's camera going almost nonstop. The *Miami Herald* photographer, Gaby saw, was not far behind.

The redhead model, apparently too dazed to scream, was now sitting in four or five inches of water with fragments of torn green plants floating around her. Chic, alarmed society women were rushing down through the garden terraces to see what had happened. A group of busboys ran past, bumping the press table. Gaby clutched at her notes.

Across the way the fashion editor of the *Herald* shouted to her, "Is that the Galanos suit she's wearing? Or is it the Ted Lapidus?"

Gaby couldn't answer. She still didn't know one designer from another without a program. She thought it was the Ted Lapidus, but the suit might have been a Galanos for all she could tell. She shrugged, and the *Herald's* fashion editor gave her a look of ill-concealed disdain before she turned away.

Gaby stared down at the metal surface of the umbrella table, feeling slightly sick. The *Herald* and *Times-Journal* were competitors. Their employees were not expected to be friendly. On the other hand, Gaby suspected she'd just messed things up again. She wiped away a drop of sweat from her forehead with the back of her hand. It was relentlessly hot under the acre of blue-and-white striped canvas, despite the luxurious portable air conditioners. After five years in Europe, she still hadn't readjusted to Miami's blistering heat, even though she'd been born and raised in south Florida.

Gaby glanced at her pad. Perhaps, she thought, she should throw away what she had written and start another lead to her story. But she was practically certain you couldn't open a fashion story with, "When the model wearing Neiman-Marcus's Lapidus suit missed her footing and fell into the lily pond . . ."

She looked back down toward the runway. The other models had come to a stop on the steps leading up to it. A woman in a large black hat, the fashion show's director, hurried up to the microphone. Whatever she tried to say was lost in the clamor of almost a hundred of Miami's Latin social elite crowding around her.

Beyond them, on the little wooden platform erected in a grove of coconut palm trees, the salsa band struck up a frantic rendition of "Guantanamera," effectively drowning out all conversation.

Gaby gazed past the fashion show's temporary stage to Biscayne Bay, its aquamarine water glittering through a curtain of live oaks and palms. Their hosts' yacht, a magnificent white power cruiser designed on space age lines, lay at anchor offshore. The Hispanic Cultural Society's brunch and fashion show was one of the most prestigious social events of Miami's summer season, a major story for the Miami *Times-Journal's* Modern Living section and Gaby's first big assignment after only three weeks on the job. Unfortunately, no one had told her what to do if one of the models fell off the runway and landed in a lily pond.

The salsa band ripped through the endless verses of "Guantanamera" but curiously enough, Gaby saw, with the exception of the photographers still snapping the floundering model in the pool, no one seemed to be doing anything. The fashion director from Neiman-Marcus's Bal Harbour store was still trying to announce a short delay, but her words were lost in the uproar.

Crissette Washington climbed out of the pond and flopped down in the chair next to Gaby. "I should have seen that coming," she said breathlessly. "That chick was wired, flying so high when she came out on that runway, she needed an air traffic controller!"

Gaby watched the sodden model try to get to her feet again. The girl's wide green eyes were rather glassy. "Isn't anybody"—she had to shout to make herself heard—"going to do anything?"

Crissette leaned close to Gaby's ear. "There's only about four inches of water in there. She isn't going to drown." The photographer paused, lifted a foot, and watched water drain from her high-heeled gold sandal. "Anyway, honey, that's men's work. They're all waiting for some *latino* male authority figure to come pull her out."

As if on cue, three men in pastel business suits hurried down the garden terraces from the main house. The band promptly struck up a Julio Iglesias tune, and the Neiman-Marcus show director reappeared at a run carrying a tablecloth.

Gaby bent toward the photographer. "Crissette, what's 'wired'?" she shouted.

Crissette gave her an incredulous look. "Lord, Gabrielle, you've been in Europe too long." She abruptly lifted her Nikon and focused it on the men arriving at the pool. "Wired, snowed. What you get when you use nose candy." Crissette looked away from the viewfinder long enough to see if Gaby understood. "*Cocaine,* Gabrielle, *cocaine.*"

Gaby felt an embarrassed rush of blood to her face. She knew it was stupid, but returning to Miami after five years working in Europe was like visiting another planet where the inhabitants spoke a baffling, unknown language. *Wired. Snowed. Flying.* Gaby wasn't so out of touch that she hadn't heard about the drug traffic in Miami, but she was still shocked. Surely, she told herself, not right out in public. Especially not a model taking part in something like a society fashion show.

From behind her camera Crissette murmured, "Here come the marines to the rescue."

The three men had rapidly crossed the garden. The tallest, in a magnificent white linen Italian suit, strode unhesitatingly into the pond, grabbed the model under the arms, and hauled her to her feet.

Gaby frowned. "How can you tell that the model was . . . uh, *wired?*"

The exquisitely dressed audience broke into a ripple of applause as the tall man wrapped the tablecloth, handed to him by the Neiman-Marcus director, around the dripping model. The redhead smiled fuzzily at him as he blotted the front of her black-and-red outfit with indifferent thoroughness.

"The look," Crissette said, focusing her Nikon on the man in the white suit. "Like crazy eyes. A friend of mine says crazy eyes are a sure sign. Nonstop talking, like wanting to do and say crazy things. Nobody flies higher than somebody on coke. Sheesh, what a tiger," the photographer murmured appreciatively as she watched the tall man hoist the model onto dry ground. "He can pull me out of a lily pond any day."

Abruptly, she lowered her camera to stare at the two squat, copper-colored men wearing beige-and-pink suits and mirror sunglasses. "Two Colombians," she muttered under her breath. "What are those cats doing here?"

"What tiger?" Gaby asked. There was still so much screaming she could hardly hear. She gazed back down at the pond as Crissette refocused her camera on the man in white. "Oh," Gaby said, staring. "Who is he, some movie actor? Is that why you keep taking his picture?"

She was thinking she hadn't seen such blatantly macho male beauty since she'd left Italy. Crissette's "tiger" was more powerfully built than his Spanish forebears, yet was still fiercely black-browed, fluidly graceful. The mobile curve of his mouth was flattened, at the moment, rather irritably.

Crissette laughed. "Eat your heart out, honey. What you're looking at is one of south Florida's great natural wonders. That's the famous Prince of Coral Gables, James Santo Marin."

Gaby watched the tall man gingerly brush the soaked front of his expensive suit. Tiger? she thought. *Tomcat* was more like it. In Italy, men as good-looking as that one were bound to be monumentally spoiled. It was almost a tradition. And all of them wanted only one thing from American women, Gaby thought glumly. That, too, was traditional.

The man's heavy gold wristwatch caught glints of the hot sun. Gaby would bet that under that expensive-looking white silk shirt was a big, flashy gold medallion on a flashy gold chain.

"Coke goes with the scenery in Miami," Crissette was saying. "You see a chick like that flying down a runway, not even looking where she's putting her feet, and you know something just went up her nose." She pointed with her

chin. "You see those two Colombian cats in the mirror
shades? You don't think they're out here just to see the
fashion show, do you? They're probably somebody's cocaine suppliers."

Gaby watched the model allow herself to be led away
by the fashion director. The Miami in which Gaby had
grown up, a slightly seedy resort city in a long decline
from its heyday in the forties and fifties, bore almost no
resemblance to this baffling present-day megalopolis. But
then, as the whole world knew, something had happened.
In just a few years the city had become what *Newsweek*
magazine called "the new Casablanca," equated with Paris,
London, and Rome. But for a native-born Miamian like
Gaby, it was like being a stranger in a strange land.

Miami still had its crushing poverty, and refugees
from South America and the Caribbean, including an
influx of Haitians, mixed with the city's own indigenous
poor in seething downtown slums. But Miami was also a
boomtown for the new Latin American banking industry,
an exploding real estate market, and a port for cruise ships
that brought a rush of European and American tourists. If
Miami's new glamour had begun with a television show,
Miami Vice, the myth had quickly become a reality. And,
as anyone could see, Miami was doing its best to live up to
all of it.

The members and guests of the Coral Gables Hispanic
Cultural Society were drifting back to their tables. The
dripping redheaded model had disappeared. The handsome man in the white suit was directing the removal of
the runway over the lily pond.

"He's not really a prince," Gaby said doubtfully.

"The way the chicks act you'd think he was," Crissette
drawled. "Voted Miami's 'most eligible bachelor,' filthy
rich, drives a Lamborghini—Look," she said suddenly, "here
comes the Queen Mother, Señora Estancia Santo Marin.
And the pale chick in the black dress is the younger
sister." She took a series of grab shots of the women.
"Gabrielle, you were born and raised in Miami. Haven't
you ever heard of the Santo Marins?"

Gaby supposed she had. But there were so many

exiles in Miami, it was impossible to keep track of them, even the wealthy, socially important ones. Yet the name Santo Marin did ring a bell.

At that moment the man below looked up. His narrowed black gaze passed over the crowd and the press table, then stopped and backed up with a flicker of interest.

"Hey," Crissette said excitedly, "you should see this cat close up, through the viewfinder. He's unbelievable! And Gabrielle, you should see him watching you."

But Gaby had turned away. The *Miami Herald*'s fashion editor, she saw with a sinking feeling, was interviewing the director from Neiman-Marcus. It was probably something she should have thought to do.

"Suppose he comes up here?" Crissette asked. "You want me to try to introduce you?"

Gaby wasn't interested in James Santo Marin; the macho peacocks she'd known in Italy had been enough for one person's lifetime. "For goodness' sake, Crissette, will you stop taking his picture?" She tore her notes and the beginnings of her story off her yellow pad and stuffed them into her purse. "Look, since the fashion show is stalled, why don't I go look for the chairwoman of this event and do an interview?"

Crissette flapped a thin, graceful black hand at her. "Wait, don't run off! These Latin dudes go mad for the Grace Kelly look. Gabrielle, he looks definitely interested!"

Gaby knew her "Grace Kelly look" was, at the moment, a sweat-shiny face surrounded by long blond hair that had been exposed for too long to the furnacelike breeze sweeping across Biscayne Bay. "Please, Crissette, I'm working! Now," she said, looking around, "how do I find the chairwoman of this event?"

"He heads up the family import business," the other woman persisted, "races a whole stable of power cruisers, wears great clothes—"

"I've got enough problems," Gaby interrupted her, "trying to learn this newspaper job without gorgeous hunks with"—she looked for the coppery men in sunglasses and pastel suits—"sinister friends."

"Hey, he likes it when you stand up," Crissette said,

unperturbed. "You've got a sexy figure, Gabrielle. You just don't show it off in those clothes."

The man by the lily pond was standing perfectly still. Without looking in his direction Gaby could feel the impact of his darkly glittering look. She gathered up her purse and stuck her notebook under her elbow, feeling irritated. "Just tell me where you think I can find the chairwoman."

"Try the main house. I think half this crowd's gone up to the ladies' room. Who are you supposed to be looking for?"

Gaby tried not to look in the direction of the lily pond as Crissette began taking the man's picture again. "Alicia Fernandez y Altamurez," she said, consulting a scrap of paper. "At least that's what it says on the press release."

The main house was nestled in a setting of sculpted lawns and palm trees, a multimillion dollar example of the new-old art deco style that was being publicized as Miami's own historic look. Smooth white concrete walls and plate glass shone through the tropical greenery, surrounded by an untouched jungle of native palmetto. A decade ago, when Gaby was still in high school, all that had been down this way south of Miami were mangrove swamps and a few mullet fishermen.

A path led through royal and queen palms and flowering oleanders, ending at an asphalt parking lot. Two women in dark-colored silk dresses, wearing almost identical Givenchy toques with fancy nose veils, strolled around a turn of the white shell driveway. A uniformed chauffeur, who had been sitting in a black stretch Mercedes limousine reading a newspaper, immediately discarded the paper, jumped out, and opened the door for them.

Gaby stared at the slender, beautifully dressed women with as much curiosity as they stared back at her. Their large dark eyes, enormous in their heavily made-up, expressionless faces, looked over her rumpled linen jacket, khaki skirt, and low-heeled sandals with the avid, baffled intensity wealthy Latin women reserved for what they regarded as Anglos' astonishingly ugly clothes.

Gaby was aware Coral Gables was now full of wealthy Latins, some of them multimillionaires, but she hadn't forgotten the poverty-stricken Cuban exiles of her childhood. Then, one of Havana's leading neurosurgeons had a job mowing the lawns at the Miami Beach Country Club. A university professor drove a Hialeah taxicab. And the convent-bred society women, once queens of sugar plantations and palatial town houses in Havana, worked as cleaning women or dressmakers. Times had certainly changed. Looking at the elegant women Gaby knew their diamonds were real by the shooting sparks of fire in the bright sunlight. So, apparently, was the heavy string of matched pearls the younger woman was wearing.

She gave them a tentative smile. "I'm looking for Mrs. Fernandez y Altamurez. Could you tell me if this is the way to the main house?"

One woman said something to the other in Spanish, then with a shrug stepped into the huge black limousine. The second woman followed her. The chauffeur slid into the front seat and started the engine.

Gaby realized she'd used the wrong language. *"Donde está el enfrente de la casa?"*

She was fluent in Italian, but her high school Spanish was not great. It was apparently understandable, though, for a hand, decorated with heavy gold rings set with rubies and emeralds, came out of the limousine's back window and pointed. *That way.*

Before she could acknowledge the help—if it was help—the Mercedes slowly drove forward and disappeared under the trees.

Alicia Fernandez y Altamurez, the chairwoman of the Hispanic Cultural Society's fashion show, was waiting in a long line of women outside one of the downstairs bathrooms. Gaby interviewed her on the spot as the queue inched forward to the accompaniment of toilets flushing. The hallway where they stood was enclosed on one side by a white stucco art deco cloister. The sun-drenched cactus garden featured a stainless steel abstract sculpture that had recently been photographed for *Architectural Digest*.

Alicia Fernandez was a member of Miami's longtime pre-Castro Cuban community. The Fernandez family were sixth-generation Floridians. Mrs. Fernandez y Altamurez spoke English with a southern accent, had graduated from Smith College cum laude, and thought she knew Gaby.

"Which Collier are you, dear?" she asked interestedly. "The Miami Shores Colliers or the William Colliers of old Pine View Avenue? A Collier girl went to Ransom Country Day School with my daughter Susan. Was that you?"

"Palm Island," Gaby murmured. She didn't miss the quick, perceptive flicker in Mrs. Fernandez's eyes. Most of Old Miami remembered the extravagant, high-living Palm Island Colliers very well. "I did go to Ransom Country Day School, but only as far as the fifth grade." If Alicia Fernandez really knew her family, she also knew that would have been about the time Paul Collier had lost most of his money.

To cut short any further conversation about her family, Gaby pushed on with her interview questions. Alicia Fernandez graciously agreed that the crowd was big, that everyone seemed to love the clothes from Neiman-Marcus, and that the Coral Gables Hispanic Cultural Society had made a lot of money. She did not comment on the model's falling into the lily pond, and Gaby didn't bring it up.

"Darling, you *are* Paul Collier's daughter, Gabrielle, aren't you?" the other woman asked. "I remember your grandfather's beautiful house. They used to have such magnificent parties there. I read about them all the time in the papers." There was something in Mrs. Fernandez's voice that said she wanted to be reassured that things were better for the Palm Island Colliers than she'd heard. "Haven't you been traveling in Europe?"

Gaby didn't look up from her legal pad. *My father is dead, and Mother is a drunk,* some perverse inner voice answered, *as nearly all of Old Miami well knows. The money is gone and the house is falling down. That's why I'm back.*

Aloud Gaby only said, "I was working in Florence, doing art research for a professor who was writing a book. It was a job I got my junior year at college."

"Ah, Italy." Mrs. Fernandez smiled her disarming smile. "I went to Venice and Rome on my honeymoon." She gave Gaby an impulsive pat on her arm. "You're such a pretty girl, Gabrielle. Did you leave a few heartbroken Italians behind?"

Gaby knew it was her own fault she froze up when people remembered her family. "Italian men are looking for *rich* American women," she said stiffly, "not poor ones."

Alicia Fernandez looked momentarily disconcerted. Then she covered it by saying, "Working for a professor, it sounds wonderful! And to be in Italy... I'm afraid Miami's going to be so different for you." She paused. "Life here has changed so, Gabrielle, it's difficult to explain. People have always come to Miami to act a little crazy and have a good time. After all, it's a resort town. But now, I swear, it's *surreal*! Life in Miami is like one of those music videos kids watch on television." She lowered her voice. "Did you see what happened today?"

So Crissette wasn't the only one who'd spotted the model's real trouble, Gaby thought, feeling uneasy. "I've got to be going, Mrs. Fernandez. I hope you'll excuse me. This is only my third week at the *Times-Journal* and I'm still learning my job."

The other woman held her arm. "Darling, I *did* know your mother and father, a long time ago. I'm sure you went to school with my daughter. Susan goes with such a nice young crowd in Miami. If we can be of any help..."

"Thank you, that's very kind of you." Gaby only wanted to get away. "I'll let you know," she promised, and fled.

Gaby reminded herself as she walked down the side path through the palm trees that meeting people who remembered her family was going to happen all the time now that she was back. It was one of the hazards of trying to live down the past. Also, dissipated fortunes were nothing new in Miami; it was her own attitude she had to work on. Especially if she was going to keep the *Times-Journal* job she needed so desperately. She went over the questions she'd asked Alicia Fernandez, worrying whether there was enough interest to make the story the features editor wanted.

She was still agonizing over the interview when she gradually came to a stop in a clump of mangroves at the edge of Biscayne Bay. "Oh damn." She sighed, rubbing her perspiring upper lip with the back of her hand. She had no idea where she was.

She could still hear salsa music and the noise of the crowd, but somehow the sandy path had turned into black Florida mud. She rested an arm against a fishtail palm and scraped the sole of one sandal against the other, trying to get rid of it.

There were people, Gaby knew, who regarded the opportunity to live and work in glamorous sun-drenched Miami, the city one saw and thrilled to in travel posters and on television, as a lifetime dream come true. In fact, her coworkers in Florence had said as much when she left.

The trouble was, Gaby was the last person on earth to appreciate what was glamorous or exciting. She'd always known she would have been much happier somewhere else—anywhere else. Running away to Europe without even finishing college had been one kind of solution.

Slowly, she picked her way back through the woods in the direction of the voices and music, pushing mangrove limbs and trailing vines out of the way. After a few minutes she came out onto slightly higher ground. She knew she had to reach the end eventually. After all, how long could anybody be lost on an estate in Coral Gables?

She found herself at the edge of a small clearing where the yellow sunlight filtered through the canopy of palm leaves. She wouldn't have expected to find anything back there in the garden's overgrown, untended wilderness, so she was shocked to see some fifty feet away, illuminated in a stray shaft of tropical sunlight, a tall man in a white suit standing with his right arm extended. In front of him, down on one knee, a figure in a beige-and-pink suit and mirror sunglasses pressed his lips to the back of the other man's hand. The figures were poised in the bright Florida sun in the attitudes of one doing homage to the aristocratic "patron" for some favor.

Or closing a deal.

Gaby stepped quickly back among the mangroves.

It was impossible not to recognize the man in the magnificent white suit—that dark, curling hair, the hard-boned features, that air of hair-trigger energy. It was the same man who had dragged the model out of the pool. *James Santo Marin.*

The damp mold under her feet gave soundlessly as Gaby moved back another step.

She'd only seen the kneeling man's back, but she knew the flashy pastel jacket. One of Crissette's sinister Colombians.

Gaby felt as though she couldn't breathe. It was stupid to be virtually paralyzed by irrational fright, when actually nothing had happened. Still, she turned and lurched away from the clearing into the woods, stumbling over the snakelike roots of the mangroves. An unseen vine caught her across the neck and she jerked up short.

What was she running from, anyway? she wondered frantically. Two men in the woods? Who hadn't even seen her?

She found she couldn't stop. She crashed through a tangled growth of flame vines and ruby red ixora. Then her feet slipped on something. She skidded, stopped, her nerves screaming, and looked down.

For a moment Gaby stared at the ground. She told herself she didn't believe what she saw there.

Crissette was waiting at the press table, her cameras packed into her bag. "What happened to you?" she asked when Gaby appeared. "Jeez, Gabrielle, you're all muddy! Where have you been?"

Gaby could only shiver. "I got lost."

The words were totally inadequate, and she almost giggled as she leaned against the table. If she weren't so breathless and shaken it would be funny. She'd gotten lost, but that wasn't the half of it!

The Latin band was still going strong. With bongos

clicking, trumpets blaring, it was playing a popular Dominican merengue. The members and guests of the Hispanic Cultural Society stood in chattering groups, making the most of the long pause before the fashion show resumed. Down the grassy slopes of the back terraces of the Santo Marin gardens, beyond the fringe of royal palms at the edge of Biscayne Bay, the magnificent yacht still rode at anchor. Reflected in the turquoise water and with the mirrored towers of downtown Miami behind it, it looked like a full-color photograph from a travel magazine.

It was all so reassuring, so different from what she'd blundered into in the mangrove jungle, that for a moment Gaby doubted her senses. "Crissette," she managed to say, "you won't believe this, but I think I just saw a drug deal being closed." She wanted desperately to sit down for a moment and catch her breath, but they were on deadline. They were probably already due back at the newspaper. "Over there." She nodded in the direction of the mangroves.

Crissette picked up her camera bag and slung it over her shoulder. Her designer jeans were wet, as were her elegant gold sandals. She was not in a receptive mood. "I think the sun's getting to you, Gabrielle," she snapped, "because you're seeing things. Maybe you ought to start wearing a hat."

"Not only that." Gaby felt like an idiot, wanting to laugh because the whole thing was so incredible. She'd really been scared out of her wits. "You won't believe this, but while I was back there I stepped into a puddle of blood that looked like somebody had just been murdered!"

Chapter 2

The old Collier house, built by Gaby's grandfather with the fortune he'd amassed on the New York Stock Exchange, was typical of the 1920's Florida real estate boom that had so altered the face of the state.

Palm Island, off the causeway that linked the island of Miami Beach with the city of Miami, was developed for wealthy residents like Bertram Collier, who wanted a unique man-made environment in Biscayne Bay since nature hadn't supplied one. Earth and rubble were dumped in the bay to form Palm Island, then planted with avenues of royal palms, hibiscus, and flaming bougainvillea, and tall hedges of oleanders that guaranteed its residents' privacy. Palm Island architecture was rigidly zoned. Most homes were built in an approved, grandiose style known locally as "Spanish hacienda." Pink and beige stucco turrets, walled gardens, a lavish use of balconies, and long driveways curving through palm-filled vistas made Palm Island a tropical delight. But in the 1950's all of that changed.

Although Miami had thrived in the forties, a decade later a crackdown on Miami's illegal gambling sent tourists, along with the famous Rat Pack, the mob, Hollywood stars, and café society on to more exciting places like Las Vegas and Monte Carlo. Palm Island, like the rest of Miami, entered the long twilight of the sixties and seventies. Many of the beautiful old Spanish haciendas on Palm

Island's Royal Palm Way were vacant and for sale, their owners having either died or migrated to trendy condominiums north of Bal Harbour. The little island became shabby, like the rest of the city.

The Collier house had needed repairs badly when Gaby left for Italy. It was even more dilapidated when she returned. Although most of the old mansions on the island were being remodeled and resold at fabulous prices, the Colliers' three-story—including a Moorish tower—Spanish hacienda stood decaying on two acres of overgrown tropical garden, surrounded by a high stucco wall that hid it almost completely from passersby.

Gaby hadn't remembered how sweltering the old house could be in August and September. The upstairs bedrooms had been designed with windows facing the bay to catch any breeze at night, and were fairly comfortable. But the only place downstairs that ever offered any coolness, especially for dinner, was the sun porch with its old-fashioned louvered glass panels that opened onto the back lawn, the boat dock, and the open waters of Biscayne Bay.

At nine o'clock, the bay lay black and mirror-smooth in the breathless dark, even though a blot of lightning-racked clouds rose over North Miami. There was an occasional pregnant roll of thunder, but the storm was too far away to stir even the faintest breeze.

Jeannette Collier lifted the old chrome cocktail shaker by her plate, refilled her martini glass, and took an unsteady sip. "I just can't force myself to eat," she complained, "when it's hot like this. I swear, if I put anything in my stomach now it will only make me sick."

Gaby looked down at the salad and spaghetti she'd hurriedly put together when Dodd Brickell had called to say he'd be there for dinner. She had to admit spaghetti with mushroom sauce out of a jar wasn't one of her better efforts.

"You don't have to force yourself to eat, Mother," she said with more patience than she felt.

Jeannette sighed gustily. "God, it's certainly not like

old times, is it?" The complaint was familiar. So was her gesture of pushing her plate away with distaste. She was wearing an old purple muumuu stained with makeup. Her gray-blond hair was uncombed, held back by Mexican tortoise shell mantilla combs, a souvenir from a long-ago trip to Acapulco. "Dodd, darling," she said to the man opposite her, "remember the parties we used to have right out here? Do you remember how we used to have hundreds and hundreds of guests? And everybody used to go out to dance on the back lawn?"

Gaby handed Dodd the silver bread basket. "Dodd doesn't remember, Mother." Silently, she thanked heaven that Dodd Brickell was an old family friend. They didn't have to keep up the pretense that it was the heat that affected her mother's appetite, rather than Jeannette's day-long consumption of booze. "All your parties were back in the fifties," Gaby reminded her, "and Dodd and I weren't even born then."

"Well, you know what I mean." Gaby watched Dodd help himself to more spaghetti. He still ate like a linebacker for the Miami Dolphins, which he had been during his pro football years, rather than the successful Miami lawyer-businessman he was now. At Gaby's insistence he'd taken off his suit jacket and loosened his tie, but even so, his custom-made shirt stuck to his upper body in dark, sweaty blotches.

"He *does too* remember," Gaby's mother said loudly. "It's true, people just fell *all over* themselves to get an invitation to our parties. Sh—sometimes we had Eddy Duchin's band to play. But ush—" She stifled a belch. "—usually it was Meyer Davis and his Society Orchestra. They always wrote it like that in the newspapers, 'Meyer Davis and his Society Orchestra.'"

Gaby looked away. She was embarrassed that her mother was bringing up the Colliers' days of lavish spending, when Dodd had come to dinner to discuss some way to deal with their present dire lack of money. Before she'd been summoned back home, there had even been terrible talk of Jeannette's applying for welfare.

"You *couldn't*," her mother went on truculently, "have

a party in Miami in those days without Meyer Davis and his Society Orchestra. That is, not if you wanted to have anybody who *was* anybody!"

Under the table Jupiter, the Colliers' ancient Labrador, gave a loud groan. Gaby saw Dodd's lips quirk with suppressed laughter. She glared at him. It wasn't funny. Listening to Jeannette night after night, Gaby felt like groaning aloud too.

Jeannette refilled her glass from the martini shaker. "Now we're so goddamned poor," she whined, staring at the withered olive at the bottom of the cocktail glass. "We don't even have any money to get the air conditioners fixed."

"Mother, please." Gaby put down her fork and closed her eyes for a second, feeling drained. After this particularly long day, she deserved something more than her mother's usual drunken complaints.

When she'd gotten back to the *Times-Journal* offices, it had taken her an excruciatingly long time to write the fashion story. Dealing with the drugged model falling into the lily pond was more difficult than most of her assignments. When she'd at last filed her copy, Jack Carty, the features editor, had kept her another hour and a half to rework what she'd done. *Inept* hadn't been the word he'd used. Gaby'd had the feeling he was searching for something stronger.

Fortunately Crissette's photographs had saved the story. Jack had taken a look at the contact prints of the model and the good-looking hunk in the white suit, and had suddenly decided to bump the story up to the lead feature in the Sunday edition's Modern Living section. Gaby still hadn't gotten over her shock.

"It's too bad your father never put in central air conditioning, Gaby," Dodd was saying. "He certainly talked about it enough."

The year Gaby's father had talked about installing central air conditioning was also the year Paul Collier had fallen madly in love with an enormous Chris-Craft Challenger. It had been no contest. The next year the money had gone to rebuilding the dock for the extravagantly expensive boat, and enlarging the terrace for bigger and better parties.

Gaby's gaze lifted to the wall above Dodd Brickell's head. It was covered with framed pictures, including the famous cover from the August 1956 issue of *Life* magazine. That elegant café-society luminary, Mrs. Paul Aston Collier, was posed on the back terrace of her fashionable Palm Island, Miami mansion. Jeannette had been ravishing thirty-odd years ago, her cool, sculpted beauty accentuated by masses of thick red-gold hair that matched her gold chiffon gown. She was already a heavy drinker then, but not yet showing the ravages.

Above the *Life* cover was a black-and-white picture of Paul Collier at the polo grounds in Palm Beach, lean, handsome, and dashing, his arms around Winston Rockefeller. There was a photo of a smiling Paul Collier and Sonny Whitney at the racetrack at Hialeah, Paul Collier and Betty Grable in a sports car in Palm Springs, Paul Collier and Senator Jack Kennedy docking a sailing dinghy on Cape Cod. In the entire collection of photographs that filled the downstairs of the Colliers' rambling old house, only a few included a small, silent, solitary child, Paul and Jeannette Collier's daughter Gabrielle. Known not-all-that-affectionately as "Mouse."

In the living room, the collection continued with pictures of Miami Beach entertainers who had become world famous: a young Dean Martin and Jerry Lewis when they were a 1950's comedy team; Arthur Godfrey and Jackie Gleason, who had streets named for them in their beloved Miami Beach; and below Godfrey and Gleason, the singing McGuire sisters with their special friend, Miami Beach celebrity and notorious Mafia mob figure, Sam Giancana.

Gaby lowered her gaze and found Dodd studying her sympathetically. "Hard day at work, honey? Are you getting the hang of it now?"

She was silent for a long moment, trying to think of an answer. She was indebted to Dodd and his father for getting her the job at the newspaper, more than she could ever say, but there were times when she was tempted to blurt out the truth: that she wasn't doing any better in her job as fashion reporter for the *Times-Journal* than when she'd started three weeks ago.

Gaby didn't dare tell Dodd; she knew he would want to *do* something. And Dodd and his father had already done enough.

"Dad had lunch with Gardner Hedison the other day," Dodd said, not waiting for her reply, "and he asked him how you were doing in the new job. Hedison said you were doing just fine. He was quite pleased."

Gaby frowned. The *Times-Journal* newsroom had seemed to know immediately when Dodd's father had had lunch with his friend the publisher. It didn't exactly boost her popularity. "I wish your father wouldn't do that, Dodd. Check on me at lunch with Gardner Hedison."

Dodd looked surprised. "Why not? From what your publisher says, you're doing a great job."

Out of the corner of her eye Gaby saw her mother's head droop forward, almost to the surface of her still-full dinner plate. With any luck, she couldn't help thinking, Jeannette would be ready for bed early. If she didn't pass out right where she was. "I know he wants to help, Dodd, but I just wish your father would leave it alone."

It was his turn to frown. "And I wish you'd stop beating on yourself, hon. When Dad told Hedison you were Paul Collier's daughter, he jumped at the chance to hire you." Dodd reached across the table to squeeze her hand. "Hey, Dad didn't have to sell you, Mouse, your background did. The paper needed you. Old Miamians are scarce as hen's teeth these days."

Gaby pulled her hand away. "Well, the newspaper certainly didn't hire me for my writing ability." She knew she sounded cross, shrewish, but she couldn't help it. "And I made it plain I didn't know anything about fashion."

"I don't see why you're complaining about that job," Jeannette broke in. She lifted the empty cocktail shaker and shook it fretfully. "Besides, I never asked you to take care of me. My father left me prov—provided with plenty of money!"

Dodd shot Gaby a warning look. "I don't think she was exactly complaining, Jeannette."

"Oh, leave her alone," Gaby muttered. "She can't carry on a sensible conversation at this hour of the night. She's too drunk."

The remark was a mistake. A mean mistake, Gaby realized at once. A look of pure venom passed over her mother's face. "You don't have to work if you hate it so much!" she cried shrilly. "God knows you could have had plenty of money if you'd married Dodd!"

A painful silence crashed down.

Gaby tried to tell herself her mother was at her worst after sundown. She was drunk, she'd been drinking all day, and Dodd knew it. It didn't help.

"If you hadn't run off to Europe," her mother persisted, her voice hoarse with liquor, "Dodd would never have married that other woman."

Gaby pushed her chair back. She couldn't bring herself to look at the man across the table.

"You ran away." There was no stopping Jeannette now that she had center stage. "You ran away, stupid little Mouse! I'll bet Dodd still doesn't know you're in love with him!"

Dodd cleared his throat, his gaze on Gaby. "Jeannette, let's talk about something else."

"And what did running away to Europe get you?" Jeannette went on relentlessly. "You took your money out of your trust account and spent it, and God knows your father and I could have used some of it. Espesh—especially those last years when he was so sick."

Gaby stood up so quickly, the dishes rattled. "Stay where you are," she said. "I'll clear off the table."

"See?" her mother cried. "You're running away again! That's what you always do!"

But Gaby had left.

Chapter 3

Gaby leaned against the kitchen sink, eyes closed. This was the worst part of coming back home, she thought. Not the shock of finding that her parents' money was gone, evaporated like mist, so that it was necessary for her to get a job in Miami, any job, to keep Jeannette from going under. Nor even the humiliation of finding, when Dodd and his father persuaded the publisher of the *Times-Journal* to hire her, that she wasn't a reporter and probably never would be, even though fashion reporting was supposed to be, outside of writing obituaries, the easiest job available. No, the worst part of coming back home was just what the problem always had been. Dealing with Jeannette.

She didn't look up when Dodd entered the kitchen.

"You know my father wasn't 'sick for years,'" she said abruptly. "Oh, Dodd, if she'd said anything about money, written to me about my father's heart condition—you know I'd have come back!"

He leaned against the kitchen table, arms folded. "I don't pay any attention to what your mother says, Mouse."

"Don't pay any attention? My God, it's been this way all my life!" Gaby put her hands over her face. "Why did you bring me back from Italy?" she asked, her voice muffled. "Why couldn't you have just let the sheriff come

28

and take possession of the house? And put my mother in some hospital for alcoholics?"

"Gaby, she's your mother." He shrugged. "And legally you're responsible."

"Responsible? My parents never knew what the word meant! *This* is what I ran away from. I ran away from *this place*!" She flung out an arm to include the entire ramshackle house. "Would you believe that when my grandfather built it, this was a famous Miami showplace? Now it's a neglected, falling-down wreck because of two people, my mother and father, who destroyed everything they got their hands on!"

He sighed. They'd been over this before. "Honey, she needs your help. That's why I sent for you."

Gaby turned to the sink and jerked at the taps, sending water gushing over the plates. "I wish I were back in Florence typing manuscripts and dealing with Italian bureaucrats!"

He picked up a dish towel. "Your mother needs to be institutionalized." It was the same advice he'd given, both as lawyer and friend, many times. "The problem right now is you can't let these decisions hang fire too much longer."

"I can't do anything about my mother," Gaby snapped. "She won't let me!"

"Yes, you can." He took a plate from the drain rack and wiped it slowly. "The solution is simple. You need to get your mother to sign a power of attorney so you can sell this place, free up the money that's left. Then we can settle the back taxes, maybe have a little left over to put Jeannette in an alcohol treatment facility somewhere."

She shook her head. "Mother's not going to sign anything. She thinks signing a paper means we're trying to do just that, get her into a sanatorium." Gaby turned to him. "My mother's right, you know," she said in a low voice. "I'm a coward. I can't deal with her. Having Paul and Jeannette for parents was—was a job for somebody stronger and braver than I!"

"Now, Mouse," he began.

"It's true! My mother and father were totally absorbed

in themselves. They never had time for me. But now I'm the one who's left," she said bitterly, "to deal with their messes!" She suddenly threw the dishcloth into the soapy water and leaned against the sink. "Oh Lord, it's so hot! I *hate* Miami. I don't want to be here!"

"Honey, just take it easy." Dodd moved to her quickly, wrapping his arms around her and resting his chin on the top of her head. "Sweet Mouse, you've been a good soldier so far," he murmured. "Don't go all to pieces on me now."

Gaby lifted her gaze to the window over the kitchen sink. The night-darkened glass reflected them like a mirror: a big man with rumpled blond hair, a rugged face that had once graced a thousand newspaper sports pages, now grown older with an unmistakable aura of success and worldly power. By contrast, she was a willowy, indistinct image whose features were less spectacularly lovely than those of her once-beautiful mother, but with Jeannette's great silvery gray eyes and tawny mane of curls.

She pulled away from him slightly. "Please don't call me Mouse. You know I hate it."

"Okay, not Mouse." In the window she could see his tender look. "You're right, it doesn't fit anymore." He paused before he murmured into her hair, "I can't believe it, how beautiful you are."

Gaby shut her eyes, not trusting herself to speak. How many times in past years had she dreamed of Dodd being there to comfort her? Holding her, just like this? He'd always been a hero to her, this bronzed, assured god of a man. He was the only one who really understood what it had been like for her as Paul and Jeannette Collier's neglected child. And Dodd Brickell had been, when she was eighteen, her first and only lover.

Unfortunately, he'd married someone else.

"Things will work out, honey." His voice rumbled through his chest reassuringly. "You'll see."

Gaby wasn't convinced. "All the ghosts are still here, in this house." She shivered. "In my life, too, since I've come back. Oh, Dodd," she moaned, "I thought I'd never come back to Miami. At least not like this!"

"Mmm," he said against her cheek.

"Don't just say 'mmm.' Your parents were kind and good. Mine weren't."

Dodd's family had lived diagonally across the street from the Colliers on Royal Palm Way in another sprawling Spanish-style mansion. Dodd and Gabrielle had been friends and played together since kindergarten. But conservative lawyer Dodson Brickell, Sr. had never approved of Paul and Jeannette, nor most of the Palm Island set. When Dodd was in high school the Brickells moved to an estate below Coconut Grove.

Gaby pulled her head back to look up at him. "Dodd, remember Willie, our chauffeur? Who drove me to school in the Cadillac every day?" She smiled tentatively. "That was something, even for Miami in those days, being driven to school in a big limousine with a chauffeur. But that was because neither my mother nor father could get up in the morning because of their hangovers."

He smiled back. "Now who's living in the past?"

There was a sudden crash from the sun porch and they both jumped. "Do you want me to go and see if she's all right?" Dodd asked.

Gaby turned back to the sink. "She only dropped her drink. She'll get another."

He cocked his head, still listening. "Your mother won't wander out the back way, will she? Or out on the dock?"

Gaby pulled the rubber plug out of the drain and watched the water whirl sluggishly away. The sink needed a plumber. So did every other drain in the house. "Jupiter follows her around. I've seen him get in front of her and sort of nudge her off in another direction if she goes toward the water."

Dodd looked displeased. "Gaby, that old dog is about in the same shape as everything else around here. How old he is now? Fifteen, sixteen?" When she didn't answer he muttered, "Jupiter's been lying out on the porch ever since I got here. I haven't even seen him move once. He's no good as a watchdog, sugar, he's dying of old age. You ought to put him to sleep."

Gaby wasn't going to consider such a thing. "Jupiter helps me. After all, I can't watch Mother constantly, especially in the middle of the night when she roams through the house with her shaker of martinis, playing old Frank Sinatra records. I've got to sleep sometime, too, you know."

"Gaby, she can't take care of herself when she's here alone."

"She's not alone in the daytime," she reminded him. "Angel and Elena are here."

The Escuderos lived in the Colliers' garage apartment. Elena did housework for families on Palm Island, and her son Angel tended yards.

"Those damned Cubans," Dodd said, exasperated. "Your grass hasn't been mowed in weeks. And while we're on the subject, Angel's probably the one supplying your mother with booze."

"You don't know that." They always argued about this, she thought. Dodd felt the Escuderos ought to be paying rent. And if they couldn't afford it, the garage apartment ought to be let to someone who could.

"Those two are about as much good around here as the damned old dog. Which brings us to another subject. Gaby, you're not going to like this, but I've got to remind you this old place isn't safe. In fact, living on the waterfront anywhere in Miami these days is dangerous."

Gaby braced herself against the sink, overpoweringly tired. "Please, Dodd, I've had a—" She caught herself just in time. There were no words to describe the day she'd just had. "Can we discuss this some other time?"

He took her by the shoulders and turned her around to face him. "Gaby, I'm serious." His craggy face showed that he was. "We've had an epidemic of waterfront burglaries where gangs pull power cruisers up to private docks, break into houses, and ransack them. It's almost like a military operation. You wouldn't believe it. They storm these places like commando teams."

She shook her head. "We haven't got anything to steal."

"They don't know that," he said grimly. "These thugs

don't think. They're too coked-up, drugged-up, to know what they're doing. With two women alone in this place—" He stopped abruptly.

Gaby felt a shiver of sudden fear. Burglary attacks like he was describing should not happen in a modern day city, but Dodd was saying that in Miami, they did. "Elena and Angel are right there in the garage," she said. "They'd call the police if something like that happened. And there are neighbors on both sides of us."

"Don't rely on the Cubans. And half the houses on this street are empty." His expression was still hard. "Honey, I know you don't want to believe all this, sometimes I don't believe it myself, but Miami was an entirely different place four or five years ago, when you left. Before we started being overwhelmed with the garbage we've got here now."

She gave him a startled look. "Oh, Dodd, that's not fair."

"Fair? There's nothing fair about it!" He turned away from her, running his fingers through his hair. "Gaby, these *latinos* are turning Miami into a damned banana republic. In another ten years they'll outnumber the Americans."

"What's happened to you?" she asked. "I've never heard you talk this way!"

"What's happened to me?" He paced the length of the kitchen. "I've been living in Miami, that's what's happened. You have to be here to realize the extent of the problem."

"But the Latins aren't the only minority group in Miami," she protested. "You can't blame them for everything. What about the Haitians, the Jamaicans, the—"

He whirled to face her. "Gaby, before you accuse me of being bigoted and intolerant, just remember—we've had a flood of refugees big enough to overwhelm any city of this size. They clog the welfare rolls, their politics are just about what you'd expect, and culturally they're still somewhere in the twelfth century."

"Dodd—"

"They have a high rate of poverty and disease," he

went on adamantly. "They're uneducated, ignorant, corrupt, and superstitious. They even practice some kind of
filthy voodoo!"

There was a silence, then Gaby murmured, "Are you
through?"

He shrugged. "I didn't expect you to agree with me.
But then you haven't been here the last five years."

"Dodd, I went to school with Cuban kids. The exiles
I knew weren't ignorant and uneducated. Most of them
were professionals, doctors and lawyers, people who'd had
money once."

"You went to Ransom Country Day," he reminded
her, "an elite private school. You weren't going to meet the
other kind."

"Maybe. But from what I've seen since I've been
back, the Latins in Miami have done very well. Why, this
afternoon I was on assignment at a fashion show at an
estate in Coral Gables—"

She stopped, dismayed, remembering the scene in
the Santo Marins' garden. It practically reinforced everything he was saying!

Dodd didn't notice her abrupt silence. "Oh, the
latinos have made money all right. I deal with them every
day. Multimillionaires big in South American banking,
export-import, Miami real estate . . ." He paused significantly.
"And the biggest drug empire the world's ever seen."

Gaby couldn't speak. She was thinking it all made
sense. And yet it was too simple. Too patently unfair.

"Look, Mouse, everything you've heard about Miami
is true. The extent of the drug traffic here boggles the
mind. There's so much money from cocaine in circulation
that the second biggest problem, after how to smuggle
drugs into the country, is what to do with all the
cash."

Gaby thought of the two men making their deal
under the palm trees. She shuddered.

This time Dodd saw it and said quickly, "Lord, I'm
sorry, honey. You're tired and I didn't mean to come on so
strong. The last thing I want to do is scare you to death.
But if you live in Miami you have to be careful."

For a long moment they simply gazed at each other in silence. The quiet of the humid night enveloped them there under the bright kitchen lights. There was so much between them that needed to be said, and neither was willing to begin.

Finally, Dodd sighed. "Gaby, your mother is right about one thing," he said softly. "It would be a lot easier if you did marry me."

It wasn't a proposal, it was a statement of fact. And so very like Dodd, she thought, to come out baldly with it like that. She didn't know the details of Dodd's marriage or divorce, but she knew he would tell her if she asked. Everything about him now said that he was willing and ready to explain.

Suddenly she wasn't sure that she wanted to hear it. That surprised her. But in the last five years she'd learned that who had loved whom—especially at eighteen—and who had not was no longer burningly important.

"I think," she said evenly, "we ought to go see if my mother's ready for bed."

A half an hour later they walked out to Dodd's Porsche. As he got into it, the storm that had been threatening all evening heralded its arrival in a wild burst of wind that made them gasp.

"I'd better help you shut up things." Dodd had to shout as a gust ripped into the trees and sent palm fronds and leaves showering down.

Gaby grabbed at her hair, pulling it out of her eyes and mouth. "No, I'll do it. I have to put out pots for the leaks."

"Hell, I forgot about that damned roof." He peered up at her through his open window. "You'd better let me help."

She only wanted him to leave. The day had been endless, and she was exhausted. "No, I'm used to it."

"Don't forget to lock all those glass doors," he shouted. "Remember what I told you about the waterfront side."

On impulse, she bent to the open car window. "Dodd, do you know someone named James Santo Marin?"

"What?" A pelting burst of rain spattered around them, almost drowning their words. "Yes." He grimaced. "Why?"

Gaby was immediately sorry she'd asked. "Nothing, just a name someone mentioned today."

"Flashy son of a bitch. Runs Santo Marin Hermanos Imports. And a bank." A roll of thunder blotted out some of his words as he put the car into gear. "—and stay away from him!"

Gaby stood for a moment watching the red dots of the Porsche's taillights as Dodd slowed for the security check at the Palm Island guard gate, then turned onto the bridge to the MacArthur Causeway. Beyond, the giant white cruise liners in the port of Miami were bathed in a pool of garish light. Lightning ripped a blazing crack in the dark sky above the ships, then died away.

She turned back to the house. The driveway was already littered with torn leaves. She made herself pick her way carefully as the wind whipped at her clothes. The lights in the Escuderos' apartment were off. There wasn't even the blue-white glow of the television set. Angel and his mother had gone to bed.

Jupiter met Gaby at the front door. The old Labrador was terrified of thunderstorms and he pressed his body close to her, whining pitifully.

Gaby shoved him away. "Oh, Jupe, don't have a nervous breakdown." Jupiter's place of refuge during thunderstorms was an old tool shed near the boat dock. "I'll let you outside in a minute."

The old dog managed to stay under her feet all the way to the kitchen. She collected an armful of saucepans and pots and carried them to the front hall.

The roof had leaked for years. She set a pan under the first ceiling stain and carried the others into the cavernous old *sala grande*. The drips in the living room had a long way to fall; the beamed ceiling rose more than thirty feet above the bare, somewhat dusty tile floor.

In Miami one was never very far from the water. On Palm Island in the middle of Biscayne Bay, the air was always moisture-saturated. Now, before the oncoming thun-

derstorm, the downstairs was like a steam room. Gaby put
down the last pot and unfastened the braid of her wind-
ravaged hair, raking it loose with her fingers. She was still
wearing the tailored shirt and skirt she'd put on that
morning for work, clothes that she'd walked in, sat in, and
sweltered in all day. Pulling down her hair, letting it swing
free, gave her a vast sense of relief.

A second later a burst of lightning, blue-white and
blindingly close, hit the island. The lamp in the living
room winked, then went out.

In the sudden blackness there was no holding Jupiter.
He threw himself at the sun porch's glass door in a frenzy,
scratching at it with his long claws and yelping. Gaby
pushed the door open. The wind promptly caught it and
slammed it away, and the old Labrador bolted into the
night.

She stood in the open doorway, savoring the sudden,
sharp coolness of the night wind. The storm was rolling
across the bay, whipping the black water into whitecaps.
Gaby hoped it wasn't going to be one of the notorious
South Florida tempests that pounded boats at their moor-
ings, tore down television aerials, and uprooted trees
before going on to set lightning fires in the everglades. If
so, there was no telling when the electricity might come
back on.

The leading edge of the storm was both violent and
spectacular. In one almost continuous electrical assault,
brilliant ball lightning hung over the whitecapped water
like a searchlight.

Gaby squinted. Or was it a searchlight? No, it couldn't
be. Certainly no one in his right mind would take a boat
out on Biscayne Bay in such a squall. Another bolt of
lightning cracked open the sky. In that brief, blinding
moment the world turned dazzlingly, starkly blue-white
and black. And what Gaby saw by its light was a huge
white power cruiser, streamlined as a space ship, cutting
through the black water right in front of the Collier dock.

The next moment it was dark again.

She stayed where she was, positive she'd been seeing
things. But another flash of lightning showed the cruiser

was really there, its ghostly white shape, its searchlight probing the churning black water. The light found the dilapidated pilings of the dock and stayed.

The storm suddenly threw the full force of its wind at the island, ripping loose palm fronds and hurtling them across the back lawn like missiles. Gaby could still see the searchlight. It *was* a cruiser, she thought, stunned. And it was putting into her dock!

In that moment, all that Dodd had said about gangs of robbers attacking waterfront homes leaped into Gaby's consciousness. It was almost midnight. She was alone except for her mother sleeping upstairs. It couldn't be happening, her rational mind tried to tell her. But this was Miami. And it was.

She turned and stumbled back into the sun porch. Hurrying through it to the lightless living room, she hit the edge of a chair in the darkness. She heard something fall. *Oh God, why did the lights have to be off?*

Another crash of lightning lit the living room. She blundered into the end table by the couch, then groped across the table for the telephone. Burglars or drug dealers were perhaps, at that moment, jumping from the biggest, sleekest cruiser she'd ever seen in her life, automatic weapons in their hands.

Her shaking fingers found the telephone's old-fashioned dial. She had to call 911. She had to be calm. She had to be able to speak when she got the operator. There was a possibility it would turn out to be nothing at all. Just boaters lost on the bay, putting into her dock to wait out the storm.

She didn't believe that.

She lifted the base of the telephone close to her face, trying to see the numbers in the darkness. Trying not to scream.

She was alone in the house except for her mother, drunk and helpless. There was no gun, no pistol anywhere. But, she remembered, there were knives in the kitchen. In the next instant she knew she couldn't use a kitchen knife to defend herself. Even to hold off robbers coming from the water. She was helpless with anything violent.

She clutched the receiver to her ear, waiting for 911 to answer, when the next realization hit her.

Just as the storm had put out the lights, the telephone, too, was dead.

Chapter 4

Outside, Jupiter began to bark.

Gaby stood trembling, rooted to the spot. She was a coward, just as her mother had said. She'd run away to Europe when the man she loved had married someone else, and she had fled in one way or another from Paul and Jeannette all her life. But now for the first time, there was nowhere to run. She was trapped!

The dog's frantic yapping rose to a frenzy over the noise of the storm. *Jupiter,* she thought suddenly. They'd kill him if he tried to protect the house!

She dropped the telephone. It hit the edge of the table and crashed to the floor, but she was already groping through the living room toward the sun porch, not even sure what she was going to do.

Violent cracks of lightning, like flashbulbs going off, booby-trapped the darkened house. One minute it was glaringly bright, the next pitch black. At the door to the sun porch she missed the step and nearly fell. She lurched into the dinner table, her cry of pain lost as a sudden downpour added to the uproar.

She knew it was foolish to panic over Jupiter if the house was being attacked, but she couldn't abandon her old pet. She threw open the sun porch door. The wind yanked the knob from her hand and slammed the door shut again. Lightning blasted the sky, going to ground somewhere on Palm Island. Beyond the porch the glare of lightning showed the figure of a man picking his way across the littered back lawn, a drenched white shape in the slanting torrent of rain, before the world went dark again.

Frozen with fright, Gaby strained to see through the storm. Had she really seen anything out there? One man? Or a whole gang of burglars with guns in their hands?

Lightning split open the sky once more, and Gaby clapped both hands over her mouth to keep from screaming. The porch door rattled, then flew open in a gust of wind.

Another stroke of lightning hit close by. In the moment's earsplitting dazzle she saw a man's white shirt, white trousers, the blur of his face. Then she was being propelled backward by an unseen hand. He slammed the door shut and leaned against it.

They tried to see each other in the dimness, breathing heavily.

"Jupiter!" she croaked. It was the only thing she could think of. "My dog!"

"He ran off." The voice in the storm-wracked darkness was husky. "Miss Collier?"

She backed away as lightning again crossed the sky. "What have you done with my dog?"

The tall figure straightened away from the door. "He ran off when the lightning hit. This is the right place, isn't it?" He turned his head, trying to locate her. "Gabrielle Collier?"

Gaby trembled violently. She was sure he was wearing the same clothes—white trousers, white shirt, and dark tie. He seemed only to have discarded the elegant suit jacket. It was the same man she had seen that afternoon, with the Colombian kneeling before him and kissing his hand. She didn't know what James Santo Marin was doing in her home, but it didn't matter. There could be a team of robbers from his boat racing for the house at that very moment!

She stumbled backward toward the door to the living room, hands held out to ward him off. Her mind wouldn't

work, it was blank with fear. The crashing of thunder and
lightning seemed to have paralyzed her brain.

She heard the shadow that was James Santo Marin
move toward her and hit the card table. "Did the
storm knock your lights out?" He rubbed his knee. "Miss
Collier?"

"W-what are you doing here?" She backed away again,
carefully. "How—how did you know where I live?"

"The newspaper." He ran a hand over his face. "I told
them I wanted to talk to the reporter who was at the
fashion show today."

Gaby's shoulder hit the doorjamb to the living room
and she winced. "The newspaper doesn't give out that
information!"

The shadow of his hand lifted to loosen his tie. "They
do to me." He slipped the tie off and pulled his wet shirt
away from his body.

His words chilled her. She remembered what Dodd
had said about drug dealing in Miami. She looked around
for something to use as a weapon. In the dark, there was
nothing. "Don't come one step nearer." It was a mistake to
sound so obviously terrified, but she couldn't help it. "Stay
right there!"

He paused. "God, don't panic. Look, are you alone in
the house?"

Gaby shuddered. With one backward step she would
be inside the living room where she could slam the door
shut and lock it, leaving him on the sun porch. Another
crash of lightning hit the island, bathing them in instant
white light.

She lunged for the living room. The shadow moved at
the same time, catching the door with his hand. It banged
back on its hinges as he stepped after her into the living
room.

In the old high-ceilinged *sala* the storm was reflected
in the mirrors and on the white walls as a bright, flickering
gloom. Gaby backed away from him and the coffee table
caught her behind her knees, painfully. If only her mother
weren't unconscious upstairs and could somehow manage

to help! If only the neighbors weren't so far away they couldn't hear if she screamed! If only—

"Miss Collier?" She could make out the shadowed planes of his face. "Miss Collier, I saw you this afternoon. You were there, standing under the trees."

She kept backing away, thinking frantically of the kitchen. The front door. A dining room window she could crawl out of. *He had seen her in the garden when he was closing a drug deal.* Oh, God, she supposed she was some sort of a witness! Had he come there now to kill her?

She stumbled into something, a chair, and doubled over it with a gasp. "I wasn't there, it was someone else!"

"You were there." He moved toward the sound of her voice. "I saw you come up from the path in the trees and then you—" A tremendous crack of lightning interrupted him. "You ran away before I could stop you."

"Not me," she cried. "It wasn't me!" Her blindly groping hands discovered the obstacle wasn't a chair. It was the couch. She couldn't seem to get around it.

She saw his white-sleeved arm lift as he ran his hand through his hair. "Do you have a towel? I'm getting everything wet."

She clutched the arm of the sofa. *Towel?* He wanted her to bring him a towel! "Get out!" She no longer cared if she sounded frightened. "If you don't go away, I'm going to call the police!"

"The police?" He stepped forward again. "Look, that's exactly what I want to talk to you about. I know newspaper people, Miss Collier," he said urgently, "and how they go after a story. I don't want you picking up on something that—" He hesitated. "—that means absolutely nothing."

She pushed hard against the couch, trying to move it out of her way. "I'm not a real reporter, I'm a fashion writer!" She knew now he was there to threaten her. "You've got the wrong person," she went on breathlessly. "I'm not interested in drug deals or any—"

The words died in her throat.

Drug deal. Oh God, she'd actually said it!

He stood perfectly still. "Jesus," she heard him say under his breath, "that's all I need."

Abruptly, lightning and thunder crashed right over their heads. Gaby had a wild, irrational thought that there was something unnatural in the way the light danced around his dimly outlined body. Her senses screamed that he smelled of rain, wet clothing, expensive cologne. Menacing. Leanly powerful. Inescapable.

There was something else, too, she realized with a fresh burst of terror. He seemed to be staring at the front of her shirt where she'd loosened a few buttons, his gaze traveling downward with an intensity that conveyed other, even more ominous messages.

"I want you out of here," she said, her voice quavering. "Whatever you have to say to me you can—you can—" What *could* he do? "You can call me at work!"

He didn't move.

"Look, Miss Collier," he said finally, "I have to talk to you now. It can't wait until tomorrow. I'm sorry if this puts you off, my coming in this way, but I can't help the damned storm."

She leaned back against the couch to put as much space as possible between them. "I can't talk to you, didn't you just hear me? I don't know what you think you're doing, bursting in here like this from a—" Her voice rose to a shriek in spite of herself. "—a *boat*! You must be crazy!"

"God, this is impossible," he muttered. "I'm scaring the hell out of you and getting no place. what you saw this afternoon was a matter of—uh, doing some friends a favor. And not, obviously, what you thought it was."

Gaby was no longer listening. Inching away, the couch at her back, she saw him move to her. "Stay away from me," she cried. "Don't touch me!"

"I'm not doing anything to you. Damn, is it because I'm a *latino*?" He was suddenly angry. "Is that what makes you so afraid?"

At that moment another blue-white explosion struck in one of the trees just outside the house. It was like a bomb detonating; the very walls shook. Gaby shrieked.

Once started she couldn't seem to stop. She gave in to pressures that had been accumulating for weeks.

"Wait!" he shouted. "It's just lightning. It'll be all right!"

Still screaming, Gaby lunged at him. In some remote part of her mind she was amazed that she, Gabrielle Collier, even threatened as she was, would attack anyone. But she sprang at James Santo Marin and heard him grunt as her fists pounded his face and chest. "Jupiter!" she screamed. "Police! Help!"

"Christ!" He tried to catch her hands, but it was dark. His wrist knocked her under the chin.

She reeled backward, seeing stars. She tried to save herself by grabbing him, but she still toppled over. He fell with her. In the next instant she found herself pressed down into the musty-smelling sofa cushions, one hand clutching a muscular bicep, her other hand trapped between their bodies.

For a long moment there was no sound except the storm as they lay stunned, trying to get their breath.

"I didn't mean to hit you." His low voice was right in her ear. "Are you all right?"

She bucked under him. She wanted to break free, but his body, sprawled over hers, held her down. And, she discovered, her hand was mashed against the lower part of his body, fingers outlining an unmistakable shape under wet cloth.

She felt James Santo Marin go very still.

The rain's hard, tropical drumming pounded the roof, mingling with the sound of drips from the *sala*'s ceiling into the pots and pans. James Santo Marin lifted his head and looked down at her, his face filled with wary discovery.

Gaby felt as though her heart were about to jump out of her chest. They were lying on the old couch in the most intimate of positions, James Santo Marin on top of her, her breasts crushed against his chest, his arm under her, partly embracing her. "Let me up," she choked.

Shadowed black eyes, inches from hers, gazed down at her with a rather abstracted expression. "Are you hurt?"

"You hit me," she cried. "Get off of me!"

"I didn't hit you." His lower body shifted almost imperceptibly against her hand. "I never hit women."

Gaby felt dizzy. She had the sudden, surreal sense of being plunged through a dimension of time that had telescoped. They were strangers, lying like this, and yet it was impossible to ignore the intimate reality of that lean, muscular body cradled between her thighs. Trapped in his groin, her hand was telling her he was growing hard.

Gaby's mind reeled with terrified thoughts. This couldn't be happening. *Sex. Force.* Her fingers contracted spasmodically.

He jumped. Violently. "Don't do that," he said breathily. "Just give me a minute."

Gaby choked back a helpless whimper. His clothes were wet. The faint aura of soap and musky male sweat tinted the soggy air. But her senses denied all of it. It was a nightmare, she told herself. There was no stranger lying on top of her in her own living room, no storm, no boat at the Collier dock. Because what was taking place was too incredible to be real. In the morning she'd wake up in her own bed and find out all this had been a bad dream.

She closed her eyes quickly, half expecting him not to be there when she opened them.

But he was.

That chiseled face was right over hers. She saw the gleam of his teeth. "You're so . . ." he murmured huskily.

His head lowered. Paralyzed, not breathing, Gaby felt the warm touch of his lips.

It was a wary kiss, yet so charged with electricity that her lips parted in amazement.

He made a soft, unexpected sound of passion, then his mouth covered hers, rough, insatiable. He kissed her throat, her temple, the lobe of her ear, as though he would get his fill of her before she made him stop.

It was like being enveloped in flames, an inferno that blazed up between them, taking them both by surprise. Gaby couldn't get her breath. Was this the famous Latin passion? she wondered crazily. The feel of that tense, powerful body pressing on hers, his ardent mouth, was overwhelming. She was drowning in it! If something terrible was about to happen, she knew she didn't have the will to resist.

He was the one who broke the moment's dark spell. He pulled back and looked down at her. "I must be crazy," he muttered, incredulous. "Jesus, I must be totally crazy, doing this!"

Gaby was dimly aware of their wet clothes, the musty smell of the old couch, her mother drunkenly asleep upstairs. She felt as though she had never been kissed, or touched, before. How could anyone put so much passion, so much *tenderness* into just one kiss? Every inch of her skin was sensitized—her swollen, tingling breasts, her arm that had crept around his shoulders to hold him, the bared expanse of her thighs that cradled him tightly. She knew he was fully aroused, her trapped fingers were telling her so.

Desperately, she tried to make her mind work. She told herself this powerful, too-good-looking man was dangerous, probably violent, probably just one step ahead of the police. But her body was going wild, she thought with a sob, actually *aching* for him! She was the one who was crazy. In this darkness, she was under some sort of spell. Yet she couldn't help the strange feeling that he was caught just as off guard by it as she.

His fingers were unbuttoning her cotton shirt. "Let me," he murmured when she stirred. The softest of touches stroked her throat, the ridge of her collarbone, then dropped to the curve of her breast. "You're so cool and lovely." His voice shook as he eased the shirt down over her shoulders. "Like moonlight." His thumb brushed the soft bud of her nipple through her satiny bra, and she moaned.

She had the most curious sensation of being frighteningly, erotically naked in the smothering darkness, even though she was clothed. And she didn't want him to stop. His gypsy black eyes, cloaked by a thick sweep of lashes, studied her intently. His mouth curved, with deep indents at the corners. She stared at him, fascinated, thinking he had a beautiful mouth. She wanted him to kiss her, and was alarmed at her own desire. The feel of his hands stroking her breasts, pushing damp clothes out of the way to press his own smooth, cool skin against her, generated a flash fire of passion between them that was unbelievable in its intensity.

She felt his damp, firm mouth touch her shoulder, then it descended to nuzzle her lace-edged bra.

In the back of her mind she realized she was going to let him make love to her. It was insane. It was inevitable. He murmured something in her ear as his fingers slid under her brassiere. Then he pulled it aside and his mouth was on her bare flesh.

Gaby's mind reeled. She wanted this beautiful man who smelled of rain and night and storm to touch her everywhere. His lips tugged at her nipples and she writhed, lifting her hips against him, a soft, throaty sound on her lips. She wanted him to hurry. She wanted to pull his clothes away, take in his hard body, his shaking, fiery hunger. Her exploring hand pressed boldly between them, outlining his sex under the damp fabric. A groan broke from him, his control stretched to the limit.

There was the sudden rasp of a zipper. Then his hand was guiding hers. "Don't say no," he whispered hoarsely. "I want you. God, how I want you!"

Gaby was beyond denying him anything. His hand closed hers around hard flesh, hot to the touch. She couldn't believe the power, the size of him. His clenched, shadowy face was right above her. She saw him as he responded to her touch with an expression of almost helpless ecstasy.

Then his mouth was on hers, claiming her in such a blazingly exultant kiss that when he stopped, she clung to him wide-eyed, breathless for more.

"Are you all right?" he gasped. He was trembling with passion. "Tell me I'm not making you do this against your will."

She stared up at him with her lips parted, not sure what he'd said.

Whatever this strange dream was about, this mad sensual fantasy there in the lightning-wracked darkness, she didn't want it to stop. *Against her will?* She was beyond everything except her own body's clamoring wildness!

When she didn't answer, his arms tightened around her. He lowered his head and pressed his forehead to hers. Several long moments passed. "Oh damn." He groaned. "Oh damn."

His lean frame was still tense with desire, yet he lay motionless. What was wrong? she wondered desperately. Why had he stopped . . . when she didn't want him to?

"I can't," he murmured, as if to himself. "Not like this."

She heard his harsh, indrawn breath, felt his body strain even more tightly against her. His narrow hips moved against her hand once, convulsively, then stilled.

Instinctively, she lifted her free hand to touch the side of his face. He lowered his head and pressed his mouth to her throat. Every muscle of his body tensed as she took his weight, his heavy, dragging gasps, for long moments. He had stopped. Passion had stopped. Everything had stopped.

She heard him sigh. Then he lifted her hand away.

In a lithe movement, he stood up by the couch, a white shadow in shirt and the trousers he hastily zipped up. He gazed at her without speaking, the expression on his handsome face indistinct. Then, abruptly, he turned away.

Slowly, Gaby raised herself on one elbow. The storm was moving off, lightning no longer lit the room. She was aware of her own open shirt, her exposed breasts, her loosened hair drifting over her bare shoulders. What in the world had happened? Her eyes strained into the darkness. Should she be glad they had stopped? But why hadn't this powerful, virile man made love to her?

James Santo Marin, she realized slowly, was leaving. Halfway across the dark *sala* his feet encountered a water-filled pan and he shied, cursed, then gave it a ferocious kick. It clattered away across the tile floor. He strode out onto the sun porch and she heard him curse again, fervently.

Then the door slammed and he was gone.

Gaby lay where she was, listening to a last low growl

of thunder receding across Biscayne Bay. Her whole body still throbbed with interrupted, unsatisfied desire. And she was light-headed with tiredness. It threatened to drag her into sleep right there on the couch. Gingerly, she touched her hands to her face. Her skin felt as though she were burning with fever.

Good Lord, what *had* happened? She wasn't quite sure.

The pressure of the last twelve hours—the fashion show with its drugged-out model, the bizarre scene in the woods, dinner with her mother and Dodd, the even stranger fantasy of James Santo Marin arriving in a huge power cruiser at her back door—had combined to make her sanity tilt a little. What was it Alicia Fernandez had said only that afternoon in Coral Gables? *Life in Miami is like one of those music videos kids watch on television.*

Gaby closed her eyes. She wasn't going to believe that for the past few minutes she'd lost her mind there in the darkness and that she, Gabrielle Collier, had turned into a wild, sex-driven wanton. Who had let a dangerous man, a stranger, undoubtedly a drug dealer, almost make love to her.

It was a dream. That was the only thing that made sense. For if it had been real, James Santo Marin would certainly have made love to her. If he'd been real, all those lean, rippling muscles, that glittering sensuality wouldn't have just faded away into the night. No, she'd made some breathtakingly handsome man she'd seen into an erotic fantasy, that was all. She'd fallen asleep right there on the couch and dreamed the whole thing.

A familiar sound from the sun porch jarred her fully awake. Jupiter was back now that the storm was fading, whining and scratching to get in.

So there, Gaby told herself, even Jupiter was all right. Nothing had happened. Nothing at all.

She sat up and swung her feet over the side of the couch. As she did so her foot touched something soggy and unresisting on the floor, and she bent to pick it up.

It was cold, soaking wet, this thing she held in her hand, a long, dark, narrow length of sodden silk.

It was no dream, she thought, staring at it. James Santo Marin had left his tie.

Let him fast who has no bread,
And sleep in the moonlight
Who has no bed.

SPANISH FOLK SONG

Chapter 5

"Now, the lead on your story," Jack Carty said as he took a pencil and slashed through the first sentence, "should match Crissette's shot of the guy hauling the model out of the pool. So change the whole thing."

In the space above Gaby's fashion show copy he wrote: "Even a spectacular, if non-life-threatening, tumble into an ornamental pool by one of the models could not diminish the luster of the celebrity-packed Coral Gables Hispanic Cultural Society's annual fashion event."

Gaby stared down at the opening he'd just written. Was that supposed to be good? she wondered. She didn't like it at all. But she'd already learned that newspaper work wasn't at all like writing synopses for art museum catalogues in Italy. Some days she felt as though she would never figure out the rules. If there *were* rules. The whole thing still eluded her.

"Are you with me?" The feature editor's freckled face wore an expression of weary patience.

Gaby nodded, fighting down the almost irrational dread that swept over her when Jack critiqued her stories.

"Now the reason," he went on, "you change the lead is that we're going to use the pool photograph as a four-column blowup on the first page of the section." He used the tip of his pencil to point out the rewritten line slowly, word by word, as though Gaby had as much trouble reading as she did writing. She had noticed Jack almost never looked directly at her. He kept his head down, speaking in a laconic monotone in the classic style of newsroom conversation. "All this stuff," he said brusquely, referring to Gaby's original sentence, "you dump. And change the rest of the copy accordingly."

Gaby still didn't believe the Coral Gables fashion show story was scheduled for the desirable Sunday edition on the Modern Living section's first page. Whenever she was at the feature editor's desk, everyone in the city room, hunched down behind their computer terminals, usually followed their conversations with barely hidden enjoyment. So far, she'd never done anything right. Only this time, incredibly enough, she had.

Crissette's pictures had been the deciding factor, Gaby knew. And not her terrible prose.

Jack took the topmost glossy print from the stack of photographs on his desk. "Nice shot. Redhead in a wading pool. Good-looking dude in a Palm Beach suit trying to keep her from drowning. Looks like a scene from *Miami Vice.*"

Gaby took the eight-by-ten print, deliberately not looking at it. She wanted James Santo Marin to go away, disappear in a puff of smoke, because she had tried, almost successfully, to forget that humiliating storm-wracked night a few days ago when she'd acted like a sex-crazed wild woman. She knew if she looked at the photograph it would set off inside her shock waves of embarrassment, fear, even inexplicable guilt, all over again.

Stop it, Gaby told herself. If she couldn't face James Santo Marin's photograph, she couldn't get any of her work done.

She held up the picture. It was a marvelous shot, even she could tell that much. Crissette's camera had caught the tall, broad-shouldered man at the moment he'd lifted the model to her feet. Drops of water, suspended in air, added a sense of action and drama. James Santo Marin had heard the telltale *szznick-szznick* of the Nikon and he'd turned, looking straight into the lens. Crissette had caught all the vivid intensity of his taut, scowling features.

He looked as real, Gaby thought, as fiercely sexy and

irresistible, as when he had fallen on top of her in her half-dark living room. Oh Lord, how she wished she could forget it! That had been the worst, the most stupid episode in her whole life.

"And write a sidebar," Jack said. He was searching through the printout of her story. "Something about the—what? The Santo Marin family," he said, finding the page. "Didn't we do a feature on them once?" The question was rhetorical; Gaby was too new to know. "Well, look it up," he told her, "and give me a couple of hundred words."

Gaby was still staring at the photo she held in her hand. The last thing she wanted was more of James Santo Marin. Now she'd just had him assigned as part of her story.

"How'd it happen?" Jack asked.

She gave him an unfocused look. She'd been asking herself that same question for days. She had no answer to the way she'd behaved that night, except that the storm and her fright had sent her into a wildly abnormal state of mind. Right there in the photograph, just beyond the man and the woman in the lily pond, were two stocky men in mirror sunglasses. If anything put James Santo Marin in perspective, it was the reminder of his sinister friends, the drug-dealing Colombians.

"It's not in your copy," Jack said. He was looking at her with leaden patience. When Gaby only stared at him, he said, "The *copy*. If you don't mind, Gabrielle, how the hell did they get in the pond?"

"Oh, the pond." She hated it when Jack treated her like a moron. She had worked in a literate, demanding job abroad for almost five years; she couldn't help it if she didn't know much about newspapering. "The model fell off the runway." Should she tell him what Crissette had said? That the model was high on something? "The model fell off this temporary runway they built for the fashion show and he—" She faltered when she saw Jack Carty was looking at her directly for a change. In fact, staring at her with exceptionally cold blue eyes. "H-he came to get her out," she stammered.

"He *who*?" he demanded stonily. "Has he got a name?"

"Y-yes, you just said it." She picked up a page of her story. And cringed. James Santo Marin wasn't identified anywhere.

"Make sure you put it in, Gaby, in the sidebar. You do know," he said carefully, "what a sidebar is, don't you?"

She looked away. She was such a wimp, she thought, letting Jack Carty browbeat her when they had these terrible story conferences. Somehow, someday, if she lasted long enough in this newspaper job, she was going to build up enough confidence to—

"A sidebar," he said, "is a little box with words, sentences in it. It goes on the side of the story, sometimes in the middle of the columns, but always in its little box. And it usually elaborates on some aspect of the copy."

"A little box," Gaby said. "Yes, I've seen them."

He took the picture out of her hands. "Go down to the morgue and look up the Santo Marin family. Go back three or four years if you have to, look up everything that mentions them. Then call the chairman of whatever it is—"

"The Coral Gables Hispanic Cultural Society," she said helpfully.

"—and ask them what Santo Marin's been doing lately, business connections, awards, all the social stuff."

"Suppose there's something..." She felt foolish, but she was remembering the reason James Santo Marin had come to her house. It was better to bring it up now. "Something that he—that the Santo Marins don't want printed," she ended lamely.

The features editor sighed. "Gaby, write a background for a sidebar. Just do it! Wait," he said when she started to get up, "there's more." He shuffled through the papers on his desk, found an envelope, and handed it to her, then bent his head. Not looking up, he said, "You've been issued a check for special expenses."

She gaped at him. "A check for *expenses*?"

"The consensus of management is that the fashion reporter has certain expenses, an image to maintain, since you . . . uh, represent the paper. So we have a new policy," he ended gruffly. "You get a clothes allowance."

A clothes allowance? Nervously, she ripped open the envelope, certain something was wrong. She stared at the piece of green paper with its official-looking numbers. The *Times-Journal* check was for five hundred dollars.

Bright color rose in Gaby's throat and flamed in her face all the way to her forehead. She sat quite still, knowing there was no need to ask for an explanation. Dodd Brickell and his father and their good friend Gardner Hedison, the *Times-Journal* publisher, had decided to be helpful again.

Gaby wondered if anyone had ever died of terminal shame and embarrassment. She also wondered what Jack Carty would do if his untalented, inexperienced fashion writer put her head down on his desk and burst into humiliated tears.

"The fashion slot probably needed it anyway," Jack said. He was studiously ignoring her, examining the backs of his blunt, freckled hands with elaborate interest. "Especially since you're picking up a following."

Gaby didn't know what he was talking about. Then she saw the editor lift his head and look pointedly across the newsroom to the elaborate bouquet sitting on top of one of the Modern Living section's file cabinets.

She'd forgotten the flowers. Four dozen extravagant long-stemmed red roses, more exotic in Miami at that time of year than orchids. There had been no card, and she had assumed it had fallen off somewhere when they were being delivered. Fashion writers were always receiving promotional gifts. The week before, a Hialeah shopping mall had sent her a basket of fruit with an invitation to something called a Midsummer Mexican Fiesta. The city room had eaten the fruit. It had been her most popular moment so far.

Now, because somebody had delivered a lot of roses, probably by mistake, Jack Carty thought she had a readership. Her "following," as he called it.

Would it be wise to deny it? Gaby gnawed at her bottom lip. To try to set him right?

"Sidebar," Jack reminded her. "I need a sidebar, Gabrielle. And hopefully sometime this year."

"Yes, yes." She jumped up hastily. "I'm on my way."

She had only gone a few steps when she heard him call out across the city room, "Not the Dade County Morgue, Gabrielle. The *newspaper morgue*. Down on the third floor."

The whole city room staff kept their heads down. But they were grinning.

The newspaper morgue, where clippings and microfilm records of *Times-Journal* back issues were kept, was a windowless, frigidly air-conditioned room that somewhat resembled the actual Dade County morgue downtown. It was made even more morguelike by bleak fluorescent lighting and a grim-faced middle-aged woman who greeted Gaby as though news of her incompetence had already filtered down.

"Photographic is looking for you," she said as Gaby signed in to use the files. "Want me to call Crissette Washington back and tell her you're down here?"

Crissette, Gaby remembered, had offered to give her a ride home because her mother's aged Cadillac was in the shop again. She told the morgue supervisor she'd appreciate the call, and went into the file room.

There were two systems in the *Times-Journal*'s morgue. Old metal bins held file folders of clippings of the newspaper's earlier issues. The daily editions since 1979 were on microfilm. Researching James Santo Marin wasn't going to be easy, she thought, sighing. She didn't even know what year to begin with. It would probably help to know how long the Santo Marin family had been in Miami.

The first wave of Cuban exiles had arrived in the States in the 1960's. But Gaby remembered someone telling her the Santo Marin export-import company had had a Miami branch office long before that. Still, looking for a story through back editions of the *Times-Journal* was a lot better than the daily struggles with her writing. At least researching was something she knew.

Gaby began with the current week's editions, but

after a half hour of monotonous sliding of microfilmed pages through the viewer she began to lose the edge of her concentration. Then the front page of the Modern Living section came up with the story she was looking for. It was four years old, she saw, checking the dateline, and the headline was something of a surprise. *"Miami Roots Still Here For Cuba's Santo Marins."*

"Goody," Gaby murmured.

Center page was a photograph of all three Santo Marins in the spectacular white living room of their just-completed palatial art deco estate in Coral Gables four years ago. The original photograph was in color; the microfilm reproduction was more muddy than usual. But James Santo Marin was certainly recognizable, tense and smolderingly good-looking in a dark business suit, standing behind the white sofa where his sister and mother were seated.

Gaby examined the women. Señora Estancia Santo Marin with her dark hair and exquisite Castilian features looked beautiful and young enough to be her son's sister. The sister herself, identified in the cut line below the photo as Pilar Antonia Santo Marin had, in spite of her lovely face, the pale, overshadowed air of one who had lived all her life in the brilliance of her mother's beauty.

She could relate to that, Gaby thought. Pilar Santo Marin was pretty, but not pretty enough. And had lived all her young life with the spotlight on her glamorous mama.

Gaby sat back in her chair and studied them thoughtfully. The two women were sleek, perfectly coiffed, with great lidded dark eyes, the very picture of upper-class *latinas*. Behind them, James Santo Marin looked down his nose at the camera with the scowling, impatient expression of someone too busy to be having his picture taken.

According to the *Times-Journal* article, the Santo Marins had been rich in Cuba, but they'd grown even richer in the States. James Santo Marin had taken over the family business on the death of his uncle and was a millionaire several times over. He had been named Young Hispanic Businessman of the Year, and served on numerous Miami area banking boards. The mansion he'd built on the shore of Biscayne Bay had been designed by a famous Argentinian architect.

The so-called "Prince of Coral Gables" played championship polo for a Palm Beach team, piloted his own Lear jet, and had acquired an Italian-built power cruiser named the *Altavida* that had won several prizes for advanced design.

He didn't, Gaby thought, frowning, have the usual fatuous, self-absorbed look of a playboy. If anything, those handsome features were too somber, too tense. Still, it was hard to picture the same man as wet and rumpled, zipping up his pants and storming out of her house. The way he had four nights ago.

Forcing that image from her mind, she returned her attention to the article. Before their exile from Cuba in the 1960's, the Santo Marin family had apparently lived in Miami as much as they had in Havana. James and his sister Pilar had been born in Miami, which made them United States citizens. In fact, he had graduated from the University of Miami.

Gaby fought down an uneasy feeling. All that money, the family business expanding into an empire, within a comparatively few years? The exiles of the sixties had been desperately poor; Castro hadn't let them take anything out of the country except the clothes they wore and one change of underwear. The Santo Marins had obviously been part of that elite, ultrawealthy Caribbean community that had once made the circuit of Buenos Aires, Madrid, and Paris, sent their young to European prep schools, shopped London's Savile Row and French haute couture houses, and contributed championship players to the international polo set. It had been a world vastly different from the one Gaby knew. Señora Estancia Santo Marin, the *Times-Journal* feature said, was Spanish-born, and the sister, Señorita Pilar Santo Marin, had been educated in convents in Madrid and Havana. They now kept busy with volunteer work for local charities.

Charity, Gaby reminded herself with a start.

She'd been so engrossed in the microfilm, she'd forgotten that Jack Carty had told her to call Alicia Fernandez.

She looked up at the clock on the wall. The *Times-Journal* was a morning paper; its deadline for the next day's editions were at nine-thirty at night, even though the Modern Living section theoretically worked from nine to five. As she rushed back to her desk in the city room, she hoped it wasn't too late to telephone Mrs. Fernandez.

The maid who answered the Fernandez phone didn't speak English well, but eventually, with the help of Gaby's minimal Spanish, Alicia Fernandez came on the line.

"Gabrielle?" Her low voice was unfailingly kind. "How good to hear from you, darling. Did you want to speak to Susan?"

Gaby was at a loss for a moment, then remembered Susan was the old school friend from Ransom Country Day School.

"Because she's isn't here," Alicia went on. "Susan would adore to hear from you, Gabrielle, but she's married now—"

"Not Susan, please," Gaby interrupted. How did you plunge right in and ask for a lot of information? It was another newspapering skill she hadn't acquired. "Ah . . . Mrs. Fernandez, I'm with the Miami *Times-Journal* now, I guess you remember," she said awkwardly. "I hate to bother you this time of night, but I'm on a deadline. I'm doing a story about the Santo Marin family, James Santo Marin, and it's important."

There was a silence, then Gaby heard a sound very much like an excited, suppressed scream. "Fernando!" Alicia cried. "Oh, my dear, have they let him out? Oh God, tell me they have!"

Gaby held the receiver away from her ear and stared at it, dumbfounded. There seemed to be a commotion on the other end with people calling out to each other. "Mrs. Fernandez, wait," she said, not sure she could be heard. "I'm calling about the *fashion show* at the Santo Marin house. You know, when the model fell in the pond."

There was another abrupt silence. "My editor," Gaby plunged on, "thought you might give me some information about the Santo Marins."

The dead air at the other end of the line was profound.

"Mrs. Fernandez?" Gaby asked.

After a long moment Alicia Fernandez said in a low, obviously strained voice, "Gabrielle, do you want to know about *Jimmy* Santo Marin? Is that what you're calling about?"

Who else could she have been calling about? "Well, yes. I have some material in front of me from a feature we did a few years ago that gives some—"

"Wait." Alicia had obviously left the telephone. When the line was picked up again she said with the same tense, almost labored politeness, "Yes, Gabrielle, what was it you wanted to know?"

In a few words Gaby explained what she needed.

"I'll tell you what I can," Alicia said with the same measured tenseness. "They're such private people, especially Estancia. She's Spanish-born, *altaclasse*. There's still that Castilian wall of *reserva*, especially since what happened last year. That poor, foolish girl Pilar." Alicia hesitated. "They've had their problems, Gabrielle, I guess I can tell you that. In spite of all the money it's been a struggle. The daughter had a terrible experience. Her engagement to one of the Dodges from Palm Beach was called off. He jilted her because I think his family wasn't happy with— with Latins. Estancia took it particularly hard."

"Oh," Gaby said, not knowing what else to say.

"Yes, but, Gabrielle," the other woman went on quickly, "people don't realize what something like that means to a girl from Pilar's background, to be dumped by a man. Even in these days."

Gaby crossed out what she had written. A broken engagement, even with a Palm Beach socialite, probably didn't go into the sidebar Jack Carty wanted. "Mrs. Fernandez, actually what I need is something about James Santo Marin. We're using a photograph of him from the fashion show, when he pulled the model out of the pond. For instance, what do people in Miami's Latin community think of him, his leadership now, his . . . uh, position socially?" Gaby was having difficulty even talking about James Santo Marin. She was strangely breathless again. "I heard they—why do they call him the Prince of Coral Gables?"

"Oh, *Jimmy*." Alicia's voice altered, "Don't call him the prince thing, Gabrielle, he hates it. As for leadership in the Latin community..." She hesitated again. "Of course Jimmy's been fantastically successful, but then he's something of a genius with all those businesses and the bank. But I couldn't say that he's a community leader actually, so much as, well, the community is... that is, many people are sort of—*protective*. No, I'm sure I don't mean 'protective' exactly, Gabrielle. It's so hard to talk about the Latin community in Miami when there are so many different parts of it. And really, I can't speak for any of them!"

"Well, how *does* the community," Gaby asked, anxious about getting any information for the sidebar, "feel about James Santo Marin?"

There was another silence. "Well, he's—popular. I guess James Santo Marin is very popular. You could call it that."

Sort of popular but sort of protected. Gaby was following something that eluded her. As did, actually, the whole subject of James Santo Marin. It was crazy. "You said his leadership—"

"Gabrielle," Alicia interrupted, "you're not going to print any of this, are you? Estancia Santo Marin would strangle me! Besides, I'm not saying the right things. Oh, darling, you picked the wrong person to call. Look, honey, contact the Santo Marins. If they want to talk to you, they'll tell you everything you have to know!"

The click on the other end said the conversation was over.

Gaby sat looking at the microfilm machine without really seeing it. Protective? Popular? The words didn't make any sense. Not when applied to what she already knew about James Santo Marin. Not the personality that went with that tense, arrogant scowl, that electric machismo in an Armani suit, handmade shoes, silk tie, and custom-made shirt.

Gaby suddenly thought it sounded like her father.

Another spoiled, sexy, beautiful man. But for Paul Collier
there had never been enough money, not in the whole
world, not the way he spent it. Maybe, Gaby thought,
there hadn't been enough for James Santo Marin, either.

Somehow he had gotten very, very rich.

She lifted the telephone directory from its rack and
found only two listings under that name. One was in
Hialeah, the other on Eighth Street in the heart of Miami's
Little Havana. Nothing in Coral Gables. She felt a rush of
relief. Undoubtedly the Santo Marins had an unlisted
telephone number.

She closed the telephone book and put it aside. She
could use what she had in the sidebar Jack Carty wanted,
and hope that it was enough. At least an unlisted telephone number gave her an excuse not to go further. She
wrote the few lines for the sidebar and left the copy on
Jack's desk.

She glanced at the telephone, realizing with some
surprise that she needed to see Dodd. She knew if she
called him he would come downtown and take her home.
She was suddenly depressed and needed to talk to somebody *normal*. She was deathly tired of the Santo Marins,
the sidebar, newspapering. She wanted not to have to
think about any of it for a long time. Like until tomorrow.
She could leave a message in photographic for Crissette
about her ride.

She had just lifted the receiver when the door to the
microfilm room swung open. A tall, slim, pretty black
woman in a tailored denim shirt, matching skirt, and gold
bangle earrings stood there with both hands on her hips,
surveying her unhappily.

"Gabrielle," Crissette said, "I've got a problem."

Chapter 6

"*I*'m kicking that turkey out!" Crissette exploded. "He thinks he's going to come home with me tonight. But I told him, you lose another job, man, you are out in the street!"

He, Gaby knew, was David Fothergill, the photographer's live-in boyfriend. From what Crissette had told her the relationship was a stormy one, mostly because David was chronically unemployed.

Crissette tucked Gaby's hand under her arm as they went down in the elevator to the lobby. "I'm glad I'm giving you a lift home, honey. I need somebody around when I go out to my car. Mister Wonderful said he was going to meet me outside after work, but I already know the message. He's out of a job again."

"Crissette," Gaby said, trying to pull her hand away, "you and David go on if you want to talk. You don't have to take me home." There was still time, she thought, to call Dodd and have him pick her up. She was hungry and the idea of dinner in some quiet, elegant place that only Dodd could afford was appealing.

But Crissette hung onto her determinedly. "That cat works for a couple of months, and then he finds out that if anybody's going to get laid off it's the ones the company's paying off the books, under the table. You know, who haven't got working papers. Especially if they think immi-

gration is going to come around the construction site and
stage a raid."

The elevator doors slid back and they stepped out
into the lobby. Gaby had seen David Fothergill only once,
a towering, soft-spoken islander with a brilliant smile.

"You mean, he hasn't got working papers?" she asked.
She was being steered to the outer door by Crissette's grip
on her elbow. "You mean your—that David is here *illegally*?"

The other woman snorted. "Honey, ain't everybody?
Gabrielle, this is *Miami*."

Gaby hung back. If Crissette's boyfriend was an illegal alien he could be arrested, she supposed, at any
moment. "Crissette, I think you better leave me out of
this. I'll—I'll just take a cab home."

Crissette wasn't listening. "My family is just raising
pure hell with me about him, and they're right. That
good-for-nothing dude is taking me for free food and free
rent! If David could swing it, he'd marry me so he could
get his green card. That's all those calypso cats are looking
for, anyway."

The humid summer night was soggy. In the newspaper's parking area a tangible veil of water drops hung
suspended in the air like fog. As Crissette pulled Gaby
along, looking for her car, Gaby couldn't believe what she
was hearing.

"He wants his *green card*?"

"Yeah, honey. If he marries a US citizen he gets to be
a legal resident. He can work steady without having to
run." The slender black woman steered her toward the
front line of cars facing the street. "My mother keeps
telling me, 'Crissette, you went to college, got a degree, a
good job on a big newspaper, just to end up with *him*?
Some bum from the islands like you can find anyplace in
downtown Miami at night, sleeping in doorways?'"

She stopped, hands on hips, looking around. "My
mother's been teaching history in the Dade County school
system for twenty years, Gabrielle. I got one brother
who's a CPA, another one who's a social worker in Fort
Lauderdale. You know what they say to me? 'Girl, what
happened to that nice intern at Miami Beach-Mount Sinai

who was so crazy about you last year? Now that cat had a future!'"

Crissette gave an abrupt scream. "I see you there!" She darted forward. "Get out of here, David!"

The muscular young man in a muddy white T-shirt, muddier jeans, and work boots, and wearing a bright blue hard hat, came out of the shadows by Crissette's Fiero GT. Gaby was sure David Fothergill had heard every word.

"'Lo, dah-leen," he greeted Crissette in his soft, lilting Trinidad accent. He gave a formal duck of his head to Gaby.

"Dump it, man," Crissette snarled. She pushed Gaby toward the passenger side of the Fiero. "You're gonna tell me they didn't even have time to pay you off, right?"

He sighed. "Honey lamb, I told you. The immigration people come up to the site with buses, they was ready to catch us and haul us away. Me, the others who got no papers, we just run like hell."

He laughed, showing white teeth, but Crissette pushed past him angrily. He followed her. "I ran back streets, back alley all the way to Miami Springs, with no time to stop to clean up, get the mud off me." He paused and looked down mournfully at his jeans and tight-fitting shirt. "And no money, love," he murmured. "I'm sorry."

Crissette opened the door to the car. "You're not coming home with me," she said in a fierce whisper. She was full of fury, her dark eyes flashing. "I told you that on the phone."

He gave her a pleading look. "Dah-leen, don't talk like that. Just let me explain."

Tactfully, Gaby turned away. She walked around the front of the Fiero, realizing that David was in love with Crissette. Unless he was a consummate actor, it was written all over him. And, Gaby had to admit, there was something in Crissette's strident anger that sounded as though she knew it, too, and was fighting it.

Gaby leaned against the hood of the car, feeling exhausted. Most people's lives were a tangled mess. She hadn't done too well herself. She wondered what Dodd was doing.

The August night was oppressive after the newspaper offices' chill air-conditioning, but the city around them was sparkling. To the south, lighted glass towers rose against a black sky. Music drifted from an all-night coffee shop in the next block, a Ruben Blades rock-blues-jazz-Latin tune, "Buscando America." The street was deserted except for a long black car that had just pulled up to the curb and stopped, headlights on, its motor running.

Thinking of the coffee shop made Gaby even hungrier. She started to walk slowly down the sidewalk, trying not to listen to the couple arguing loudly behind her. Reading about James Santo Marin had depressed her. So why couldn't she just forget it? Why worry about someone who'd found a particularly loathsome way to get rich?

The black limousine idling across the street was a custom-built stretch Cadillac, probably driven by a chauffeur. Since the windows were tinted Gaby couldn't really tell. Perhaps it was waiting to pick up someone from the *Times-Journal,* she thought. But not Gardner Hedison. The publisher had gone home hours ago. Yet it was possible somebody had a late date. A *rich* late date.

A rich late date? She mentally ran through all the newsroom personnel, including the food editor and even the rewrite desk, and rejected them all. When she came to dour Jack Carty, the idea that the features editor might have a wealthy lover in a Cadillac was so ludicrous she almost smiled.

Then she frowned. Actually, she mused, a long black limousine had been in the same place the night before. It had left abruptly when she'd gotten into her car to go home. She also remembered that she'd had to wait when she was pulling out of the parking lot to let it pass. Feeling a little chill of apprehension shiver down her spine, she turned back toward the lighted parking area, quickening her step.

There was no reason, she told herself, to think someone inside the car was watching her. But now that she thought about it, the black Cadillac, or one that looked exactly like it, *had* pulled into that same space, just past the corner of Fiftieth and Biscayne Boulevard, the night before at approximately the same time, nine-thirty. And two nights before that it had been sitting there when she came out of the *Times-Journal* building. Why hadn't she paid attention to it before this?

Gaby broke into a little trot. She wasn't frightened, she told herself, she just wanted to hurry. But wasn't it true that you could literally feel someone's eyes on you when you were being watched?

She was not going to run, she thought. She could see David and Crissette from there. She was not going to do anything crazy. But her thoughts were churning. If she had witnessed some sort of deal that afternoon at the fashion show and the Colombians thought she was a newspaper reporter—a *real* newspaper reporter—what would they do? And how about James Santo Marin, rich, powerful, inscrutable. Was that his limousine? Would he sit there at night, waiting for her to get off work, not making himself known?

Gaby cut around Crissette's Fiero at a run. The photographer and the Trinidadian stopped their arguing as she skidded to a halt. "Let's get out of here," she gasped. "That car is following me." When they only stared at her she almost yelled, "It was here last night too!"

Crissette and David turned toward the street. As they did, the limousine's motor revved up and the car slid away from the curb. Without undue speed it continued down Fiftieth Street, around the corner onto Biscayne Boulevard, and disappeared.

"There's somebody in that Cadillac following me." Gaby was beginning to feel like a lunatic. "It's been here three nights this week and I didn't even notice it. Let's go before they come back!" She took Crissette's arm and tried to pull her to the door of the Fiero. "Please, please," she begged her. "Let's get out of here!"

The other woman looked amazed. "What's with you anyway? Are you seeing drug dealers again?"

"Yes. No! They've been watching me. Either that, or I'm losing my mind! Can't we—"

"Gabrielle, are you trying to drive me nuts?" Crissette

freed herself. "You're working too hard, baby, but you just can't freak out like this."

David Fothergill put himself between them. "Easy, love." He took advantage of the moment to open the Fiero's passenger door and shove Gaby into the back seat. Then he jumped into the front himself and slammed the door.

"Oh, no, you don't!" Crissette shouted. "David, you get out of there!"

He stuck his head out of the window, smiling angelically. "Dah-leen, I got to get my clothes and things from your house, don't I now? Let's take lovely Miss Collier home first."

Gaby leaned over David's shoulder to the front window. "Crissette, *please!*"

"I'm going to kill you, David," the photographer said between her teeth. But she went around to the driver's side and got in.

The Fiero sped down Biscayne Avenue to the causeway with Crissette at the wheel, flying through a number of traffic lights just turning red. Gaby huddled in the back seat, hardly noticing. She knew she'd just made a fool of herself in the newspaper parking lot, but at this point it didn't seem to matter.

"Anything's possible, love," David was saying. "Now, Miss Gabrielle say she sees two men in a garden making a drug deal—"

Crissette cut him off. "The whole thing's in Gabrielle's head. It was a fashion show, man, *a fashion show*. Drug pushers are not going to be making deals in the woods while the biggest *latino* society bash of the summer is going on, with photographers and reporters crawling all over the place. Gabrielle's got a case of culture shock from being in Europe too long."

He shook his head. "Love, in Miami drug dealing is all over, you can find it anywhere."

"Listen, you don't know how strung out this girl is." Crissette looked at Gaby in the rearview mirror. "She comes back home and finds out her family's money's all

gone, her mother has a terminal drinking problem, and
she has to find work quick to keep them off welfare.
Gabrielle is a nice chick, but she hasn't got any self-
confidence. She's seeing things."

"I'm not neurotic," Gaby said listlessly.

"I didn't say that, did I?" The other woman stared
hard at her in the mirror. "What you saw at the Santo
Marin place was a Cuban and a Colombian doing something you didn't understand. But Gabrielle, in a newspaper job you see a lot of strange things. You can't let your
imagination run away with you. If you do, you're in big
trouble."

"But they *did* look like they were involved in some
sort of a deal." Gaby was tempted to go ahead and blurt
out everything. But, she reminded herself, David was
there.

"Forget the whole thing, will you?" Crissette sped
through another red light near the port of Miami. "Just go
home and get a good night's sleep."

Gaby sank back into the seat. She was turning over in
her mind the idea of telling Crissette about James Santo
Marin's visit. How he had arrived in a huge power cruiser
in the midst of a thunderstorm to threaten her. And then
started to make love to her, yet stopped. She bit her lip.
Not a wise move. Crissette already thought she was pretty
strung out.

"Gabrielle, honey," Crissette went on more gently,
"you shouldn't let Jack Carty and the newsroom staff bug
you. They do it to everybody." She turned onto the old
Palm Island bridge with its concrete balustrades and
1920's-style globe lampposts. "How's your mother? Things
any better?"

James Santo Marin had warned her that she hadn't
seen anything that afternoon in Coral Gables. On the
other hand, why would he come to her house in the
middle of a raging storm just to tell her that, unless she
had seen something important? Was it James Santo Marin
in the big Cadillac? Gaby knew he was dangerous. Could
he be unbalanced? Oh God, a drug user himself? She

closed her eyes for a moment. "My mother's not much better. If you mean the drinking."

The Fiero turned into Royal Palm Way, tires screeching, and stopped abruptly at the Collier front door in a shower of crushed shell.

"Lord, what a beautiful house." Crissette leaned out the car window to look at the shadowy Moorish-Spanish outlines of the old mansion. In the moonlight, the towers, tangled bougainvillea vines clinging to the stucco, and myriad wrought-iron balconies were mysterious. "Even if it does look like the Munsters live here." She turned to Gabrielle in the back seat. "Let David see you to the door, hon."

David didn't move. "I been think-een, love, maybe you should ask our Miss Gabrielle why someone could be following her. Those two men in the garden could have been dealing drugs, yes. It's possible."

Crissette glared at him. "Will you stay out of this?"

But David Fothergill's expression said that he, at least, took Gaby seriously. "If things keep happening," he told her, "you keep track. Like, if anybody bothers you, Miss Gabrielle, you let me know."

He got out of the car and helped her from the backseat. "You don't have to see me to the door," she said. "I'll be all right. And thanks for the ride."

They waited as she walked the few feet to the front door. Just before the entranceway she ducked under the overgrown hibiscus bushes. As she did, she almost stumbled over something lying on the path.

She bent, peering in the moonlight, trying to see what it was. "Jupiter? What are you doing here?"

The old Labrador lay stretched out on the path, his body flattened, legs extended in a curious attitude.

She supposed she already knew Jupiter was dead before she touched him. His fur felt dusty, lifeless. Gaby fell to one knee with a muffled cry. There was a cord around the dog's neck, twisted tightly.

She lurched back to her feet. Instead of turning back to the car where Crissette and David were still waiting, she ran up the front steps and pushed at the door so she could reach into the hall and turn on the outside light. She had to look at Jupiter. He couldn't be dead. Not with a twisted cord around his neck. There was some mistake.

The door wouldn't yield. Something inside was holding it shut. Numbly, she bent to look through the letter slot. A body was lying on the floor just beyond.

Her mother, she realized, peering through the slit into murky dimness. Something had happened to her mother too.

Chapter 7

$\mathcal{G}$aby sat on the living room couch beside Crissette, listening to Detective Sergeant Antonio Lopez tell Dodd Brickell what the police had found. It was the third or fourth time Detective Lopez had gone through his summary, once to Gaby and Crissette and at least once over the telephone to headquarters, and Gaby's head was pounding. She really wanted to ask Crissette about David Fothergill, but when she turned to the photographer, Crissette gave her a warning look and shook her head no.

Gaby sighed. She supposed Crissette was right. It was no time to discuss David, not with the police around. Crissette had hustled the big Trinidadian out of the house before the patrol car arrived, and Gaby wondered if David was lurking around somewhere on Palm Island. And whether some of the more security-conscious residents, seeing a gigantic man in muddy clothes and a hard hat who obviously didn't belong there, would call the police. She choked back an unhappy urge to giggle. All the police, the squad car with two uniformed policemen and another car that had brought two plainclothes detectives from the robbery detail, were right there, in the Collier house. They probably couldn't answer another call in the neighborhood if they wanted to.

Crissette heard the muffled sound. "Let me get you a drink," she whispered. "You look like you need it."

Gaby shook her head. *Drink* was a dirty word in the

Collier household. To find a bottle of booze they'd have to ask her mother. And Jeannette was in no condition to tell them anything.

"God," Crissette muttered under her breath, "I wish this was over." Across the room a policeman and the Brickell family doctor, whom Dodd had called, were leaning over Jeannette Collier. She was propped upright in one of the *sala's* faded armchairs. "Let them take her to the hospital," Crissette said to Gaby. "Just tell them."

"She doesn't want to go." Gaby was so tired she was light-headed. Fright, revulsion, the awful excitement of the police searching her house for intruders, had drained her. "You heard what the doctor said. He can't forcibly admit her. Maybe," she added, not really caring anymore, "Dodd can reason with Mother."

Jeannette, they'd discovered, was not injured in any way, only drunk enough to pass out in the front hall by the door. According to the police, her mother might have heard a disturbance outside and gone to see what it was. Now, conscious but hardly sober, Jeannette was making life miserable for anybody who tried to persuade her to go to the hospital, even overnight for observation.

Dodd was waiting, Gaby knew, to tell her that this was their chance, at last, to get her mother hospitalized for an evaluation and possibly treatment. Gaby supposed it was, but at that moment it was wildly unreal to be sitting in the living room at well past midnight, surrounded by uniformed policemen, detectives, the ambulance crew, the Brickell family doctor, listening to Detective Lopez explain to Dodd what the police believed had happened. From what she gathered, it was all being blamed on the Escuderos, Elena and her son Angel.

The night was still sweltering. Detective Lopez, in a rumpled business suit, was perspiring slightly. He'd learned, early on, that the call to investigate a suspected breaking-and-entering involved two employees of Miami's second largest newspaper—one of whom was the daughter of the once very well-known Paul Collier—and an angry family friend who had just driven up to find out what in the hell was going on.

Detective Lopez had instantly recognized the family
friend as an influential Miami lawyer and businessman,
the son of a former city councilman, a partner in one of the
city's most prestigious law firms, and a descendant of a
Florida pioneer family that had virtually founded Old
Miami society. Dodson Brickell III also had an honorary
VIP police pass. And he was, he told Detective Lopez
immediately, shocked, angry, and disturbed about the
effect of the night's events on Mrs. Collier and her daughter. Especially the business about the dead dog.

"We run into this every once in a while," the detective explained. "Last year we had a regular epidemic. It
turned out to be some sort of fight between rival priestesses."

He looked across the brightly lit *sala* to where his
partner, Detective Andriado, was kneeling beside the
living room coffee table, putting chicken feathers taken
from the Colliers' back door into small plastic sandwich
bags. The alleged victim, Mrs. Jeannette Collier, was
sitting up in the armchair as the doctor checked her blood
pressure again.

"Usually," Detective Lopez went on, "the complaints
are about the goats and chickens and stuff used in the—ah,
the rituals. The Department of Health forwards them to
the Miami P.D., and then we go in and clean out the
premises where the alleged problem exists."

Dodd only stared at him. The detective continued, a
little uncomfortably. "Officially the city's attitude is that
Santería, voodoo, *shango*, whatever these people want to
practice is harmless, just so long as it doesn't create a
health hazard."

"You call this harmless?" Dodd was incredulous.
"Women scared out of their wits, the house smeared with
blood and garbage, a family pet strangled?"

"Allegedly strangled," the detective corrected him.
"Mrs. Collier's not able to state that she heard or saw
anything. The dog wasn't a nuisance, there've been no
complaints from the neighbors, so we can probably rule
out that someone would want to do away with it."

Gaby watched the second detective stack his sandwich bags in an ordinary brown paper grocery bag. There

had been chicken feathers and blood smeared all over the sun porch door, but the police had found no evidence of forced entry. No one had come inside the house and nothing, as far as anyone knew, was missing. Her mother was not hurt, only embarrassingly drunk.

"Nobody around here would kill an old dog," Dodd said. "People know the Colliers. They don't have any enemies." He gazed around the room. "What the hell else did you find?"

Detective Lopez indicated the sun porch. "You can look outside if you want to. They killed the chicken, spattered the blood and feathers out there."

Gaby wrapped her arms around her body and shivered. It had been hours since she'd had anything to eat and she was exhausted. She was still worried about David Fothergill. When the police had arrived, they'd asked for her identification and Crissette's, even their *Times-Journal* employee passes and their driver's licenses, almost before they did anything else. If David had been there they would have arrested him, surely, as an illegal alien.

She could hear Detective Lopez on the sun porch explaining that the black chicken feathers and blood were being taken downtown to Miami police laboratories to be tested, but there was no reason to believe it was other than what it appeared to be—animal blood, not human. And they were certain now Mrs. Collier's collapse was due to alcohol intoxication, not foul play.

Gaby wanted to put her hands over her ears. She knew what was coming next. Detective Lopez was going to tell Dodd that Jupiter's death and the bloody mess at the back door probably somehow involved the Escuderos living in the garage apartment.

Santería. She'd heard of it before. After all, she'd grown up in Miami. In Little Havana there were shops called *botánicas* full of plaster statues and ingredients for voodoo charms, but she had never paid much attention to something so far removed from her own world. It was nothing short of grotesque to find it there, now, in her own house on Palm Island.

Worse, Elena and Angel Escudero were gone. An

examination of the garage apartment showed they had
taken a few clothes with them, but not much else.

Detective Lopez came back into the living room.
Dodd, wearing jeans and an old jogging top he'd obviously
thrown on when Gaby had called him, followed, looking
angry and frustrated.

"It's voodoo with the Haitians," Detective Lopez was
telling him. "Everybody knows what that is, I guess, from
the movies. We have problems with that too. The Cubans
and Puerto Ricans are into *Santería*. The Jamaicans and
the other islanders practice what they call *shango*. Down
in Brazil they tell me it's *macumba*. It's all related."

Dodd rumbled a question Gaby couldn't hear. "Not
me," the detective said quickly. "I'm third-generation
American. I don't even speak Spanish. But you'd be
surprised at the people who really believe in this stuff."

Crissette took Gaby's hand in hers. "Tired? They look
like they're winding it up."

Gaby watched the second police detective pick up
more bloodstained black chicken feathers from his pile and
stick them one by one into yet another plastic bag. She
fought down the same feeling of panic she'd had when
she'd seen the black limousine pull away from the curb a
few hours ago.

No one would believe any of this, she thought. She
needed so badly to confide in someone without sounding
like a mental case. Luckily, she'd known better than to
blurt out anything about drug dealers and being followed
to Detective Lopez.

Now she wasn't so sure even telling Dodd was such a
good idea. His reaction would probably be the same as
Crissette's: a comment about how hard she'd been working
and worrying about her job, about her mother. That she'd
been under lots of stress. And that people saw strange
things every day in Miami.

"Ordinarily," Detective Lopez went on, "you wouldn't
find *Santería* in a residential area like this. Except, of
course, that there are Hispanics living on this property.

Dodd scowled at him. "What's that supposed to mean?"

The detective's expression was bland. "Well, *Santería*

is used for a lot of things. Revenge, coercion, threats, sometimes just a spell to get lucky and win at the horse races or jai alai. Or a lover. The bad stuff, like the black feathers and chicken blood, is supposed to be very powerful. The red cord used to strangle the dog is really big magic. Something like this isn't for an amateur. A *santera*, the priest or priestess, usually sets it up."

Dodd rubbed his forehead, exasperated. "There ought to be some law to take care of this nonsense!"

"For some of these people it's a religion, Mr. Brickell. Any law against it would be a violation of the Bill of Rights. Freedom of worship, specifically." Detective Lopez turned away. "Anyway, even if the mother and the boy show up there's nothing to charge them with. They might have been the targets, not the perpetrators."

Dodd planted his hands on his hips, his big head thrust forward. "I never see a damned police patrol car out here on Palm Island. If you people can't get a regular patrol in here to keep this from happening again, I'll damned well go through the mayor's office."

The patrolman and the detective exchanged looks. "Mr. Brickell," Detective Lopez said, "I'll be glad to file a report of trespassing and malicious mischief by person or persons unknown. I'll even leave a number where I can be reached if Mrs. Collier and her daughter are bothered again. I don't know about a regular patrol out here, but in my judgment if the Cubans are gone, they probably took the problem with them."

"That's not good enough."

Detective Lopez actually smiled. "I'll tell you one thing I can do. If Miss Collier can find a plastic garbage bag, I'll have one of the officers put the dog in it. Just leave it out by the curb and Animal Control will pick it up in the morning."

When she and Gaby were finally alone, Crissette was adamant. "I don't want to hear it, Gabrielle." They were sitting at the kitchen table drinking hot tea in the hope it would help them to sleep. "I don't want to hear about drug dealers and you being followed by weirdos in big

black limousines. What you got here," she said decisively,
"is a bunch of crazy Cubans playing with voodoo. You told
the detective yourself, you and your mother offered to let
some of the Marielitos live here years ago through the
church program. You know there's no connection with all
that stuff that's been bugging you. Unless you really are a
paranoid chick."

Gaby knew Crissette didn't mean it, but the intima-
tion that this might just all exist in her head was making
her feel worse. Shock, horror—it had all had its effect on
her. During the past few hours while the police filled the
house, she had had wild thoughts about the men who
dealt in drugs who might have done this obscene thing to
frighten her, to seal her lips about what she'd seen in the
Santo Marins' garden.

Or, she thought with a shudder, it might have been
James Santo Marin himself.

Before she could answer Crissette, they heard David
Fothergill scratching at the kitchen door.

"You must have been watching the house," Crissette
said, letting him in, "to get here this quick."

"I'm develop-een skills, love, I never knew I had."
The big Trinidadian came into the kitchen, smiling his
good-natured smile. Which faded when he saw Gaby
sitting with her head propped in her hand, staring numbly
into space. "How's lovely Miss Gabrielle? She all right?"

Crissette rummaged in the cabinets for another cup.
"We just got back from the hospital. I asked some creep in
admitting to give Gabrielle some sleeping pills, but he
wouldn't do it."

"I'm all right," Gaby said. "I'm just too tired to be
sleepy, that's all."

David eased himself into a kitchen chair. "It was a
very bad thing, this. I'm sorry it happened to you. How is
your mother?"

"All right. She'll be in the hospital overnight for
observation." Gaby was still trying to come to terms with
her last sight of her mother, looking strangely old and
wasted against the white sheets of the hospital bed. "Crissette
is going to stay here tonight. It was the only way we could

get rid of Dodd." When he looked at her inquiringly, she said, "The man you call my boyfriend."

"Good," he said promptly, "I'll stay, too."

Crissette whirled on him. "Now wait a minute, David—"

"I'll sleep downstairs on the sofa." He kept grinning. "There is a sofa, yes, lovely Miss Gabrielle?"

Dodd had tried hard to persuade Gaby to spend the night at his condominium in town. He'd only given in when Crissette volunteered to sleep over. Now Gaby found the idea of big, soft-spoken David Fothergill staying downstairs strangely comforting.

"Is Dodd the big man who came in the Porsche car?" David asked. "He looks very rich, love."

"I grew up with him." It was beyond Gaby, at the moment, to explain about Dodd. "He's an old childhood friend."

"But not a lover?"

"David, will you leave her alone?" Crissette said. "I'm trying to get her calmed down so we can all go to sleep."

Gaby looked at David through a fog of fatigue. She had always loved Dodd. It was impossible to think of him any other way, and it was too hard to explain. "David," she asked softly, "do they have voodoo in Trinidad?"

For a moment he looked startled. "Ah, so they know what the blood and the feathers mean, the police."

"You knew right away, didn't you? You knew when you saw poor old Jupiter. Oh, David, why didn't you *say* something?"

He glanced at Crissette. "I thought somebody only plays jokes," he said uneasily, "notheen serious."

"David, they killed my dog!" Gaby burst out. "Don't you call that serious? The detective said it was because somebody was trying to put black magic on the Escuderos, the Cuban family who live over the garage."

"Do not say black magic," he said quickly. "That could mean anything. This is African religion, very old, very mysterious."

"Tell her about it," Crissette said, dropping wearily into a chair. "She still thinks it's drug dealers."

"It is real religion," David said almost somberly. "In the bad old days when the slaves were brought to the islands they want to worship their own gods, but the white masters say no, that is dangerous, they don't like it. Then black people worship their gods in secret because the white masters punish them very severely if they don't be Christian."

David pulled the cup of tea toward him. "Must we drink hot tea, love, in this very warm weather? Have you no cold bottle of beer, not even a little one?"

Crissette gave him a hard look. "Water or tea, man, take it or leave it."

He sighed and lifted his cup. "In Haiti, the priests of voodoo had to hide in the forest, play the big drums that call the gods to come down. So the voodoo it stay in the hills very hidden from the white man. But in Cuba the slaves are more clever. They don't go into the woods. They take the Catholic saints from the churches and make them same as their old gods. So if the white masters come around looking for African religion, the slaves say they are doing nothing wrong, only praying nicely to Saint Barbara, Saint Lazarus, the Holy Virgin, all of them. But the Cubans will tell you Saint Barbara is really Chango, who is god of fire and lightning. Saint Lazarus is Babalu-ai-ey, the healer of the sick. And the Holy Virgin is sometimes Oshun, the goddess of love and money, and sometimes Yemaya, who is Mother Goddess. Depending if she is Nuestra Señora de la Caridad or la Señora del Asunción."

Both women were staring at him. Crissette said, "Man, you don't believe in all that, do you?"

"But they do practice black magic, don't they?" Gaby said quickly. "The detective said killing poor old Jupe was some sort of spell, to threaten the Escuderos."

David lifted his eyebrows. "I don't know none of that, love. *Santería* is not a Christian religion, it is African, and the gods are very different." He looked away. "The *iyalochas,* the priestesses, will make spells and charms for you that be sometimes good, like if you want luck to gamble. Or sometimes bad, if you want to hurt an enemy."

"David, you jungle bunny," Crissette sputtered, "you

were really into this down in Trinidad, weren't you?" She reached over and grabbed his cup and saucer. "My family's right, I must have been out of my mind to ever have anything to do with you!"

"Please, you two." Gaby couldn't bear to listen to them wrangling again. "Do you suppose Angel and his mother were in some sort of trouble," she said musingly, "and we didn't know anything about it? I wish they had said something. Maybe we could have helped."

Suddenly, she couldn't hold back a convulsive yawn. She looked at them sheepishly. "I'd better look for some clean sheets so we can make up a bed for David down here." When Crissette turned to her, frowning, Gaby said, "I want David to stay. I'd really feel a lot safer with him down here."

Crissette looked around one of the Colliers' usually closed-up guest bedrooms, this one with Scalamandré gauze curtains that were virtually rags, and a Louis XIV four-poster bed with a tufted satin spread.

"This is some place, Gabrielle," she said appreciatively. "It blows my mind. I'd like to get in here sometime and set up my cameras, do a photo-essay on this old house." She fingered the satin spread thoughtfully. "And maybe some others on Palm and Star islands, too."

Gaby yawned again, her eyes drooping. "My mother loves satin and mirrors. This room used to have a wall-to-wall white fur rug. My father always said the upstairs bedrooms were decorated in 'Jean Harlow Ultra-Baroque.'"

Crissette kicked off her shoes and sat on the edge of the bed. "It would be kind of strange to live in. Listen, if you get scared, Gabrielle, you can come sleep in here with me. Or I'll go down to your room, it doesn't matter."

"Scared?" Gaby hadn't even considered it. "I think I'm so exhausted I've blanked out. I'm not feeling a thing."

Crissette followed her to the door and stood there, watching as she went to her own bedroom down the hall. "If anything bothers you, Gabrielle," she called after her, "just yell."

* * *

Once in bed, Gaby shut her eyes, positive sleep would come quickly, she was so tired.

It didn't.

The box fan in the window whirred noisily, sucking in the moist night air from the bay. The bedsheets were sticky and burdensome. Finally, after tossing and turning for a good part of an hour, she threw the cover back and lay there with her old batiste nightgown pulled up to her hips, one arm thrown over her eyes.

Time seemed interminable in the breathless dark. Gaby rolled over and looked at the luminous dial of the bedside clock. It was quarter to four.

Groaning, she got up and crossed the Spanish tile floor that was delightfully cool to her bare feet, then closed the blinds so the light of the full moon wouldn't fall across her bed. As she stretched out again she told herself, Stop thinking about poor old Jupiter.

The restless exhaustion was like a fever. Sometimes it seemed her body would never adjust to being back home again, to Florida's humid heat. But Italy had been almost as hot, she thought fretfully. What was the matter with her?

Voodoo. Santería.

She rolled over onto her stomach. The blood in her temples was throbbing. When she closed her eyes it was strong enough to make the whole darkened room vibrate. Like hearing one's own heart thrumming and pumping, magnified a thousand times.

Gaby knew in some curious way she'd fallen asleep. She was back in Florence, in her room in the *pensione* on the Via Strattore, above the street where the little Vespa motor scooters always woke her in the morning with their popping and thundering. Motorbike engines had that same pounding beat.

She knew, after a while, that she was lying in someone's arms and he was holding her tightly. His body was muscular and warm, his satiny skin irresistibly sensual, but his heart was beating so loudly that she tried to pull away from him. Every inch of her reacted to the feel of that desirous power, the hard pressure of him against her.

There was such a desperation in him, a sense of need, that it frightened her. He wanted her. She knew that without being told.

Whoever he was, he held her as though he would never let her go, so close, so desiring, she felt the warmth of his breath against her lips. That terrible desperation that she sensed in him grew, and with it her fear. No one could want, could *need* someone else as fatally as this! A smothering, breathless feeling of pure panic attacked her again.

No, she cried out soundlessly as she struggled.

Suddenly a strange roaring that seemed to come from a leaping ring of fire burst into the dream. The sound crashed through her, overriding the measured sound of her heartbeat, a skull-bursting scream. A dazzling flickering like lightning. The shriek of violently compressed air.

It brought Gaby awake, bolt upright in bed, a barely stifled scream on her lips.

She was home, she realized, shaking. In her own bedroom. She was wringing wet. Bright slivers of moonlight spilled through the blinds and across the sheets. What had she been doing dreaming of Florence, she wondered groggily, of motor scooters? Of someone who wanted her, with arms like steel bands that wouldn't let her go? Of something that screamed like airplane jet engines?

Then she listened. The hot dark night quivered faintly. It was not the wind, nor a window fan. Nor the refrigerator downstairs. But it was there, thrumming in the walls.

She swung her feet over the edge of the bed and padded out into the hall, the gallery above the *sala grande*. She was following the strange beating, drumming sensation that seemed to hang in the sultry air.

Down below, David was sleeping on the couch. She could make out the tumbled white sheets and the shape of his big body in the moonlight.

Shivering, her arms wrapped around her, she tried to tell herself that she'd had a nightmare. But if she'd been dreaming, why did that mesmerizing half sound, half mental throbbing go on, now that she was awake?

There was a scent, too, stronger here in the gallery. Burnt wood, green jungle. Sunshine. Hot, pungent cooked food.

She saw David stir, open his eyes, and look straight up into the darkness. In one abrupt, catlike movement he slid from the couch and to his feet. He wore his jeans, his upper body gleaming bare and muscular. He slowly turned to gaze up at her as though he'd known where to look, perhaps even whom to look for, there in the middle of the night.

Gaby stared down at him. There was a gleam, almost forbidding, in his shadowed eyes. She knew how she appeared to him at the gallery railing, in a ragged old nightgown, her hair drifting around her shoulders, bathed in the light of the bright full moon.

The faint throbbing like jungle drums enveloped them. The scent grew stronger, evoking tropical islands and the sea. And hot, baking landscapes. With a thrill of fear Gaby knew that David heard it, smelled it, too.

"David," she whispered. The vast room echoed her words. "This has nothing to do with the Escuderos. It's directed toward *me*, isn't it?"

He didn't have to answer. She could see from his expression that she was right.

Chapter 8

*T*he bumper sticker on the car ahead had a picture of the Stars and Stripes and read: WOULD THE LAST AMERICAN TO LEAVE MIAMI PLEASE BRING THE FLAG?

Crissette swung the newspaper's rental car onto Miami Beach's thoroughfare, Collins Avenue. "I haven't seen one of those stickers in a long time," she said, "but I'm not surprised. *Anti-latino* feeling just doesn't lie down and die in this town. It's not only rednecks, either. The black community has a lot of problems with Hispanics, too."

Gaby stared out the window at the renovated hotels and apartment buildings of the Miami Beach National Historical District. It might seem presumptuous to declare "historic" the area that stretched north on Collins Avenue, an improbable vista of 1940's lavender, pastel pink, lime green and baby blue. But the Beach had done it, and immortalized its garish art deco buildings. "Maybe there's just too many Latin Americans," she said thoughtfully, "for one city to absorb."

Crissette shook her head. "Hey, *latinos* work hard and believe in the American Dream—like all of us used to, once. And not," she added, "like this cat we're going to interview this morning, General Rodolfo Bachman, the South American politician-you-most-love-to-hate." She shook her head again. "I'll bet you the *Times-Journal* is going to get a bunch of hate mail just for interviewing him."

"His wife," Gaby corrected her, staring through the

89

windshield as a hotel in beige and magenta with chrome trim flashed by. "I'm going to interview Señora Bachman about her shopping trip and the clothes she bought here, not the general."

General Rodolfo Bachman was notorious for torture of political prisoners under his country's past regimes. But he was admired, unfortunately, by a good number of right-wing U.S. congressmen. When the general stayed at the Fontainebleau Hilton Miami Beach, his party took up two hotel floors and included half a hundred aides, staffers, and bodyguards.

Gaby looked at her wristwatch. "Crissette, we're running awfully late."

The photographer promptly stepped down on the gas pedal. "Don't worry, honey. This fascist pig is running on 'Latin time.' Ten o'clock sharp means ten-thirty or maybe eleven o'clock, depending on how long it takes everybody to eat breakfast and get dressed, do a couple of tangos, and watch the señora put on her jewelry."

Gaby's interview with Señora Constanza Bachman had nothing to do with politics. The *Times-Journal* wanted a fashion story on Señora Bachman's annual spending spree in Miami. Midsummer in the northern hemisphere was, in South America, the depths of winter. In July and August thousands of South Americans descended on Miami to enjoy the warm weather and shop for bargains in malls and department stores. Jack Carty had decided an interview with the general's wife was well worth doing, if only to have on file. Just as it would have been worthwhile doing a story on Evita Perón in her heyday.

"Good Lord," Gaby cried suddenly, "what is that?"

They were driving straight down Collins Avenue toward a gigantic marble Greco-Roman archway flanked by towering, vaguely Egyptian female statues that straddled the thoroughfare. Gaby couldn't ever remember seeing anything like that in Miami Beach.

Through the four- or five-story gateway could be seen the curving white bulk of the Fontainebleau Hilton Miami Beach and its famous swimming pool. Built to resemble the Blue Grotto of Capri, it even boasted an outsize artificial waterfall. Over the Fontainebleau in a typically azure blue Miami Beach sky floated two white puffy clouds.

Gaby gasped and clutched the dashboard with both hands as Crissette abruptly wheeled the rental car to the left. They passed the gigantic arch instead of going under it. The car doglegged a sharp right and drove up into the driveway of the real Fontainebleau Hilton and stopped.

Crissette turned and grinned at her. "I didn't think you'd seen the famous fool-the-eye mural. There's no archway there. It's a fake, painted on the side of the building."

It was, Gaby realized, a giant trick in Day-Glo colors just where Collins Avenue took a sudden left northward. It had looked exactly as though they were going to drive straight through. "Good heavens, how big is that thing, anyway?"

"I don't know, a couple of hundred feet maybe. It was Steve Muss, the hotel man's, idea." Crissette turned the car over to the Fontainebleau's uniformed parking attendant and unloaded her cameras from the trunk. "Hotel developers are into a campaign to make the Beach look like fun again. Kitsch was always high art out here. This is sort of the big bang, a gigantic mural on Collins Avenue."

Gaby followed Crissette through the Fontainebleau's crowded reception area. The garden side of the hotel was still as she remembered it, but the old lobby was now a vast room with a bar and lounge that overlooked the famous Blue Grotto swimming pool, palm garden, and artificial waterfall—just as the gigantic trompe l'oeil mural on Collins Avenue depicted it. The place was packed with noisy, expensively dressed, vacationing Venezuelans, Chileans, Argentinians, and even a number of Portuguese-speaking Brazilians.

"We go to the Dining Galleries," Crissette said, and steered Gaby in the direction of the hotel's premier restaurant.

The interview had been set up for breakfast at the not unusual hour, for South Americans, of ten A.M. But Gaby hadn't expected to find the general's party had com-

mandeered the entire restaurant. A pair of muscular bodyguards in military uniforms were at the oak doors.

Crissette pushed Gaby ahead. *"Estamos aquí,"* she
announced. *"El Miami Times-Journal,* dudes. Open the
door!"

The paramilitary guards looked over the black photographer in a lime silk jumpsuit and high heels, her camera
bag slung over one shoulder, and registered monolithic
impassiveness. *"Identificación,"* one uttered, not moving
his lips. *"Carnet."*

Gaby fumbled in her pocketbook for her press pass,
but Crissette demanded loudly, "Are you kidding, Jack?
For a bunch of you cats in *your* country maybe, but *no
aquí!"*

With an imperious sweep of her arm Crissette reached
between both men and grabbed the doorknob of the big
oak doors. Fortunately, the doors opened inward.

Over her shoulder she ordered, "Let's move it out
quick, Gabrielle."

Gaby scurried after her, holding her breath. But
Crissette's breezy authority had gotten them through. The
guards only stared, open-mouthed.

They paused at the top of the steps to the restaurant.
The Dining Galleries' decor was plum-colored velvet, with
imitation Louis XV furniture and outsize crystal chande-
liers. Each mauve damask-covered table was set for lunch,
with massive two-foot-tall silver epergnes brimming with
real fruit and tropical flowers. Life-size bronze statues of
Greek and Roman gods and goddesses stood knee-deep in
living greenery at points around the room.

At a large table littered with the remains of an
extensive breakfast, the whole Bachman family waited
expectantly: General Rodolfo Bachman in a spectacular
gold, red, and green dress uniform holding a croissant and
a cup of coffee; and beside him a small, plump woman in a
gorgeous Christian La Croix turquoise chiffon cocktail
dress with silver sequins. Standing around the general and
his wife were secretaries and aides. Beyond them were at
least twenty uniformed bodyguards. At the center of this
picturesque group were half a dozen well-dressed chil-

dren, including a toddler playing with an empty silver creamer on the restaurant's purple carpeting, and a surly-looking teenager wearing a T-shirt with a picture of a silver Rolls-Royce on the front. The Rolls's headlights were red glass, battery operated, and blinked on and off, nonstop.

"Jeez," Crissette said under her breath.

The Bachmans beamed at them happily. Crissette and Gaby stared back.

This was supposed to be, Gaby reminded herself, only an interview on what clothes the general's wife had bought this trip, but it looked like a state-of-the-union press conference. She felt her knees buckling with apprehension.

Just then a totally unknown emotion seized her. Gaby was aware that she couldn't go on like this any longer, being scared to death, immobilized by her own feelings of inadequacy. Crissette was looking at her with a concerned but impatient expression that said she might as well get her act together. Or quit.

Gaby knew at some point she had to stop expecting the worst of herself. Right now dozens of dark, gleaming South American eyes were fixed on her, waiting.

Conscious of Crissette watching, Gaby squared her shoulders.

The interview, Jack Carty confirmed later, was just one of those things reporters encounter every once in a while. The general treated his wife's fashion interview as though it were intended for world circulation. All that was missing were the television cameras. For the first time so far in her newspaper career, Gaby wasn't hamstrung by self-consciousness. The Bachmans were so strange, at least by American standards, it probably didn't matter how she wrote them up.

An interpreter, a slender, nervous young woman who spoke perfect idiomatic English, introduced herself. While Crissette set up her tripod Gaby perched on the edge of a purple velvet chair with her notepad in her lap, smiling determinedly. It was the only thing to do. The entire group was beaming back at her.

"Señora Bachman is very happy you want to interview her," the interpreter said, leaning over Gaby's shoulder. "Reporters usually only interview the general."

Gaby had to admit there was something very impressive about the Bachmans. The general might be a despotic military-political threat in his home country, but he was undeniably a big family man. When his youngest grabbed him around the knees and drooled on his impeccable trouser leg, the general picked up the baby and held him in his arms while he wiped the child's face with a mauve napkin. The teenage son, leering at Gaby lasciviously, jumped to respectful attention when his father spoke to him. And little Señora Bachman, tightly squeezed into her elegant La Croix pouf, beamed on Gaby as though she were making a lifelong dream come true.

"I'd like to start," Gaby told the interpreter, "by asking Señora Bachman her favorite places to shop in Miami."

"Señora Bachman has been to Rive Gauche at Bal Harbour and Martha's," the interpreter said promptly. "Señora Bachman also goes up to Worth Avenue in Palm Beach at least once to shop." Aides had started displaying boxes, packages, and shopping bags with expensive boutique labels.

"Señora Bachman," the interpreter went on, "is very discriminating. She likes Cardin and Dior." The aides held up an evening gown and a sweater suit. "Also Lenox china and crystal." A secretary dove for another box. "And also shoes from Gucci which is in—" The interpreter consulted a card. "The Trump Plaza of the Palm Beaches."

Speechless, Gaby wrote it all down. From time to time the plump little señora broke in to proudly tell the price of her acquisitions. If the señora was telling the truth, and Gaby had no doubt she was, the cost of her purchases sounded like the national budget.

Gaby had counted at least eight offspring milling around, and she couldn't help thinking the general's wife probably deserved a hobby. "The señora's wearing a Christian La Croix, isn't she?" she asked.

"Oh, yes," the interpreter said. "Señora Bachman

prefers only the best, the most expensive, the most exclusive fashions. She shops with exquisite taste." She raised her voice because the señora was interrupting, waving her hands and shaking her head violently.

"Señora Bachman wants to say something," Gaby pointed out.

The señora spoke rapidly, while the interpreter put in a word or two. The general interrupted, obviously displeased. Everyone stopped smiling.

Gaby watched in astonishment as the general launched into a lengthy complaint. He actually stamped up and down the restaurant, shouting. The bodyguards looked uneasy. The plump señora pursed her lips, her back straight, looking stubborn. The interpreter pleaded with them both.

The señora, Gaby saw, was the winner. Everyone started smiling happily again.

The interpreter sighed. "Señora Bachman wants you to know," she said, "that above everything else..." She looked as though she could hardly bring herself to say it. "The señora's biggest favorites are K Mart." She made a little strangling sound. "And Toys-R-Us."

When Gaby arrived for lunch at the French restaurant at the top of the Brickell Banking Tower, Dodd was already at his table. He stood up to greet her, then froze, surprise clear in his eyes.

"Am I late?" she asked breathlessly. "It looks like I'm going to spend my day in restaurants." She slid into the chair the maître d' held for her. "I've just come from the wackiest interview at the Fontainebleau, I still don't believe it. All I can hope is those people don't manage to overthrow the Argentinian government."

Dodd stared at her, napkin still clutched in his hands. Finally he signaled the waiter to bring them their menus and sat back down. "Gaby," he managed, "what have you done to yourself? You look—you look so completely different." His face showed a stunned admiration. "My God, you're incredibly lovely."

Gaby, caught up in the hurry of the Bachman interview that morning, had almost forgotten. The restaurant on the twenty-fourth floor of the Brickell Tower was surrounded by two-way mirror glass. She had only to turn her head to see her reflection: her hair cut considerably shorter, barely shoulder length, sparked with coppery highlights from the rinse she'd let herself be talked into in the Mayfair Mall salon.

"I forgot to tell you." She couldn't bring herself to mention the "expense" allotment for the fashion writer. The new coral linen suit, its unstructured jacket worn over a flowered shirt, was pure summertime Miami, tropical, blindingly bright. The lipstick she'd bought to go with the suit had led to all sorts of things: blusher, foundation, dark brown eyeshadow. When Crissette Washington had seen her for the first time in the city room, the photographer had staggered back in exaggerated shock.

"You know," Gaby said, "I think I'm on a roll. Is that what they call it, a roll?" Dodd's eyes were fascinated. When he didn't answer she rushed on. "I think I did something right at this crazy General Bachman interview."

Jack Carty had actually laughed when she described it to him on the telephone afterward. She still couldn't believe it. "Write it up just the way you told it to me," the features editor had said. "It's good."

Dodd was watching her intently. "I'm glad you could get something out of those idiots. Don't give them an inch, they don't deserve it." He paused, then went on in a different tone, "I saw your mother this morning."

Her smile faded. "Yes, I did too, before I went to work." Gaby took the menu the waiter handed her and bent over it. Visiting Jeannette was becoming more and more difficult. Some of her mother's famous beauty had revived with her hospital stay. Jeannette was not yet fifty; there still could be many good years ahead. What was worrisome was that her mother merely sat and stared as though preoccupied with other, more pressing thoughts. Not unhappy, but not happy either.

Dodd was gazing absently out the restaurant's windows to the breathtaking sweep of Miami's bayfront, the islands of Miami Beach and Key Biscayne beyond. "The hospital can't hold her much longer without beginning some sort of treatment."

"My mother's changed." Gaby found it hard to describe in what way. "Did they tell you they'd tested her for stroke?"

Dodd scowled. "Damn that criminal nonsense the other night. Subjecting both of you to a dead dog and that mess. I don't know what in the hell your parents were thinking of to let those Cubans use the garage apartment."

"But we don't know that the Escuderos had anything to do with it," Gaby protested.

"Well, who else? Who would want to lay some damned voodoo spell on you or your mother? Twenty years ago Miami didn't even know about these things," he said, disgusted. "But then we hadn't become an outpost of Latin America, either!"

Gaby remembered the bumper sticker she'd seen that morning. She couldn't believe Angel and his mother were practicing *Santería*. The Escuderos were so hard-working, so cheerfully determined to make it in a new country. Angel made good grades in high school, Elena was struggling to improve her English. Ugly superstitious practices didn't fit them at all.

But then what *did* fit anything, she wondered, here in sun-drenched, dream-worldly Miami?

Gaby looked down blindly at her menu. She should tell Dodd that she was being followed, that strange, inexplicable things seemed to be happening to her, but she didn't know how to begin. It all sounded so crazy. Instead, she tried to defend the Escuderos again.

"My father volunteered the old chauffeur's apartment. A church group was looking for living space for the Marielito refugees, and no one was using it. The Escuderos had had such a bad time, Dodd. Elena and Angel were practically thrown into a little motorboat in Mariel harbor by Castro's people during the exodus. They were scared to death they were going to drown before they got to Miami. And then halfway there the man who owned the boat tried to hold them up for more money. Poor Elena, she was a widow with a young boy to look after. She wanted to go to

America because some of her relatives had been in the Bay of Pigs invasion and she thought the Castro government held it against her. I just can't believe they'd do anything to hurt any of us." Gaby sighed. "They've been through such a lot themselves."

Dodd said nothing, wouldn't even look at her. They weren't going to agree on it, Gaby could see. She stared down at her menu again.

"While I was at the hospital," he said, "I talked to your mother about what she'd said the other night at dinner, about our getting married. I told her that I loved you and wanted to marry you."

Gaby looked up at him quickly.

"Unfortunately, I don't think she understood much of what I was trying to tell her."

"Oh, Dodd." Gaby's thoughts were in confusion. Why had he picked now, of all times, to tell her this? "Don't you think you should have asked me first?"

He sighed with considerable frustration. "Gaby, I don't seem to be getting through to you lately. You don't listen to anything I've got to say. I've been sick with worry this past week thinking about you alone in that house when I have a perfectly good guest room at my condo. Look," he said, when she opened her mouth in protest, "it's not like we're—well, damn, Mouse, you're not a vulnerable seventeen-year-old this time!"

This time? Was she seeing doubt, confusion . . . guilt, in Dodd Brickell's eyes?

The big man sitting across the table in his conservative dark blue linen suit and white shirt with surah silk tie was handsome, wealthy, and successful, Gaby told herself. Even though she'd known him all her life, she had to admit Dodd Brickell was the most attractive, solid, desirable man any woman could find. Why was she suddenly so uneasy?

He moved his silverware around, abstracted. "What happened was a long time ago, Gaby, and you were just a kid. That night of the dance, what you were feeling for me was something considerably more than I was feeling for you." He jerked his head up, "No, God, I don't mean it that way! But do you know what happens when a man realizes he's lost control and taken advantage of a very young virg—" He caught himself. "I hoped like hell you'd forget the whole thing. I never intended to touch you, Gaby. I'd had a few drinks. Afterward I couldn't bear to face myself. I wanted to forget it and I hoped, prayed, you'd do the same. You were only seventeen—"

"Eighteen," she murmured.

"All right, eighteen. But I was playing my second year of pro ball with the Dolphins. I'd been around. And I was engaged at the time." His voice faltered. "You couldn't have known about the engagement. We hadn't told anybody."

Gaby stared out the window. Forget about the whole thing? Is that what he'd thought? "No, I didn't know about the engagement," she said softly. "That's true."

He groaned. "Oh, Mouse, I take responsibility for everything. Look, does it make any sense to you when I say I was a pro star, I had it made, I was set to marry the reigning campus beauty queen . . . ?" He bent his blond head, not able to look at her. "You come down hard at twenty-five when you find out you're not king of the world, God's gift to pro ball," he said bitterly. "When a little thing like a busted bone in your knee brings an end to the glory in a hell of a hurry. That's when I came back home."

"Dodd . . ." Gaby began uncertainly.

"Wait." The waiter showed Dodd the label of the bottle of Reisling he'd ordered. Dodd impatiently waved him to fill their wineglasses. When the waiter had gone, he said in a calmer voice, "You were in Italy by then, and my football career was behind me. I took my bar exam, joined the family firm, and opted for what the Brickells had been doing since they sold their first piece of Dade County swamp to a Yankee—making money. But when things changed, so did my marriage. It wasn't the big-time, exciting lifestyle of pro-football Trish had expected, and she told me so."

Gaby wasn't going to ask him when things had changed so much that he realized he wanted her. But her heart was pounding. She'd spent years hoping that something like this would happen. That Dodd would finally come to know that she was there, waiting for him.

Now he was saying that he wanted to marry her. He'd even gone to the hospital to tell her mother. She told herself she needed Dodd Brickell terribly. She wasn't brave, assertive, independent like Crissette. She had to have someone to talk to, to confide in, if only to convince her she wasn't going crazy. But where to begin?

"Dodd," she said, "when you were at the U of Miami, did you know James Santo Marin?"

He waited until the waiter had served their lunches. "Didn't you ask me this before?"

"I just finished a story about—about the Santo Marin family," she faltered. *Tell him,* a voice deep inside screamed at her. "I—I was just curious."

He looked puzzled. "Curious?"

"Yes, I was doing a sidebar for a story." *Help me,* she appealed to him silently. *You're my friend, you say you love me, help me tell you this.* "I've been calling around, talking to people. I need to know more about . . . things."

"Santo Marin?" He took a sip of wine and lifted the glass to the light. "Gaby, do we have to talk about this right now?" When she nodded, miserably, he growled. "Good God. Okay. Ah . . . rich, upper-class. Longtime connections in Florida."

"You know them?"

"The Santo Marins?" He smiled a little sourly. "Well, they aren't exactly your typical shirtless exiles. The upper-class Spaniards who migrated to the New World kept their grip on their power, their bloodlines, their money, in Cuba just like everywhere else in Latin America. According to Castro, that was the point of the revolution, wasn't it? To kick out the corrupt upper classes and the Mafia? You," he said abruptly, "don't want to know them."

"Why not?"

"Because Santo Marin's business may look legitimate from the outside, but the big cars, the boat, the lifestyle are a dead giveaway. He's one *latino* stud who's too rich and too visible not to have his hands into something. Gaby, are you going to let me say what I'm trying to say?"

He reached across the table to take her hand. "Mouse, darling," he said huskily, "I want to take care of you. I want to give you the world if I can. I messed up my life once and I hurt you terribly. Please let me make it right."

She gazed at the man across the table who clutched her hand so tightly. She was startled as a sudden need to love broke through her apprehension. Dodd was safety, comfort, *love*, and always had been. And oh, how much she needed those things at that moment! She wanted to give him all of that, too, in return. Wasn't this what she'd always dreamed of?

Impulsively, she leaned across the table and managed, in spite of their food and wineglasses, to place a kiss on Dodd's lips. For a second she thought he was going to jump up and take her in his arms and passionately return the kiss right there in the middle of the restaurant. He didn't, but his blue eyes were glittering as she sat back in her chair.

"You know what I want to do, don't you?" he muttered.

"You won't do it," she teased. "You're too Old Miami and proper for that." She added quickly as he started to get to his feet, "And so am I."

He sat back down, grinning. "Gaby, I want to announce our engagement right away. But your mother—"

"—can't do it right now, I know." Things had suddenly taken a new turn, Gaby realized with a slight rush of alarm. An impulsive kiss was now a commitment. Did she really want to do this? It meant so much to Dodd, to all the Brickells, to have formal engagement announcements, the whole social program of showers and parties and, inevitably, a very large wedding. Why was everything suddenly so real, so imminent?

"I suppose I can announce it myself," she said uncertainly. "I can give the announcement to the bridal desk at the paper in Mother's name. You know, 'Mrs. Paul Aston Collier announces the engagement of her daughter Victoria Gabrielle, et cetera, et cetera.'"

His hand almost crushed hers with happiness. "Then let us give the engagement party. It's the least the Brickells can do since your mother is hospitalized. God, Mouse," he said fervently, "one of the first things I want to see you have is a little money. Once we get these damned affairs wound up, get your mother's power of attorney and sell that mausoleum on Palm Island . . ." His voice trailed off as he stared at her. "Do you have any idea how incredibly beautiful you are in that suit? I'm glad you spent the money—"

In the next instant he knew what he had given away. "Ah, darling, I hope you're not angry. My father was only trying to help."

Gaby let him see that it was really a sore spot. "Dodd, no more money through the newspaper, even for clothes. You'll have to promise me you and your father will stay out of my job." The words suddenly rang a bell. Gaby shot a glance at her wristwatch. "Oh, Dodd, I have another appointment. I've got to run!"

"But you haven't finished your lunch." He stood up and threw his napkin down on the table. "And about the newspaper job, that's another thing—"

"Later," she said hurriedly, "later. I've got to go!"

She was halfway across the restaurant before she remembered that now that she was engaged to Dodd she should have kissed him good-bye.

Twenty minutes later, David Fothergill stepped out of a doorway on Eighth Street in Miami's Little Havana. The big Trinidadian's first words were, "Miss Collier, I don't think we want to be doing this."

Chapter 9

*I*n August's ninety-five-degree heat Little Havana looked like some flat, dusty suburb of its namesake. Eighth Street, *Calle Ocho* in Spanish, was lined with insurance offices, furniture stores, cut-rate dress shops, a few expensive Spanish-style restaurants, and a lot of open-sided *cafeterías*—coffee stands, not what the word meant in English—that sold Cuban sandwiches and thick, hot black espresso coffee in thimble-size paper cups. Little Havana's one tiny urban park was filled with elderly exiles, all men, playing endless games of dominos on concrete tables. Eighth Street was quiet, sunbaked, shabby; not at all what one would expect, considering its publicity.

David Fothergill, too, looked quite seedy, Gaby thought. He had the air of someone who did not have a permanent place to sleep. Which was probably the case. David had moved out of Crissette's apartment several days before.

David also looked unhappy. "Miss Gabrielle, I don't think you should be doing this. I know you want to get someone to explain to you what the *Santería* at your house meant, maybe even find out who might be doing it. But I think this is dangerous."

She held her hand up to shade her eyes against the street's hot glare. "David, I just want to ask some questions. Surely somebody ought to know something. Voodoo—*Santería*—is never done against Anglos. That's what the police said."

103

"I don't know about that." His eyes were troubled. "This is very hard for white people who are used to the Christian God to understand. African gods are capricious, they have no ethical systems. What the *Santería* gods do is mysterious, sometimes you would say even cruel."

Gaby stared at him. David's lilting calypso accent was still evident, but his tone of voice, his choice of words, especially phrases like "ethical systems," were not what she expected. Suddenly she knew David Fothergill was much better educated than he wanted the world to know.

He saw her expression and smiled, a trifle ironically. "Sorry, Miss Gabrielle, I think I'm in too much of a hurry to convince you not to do this. Forget the sociological observations. My point is that you may find that what the followers of *Santería* accept and believe in deeply might . . . ah, alarm you very much."

"Good Lord, I already *am* alarmed! Killing Jupiter and putting that *Santería* mess at the back door was meant for me, not the Escuderos, I'm sure of it." They were standing in burningly hot sunshine, but Gaby couldn't suppress a slight shiver. "You said to get in touch with you if anything else happened, didn't you?"

He frowned. "Something else?"

"Someone's still following me, the same black limousine. Only it doesn't park in the street across from the newspaper anymore. It starts after me when I take the causeway to go home. Whoever it is, they know I'm aware they're following me. When I turn into Palm Island they just keep on going. They never follow me all the way to my house."

"Is it the same car? You're sure?"

"Yes, I'm sure." Another shiver raced through her. "Who could miss a stretch Cadillac with tinted windows? It's careful to stay some distance behind me. I never get a chance to see the license plates. The other thing," she said, even more hesitantly, "is still there, in the house." She felt foolish blurting all this out in broad daylight. She hoped David believed her. "Night before last I heard that thumping or beating like drums again and it woke me up. It was all I could do to keep from running outside."

He regarded her thoughtfully. Then he took her hand in his own huge one and steered her rapidly along the sidewalk. "Miss Gabrielle, I don't think visiting a *santera* will find out much for you. You are an outsider, remember. You don't believe in these things."

"But David, you said you'd find one!"

"Oh, I have found someone. It is not all that difficult to find a priestess in Miami. But I am think-een," he said slowly, "if you don't know what this is all about, maybe the priestess won't either. Strange business like this just don't happen to lovely young ladies, who"—he looked pointedly at Gaby's expensive suit, her newly styled hair—"who live on Palm Island, have rich, important boyfriends, and work for a big newspaper."

Gaby hurried along, trying to keep up with his long strides. "But somebody came to my house, killed my dog, and frightened my mother so that now she's in the hospital. I don't know why that happened, but I want to find out. The police don't seem to be any help." Gaby remembered something else. "David, the priestess, she . . . this won't involve killing anything, will it? If somebody's going to sacrifice a live animal, I don't think I can take it!"

"No, nothing like that. We come only to ask a few questions."

But Gaby pulled him to a halt. "Did you ever consider that somebody could be just trying to frighten me? Do you think somebody could rig up a tape machine or something, and put it in the walls at my house to make that sound?"

He was silent for a moment. "No," he murmured finally, shaking his head, "it is no tape recorder."

"How can you be sure? Suppose it's the same people who are following me in the black limousine."

"Maybe people are following you, that could be. But what we have heard in the house is something else."

He seemed very sure, and Gaby sighed.

"Well, then," she said. "Let's go visit this priestess. My car's parked—"

"But we are here."

They had stopped in front of an entrance sandwiched

in between an H & R Block tax office with signs in Spanish and a tiny *joyería*, a jewelry store. David guided her through a narrow hallway and up a flight of stairs. At the top was a door to what seemed to be an apartment. David entered without knocking, and Gaby saw they were in a tiny waiting room with several plastic chairs and a coffee table with old magazines scattered on it. It looked like the very shabby office of a dentist.

"Shouldn't we ring a bell or something?" she whispered. Her nostrils were registering a faintly familiar odor of spices and smoke, and heavy, tropical food.

He pushed her ahead of him. "I think the *iyalocha* is expecting us."

The inner room was blindingly dark after the sunlight of the street. It took Gaby's eyes several long minutes to adjust. When they did she saw one wall of the room was almost solidly covered with silk flowers, bits of tinsel that winked like mirrors, fishing nets and seashells, and swags of red, green, and purple velvet and satin, some with glittering gold fringe. The wall seemed to be one gigantic, floor-to-ceiling, stupendously gaudy altar.

In front of the wall, on red and blue velvet-draped stands, were brightly painted plaster statues of Catholic saints, big pottery vases and earthenware pots, cheap plastic dolls dressed in gold and satin costumes, and several varieties of knives, including machetes and replicas of two-headed ceremonial axes. On the floor were pottery dishes filled with pastries, and baskets of tropical fruit—pineapples, mangoes, guavas, papayas, red, green, and yellow bananas, and a number of coconuts. Beside the baskets were three huge primitive drums decorated with black symbols. Through the draped satin and velvet, the tinsel, the artificial flowers, and the statues flickered the flames of a hundred candles.

Gaby stood transfixed. That same haunting odor had followed them: heavy sweet perfume of tropical flowers mixed with spices and garlic, cigar smoke, and something that could only be the pungent stink of raw, heady rum.

The room was not only dim but suffocatingly hot. Windowless, and obviously without air-conditioning. The humming dark, the cluttered space, the myriad tiny candle flames, and the heat all made Gaby dizzy. Something in the pit of her stomach, too, responded with an ominous tremor.

"*Iyalocha*," David said softly behind her.

A small figure that Gaby had taken for another plaster statue, it was so still and unmoving, suddenly nodded its head. An incredibly tiny black woman, wearing a long scarlet dress of magnificent taffeta silk decorated with heavy festoons of lace, and a green satin head kerchief knotted in the front, African style, was the priestess, the *santera*, of the temple. Her face, with a slightly beaked nose, had the blackest eyes Gaby had ever seen.

"Miss Gabrielle, this is the *iyalocha*, Señora Ibi Gobuo." In the stillness David's voice seemed unnaturally loud. "You don't call her *santera*. This priestess is African. You call her what I said, *iyalocha*."

The little figure in front of them did not move.

"Now," David said, "we must wait to see if she will speak to us."

The black eyes under the green satin headcloth unhurriedly looked Gaby over from the top of her hair to her shoes. It was quite an inspection. Gaby felt herself raked with a strange, dark intelligence that measured her looks, the way she was dressed—and much more than that—very thoroughly.

"Come." The old, strangely disembodied voice was so commanding, Gaby jumped. She moved forward, thinking the priestess was so small she would almost have to crouch down to speak to her.

"*Iyalocha*," David began, "this—"

An impatient hissing sound cut him off. The *iyalocha*'s old, bony hand, so black it seemed a shadow, extended toward Gaby, index finger pointing.

Watching it, Gaby felt a trickle of perspiration snake down her back. The smoke, the heavy odors of food, the dark and fragrant flowers were having their effect. She could hardly keep her eyes open. She stared at the hand with its pointing finger. Something was flowing from it straight into her. She would swear it.

"I know why you come," the *iyalocha* said in a strange little parrot voice. Her pointing finger held Gaby pinned. "You are changing, *mundele*, you will change more. Oshun likes pretty clothes. She makes herself beautiful for Chango."

Gaby took a deep breath. Was it her turn to say something? "Excuse me, *iyalocha*," she whispered, "but I came here to ask you—"

"He comes with the lightning all around him," the old woman said, ignoring her. "In the thunder and the storm. That is Chango's sign."

Gaby watched as the gnarled black hands rose to shape a circle. "In the big storm and the lightning," the priestess crooned, "Chango come to you. He is so beautiful and strong. *El arena del fuego*. He brings the ring of fire."

Gaby gaped at her. This much hit home. The little priestess couldn't know the ring of fire was a part of that nightmare Gaby hoped she'd never dream again. When she turned to look at David, he only shook his head.

Instead of answers, they were finding more questions. Who was Chango? And what did this have to do with anything?

The stiff red taffeta gown rustled and whispered as the *iyalocha* turned away. "I speak Yoruba," the tiny woman said, "the true language of *Santería*. But for you I will speak your language, maybe sometimes Spanish, a little."

Gaby was growing even more uneasy, wanting to get it over with. "Señora—*iyalocha*, I want to know why my dog was killed. The police said someone was practicing *Santería* at my house, but they thought it was meant for the Cuban family who lives in our garage apartment. Who *used* to live in our garage apartment," she corrected herself. "The Escuderos have disappeared."

The old woman wasn't listening. In a high, sweet, trancelike voice she said, "Your mother loves you, *nina*, even if you think she don't. She took the bad things what was meant for you." She paused, her black eyes unseeing. "But she will be better. That is so."

Gaby's mouth went dry. For a moment the voice had

been, incredibly, Jeannette's voice. A long time ago, when her mother had been young and vital.

She was still telling herself she was mistaken when the *iyalocha* said imperiously, "*Ven aquí, mundele. Quiero explicarlo.*"

Come with me. I want to explain.

The *iyalocha* stopped in front of a large mahogany cabinet and pulled open the doors. "This is the *canasterillo,* the cabinet where the *otanes* of the gods are kept. These are great African gods of *Santería.* I will explain and you will listen, *mundele,* because I do not do this again."

An old black hand touched the top shelf lightly. "Here is the place for Obatala, a very great god for peace, purity. He is *orisha* of the sky. Obatala is like Jesus Christ. His color is white, is sign of the white dove."

The gnarled fingers moved to the second shelf. "Here is Oshun, the *orisha* of the river waters. Oshun is beautiful young goddess. *Su color es amarillo y rojo*—yellow like gold, red like love."

The shelf, Gaby saw, was filled with fans, bottles of perfume, a jar of Sioux Bee honey, coral necklaces, and several tiny toy canoes made of plastic.

She watched the old black hands lift the jar of honey and open it. Then, moving too quickly for her to pull back, the hand reached out and the priestess dabbed sweet sticky stuff across her lips.

Startled, Gaby licked her mouth, tasting the honey. The more she tried to get rid of it, the more the honey clung to the inside of her mouth and her lips. It had a bitter aftertaste. The *iyalocha* watched her closely. "You like, you like?" she asked.

Gaby swallowed with difficulty, longing for something to wipe the honey away. "Nice," she said, untruthfully.

The *iyalocha* turned back to the cabinet. "Third is Oshun's sister who is Yemaya the ocean waters. Oshun is *orisha* of love, rainbow, rivers. Sister Yemaya goddess is woman, mother. All the house belong to Yemaya and women who carry baby and have childbirth. They pray to her."

The hand moved down to the last shelf. "Is Oya here,

the *orisha* of cemeteries and the dead." The *iyalocha* shut the cabinet door abruptly. "We don't talk about Oya of the people of the dead now. Maybe later."

The little figure moved to another, smaller cabinet. "Here live more *orishas,* very powerful, Ogun who makes iron, Eleggua who tells the future and past, Babalu-ai-ey who heals the sick, plenty more. But here in his own place, I show you—Chango!"

She opened the doors of the finely carved cabinet to reveal several shelves scattered with candles and bowls, a miniature two-headed ax, a handful of dried okra and cornmeal, two apples, a dark, overripe banana, and gold coins. Behind these stood a small statue of a woman dressed in medieval red and white robes. She held a sword, and at her side was a miniature castle tower.

"Santa Barbara is saint for him," the *iyalocha* said, touching the plaster statue of the Catholic saint. "But Chango is man *orisha,* very beautiful, god of fire and lightning, very powerful, mysterious." She paused. "And *mucho* sexy. Chango make very good love."

Gaby held her hand to her mouth. She couldn't get rid of the honey's terrible taste. "David, what is she talking about?" she whispered.

He stirred. "*Mundele* is white person in Yoruba, Miss Gabrielle," he whispered back. "The *iyalocha* says an *orisha,* an African goddess of *Santería,* claims you. Even though you are a *mundele.* One of Oshun's manifestations is *Ye Ye Caridad.* Sort of like Venus, only more so."

The *iyalocha* was rummaging in one of the baskets of fruit on the floor as though her visitors weren't there. Gaby was feeling slightly nauseated. "We'd better go," she told David from behind her hand.

The priestess lifted a coconut and sniffed it. "We must make the *dar coco al santo.*" She held out the coconut. "When we do that, the *orisha* will answer your questions."

Gaby swallowed again. "We weren't going to stay, for any sort of ceremony, really."

But the tiny black figure in the flame-colored dress had begun chanting. "*Illa mi ile oro illa mi ile oro vira ye yeye oyo ya mala ye icu oche oche oye ogua ita . . .*"

"David," Gaby murmured. Her stomach was rebelling. The room's overpowering heat made her dizzy. David apparently didn't hear as the priestess continued chanting in Yoruba. She took down a machete from the altar wall and, placing the coconut on a stand, she hacked it quickly into several pieces with the big knife.

Gaby fixed her gaze on a bunch of artificial poppies to keep down the growing uproar in the pit of her stomach. She never liked the smell of coconut. Why couldn't she get David to do something?

The *iyalocha* gathered up the coconut pieces in both hands and shut her eyes. Then she violently scattered them on the floor around her. All the broken pieces of coconut landed with the dark sides up. The black woman gave a little indrawn hiss.

"*Oyekun!*" the *iyalocha* rasped.

They were just pieces of fresh coconut, Gaby told herself, trying not to look at them. The odor of coconut milk drifted up to her. Somehow, she thought grimly, she didn't need to be told that the message was not good.

"*Yo veo todo es oscuro. Muy loco,*" the old voice intoned "*Pero, oiga—yo veo una mujer muy mala!*"

For a long moment the *iyalocha* stood poised on the tips of her tiny feet like a little bird ready for flight. Then she settled back on her heels.

"Is too much for me," she announced matter-of-factly. "We need go see the *babalawo* right away."

"Miss Gabrielle." David's voice seemed to come from far away. "She wants to take you to the high priest."

Gaby was bathed in a cold sweat. Something was wrong. She felt sick but she couldn't seem to do anything about it.

"Miss Gabrielle, are you listening?" That was David's voice again. "The cocos fell in the pattern of *oyekun,* which is bad. The worst."

The little *iyalocha* stepped in between them, pointing a gnarled finger at David's chest. "*No queremos poetas aquí!*" she said shrilly. "Your friend is not what he seem!"

Gaby was seeing only a dirty gray mist. "David . . ." She had to struggle to speak. "Did you understand that?"

It was like a nightmare. She couldn't shake the feeling that she was fading completely away. "It's crazy. The *iyalocha* thinks you're a poet!"

In the next instant Gaby realized she should have told David to get her out of there. Quick. She was either going to be sick to her stomach, or she was going to faint.

She felt David's arms go around her. "Oh, Miss Gabrielle!"

No, not sick to her stomach, Gaby thought dimly. She was definitely going to faint.

Chapter 10

The hot afternoon sun seeped in through vertical blinds and fell in stripes on the *babalawo*'s office carpeting. The room was frigid, typically, for Miami in late summer. The air-conditioning was set at near-freezing, but this was also, the high priest had already explained, for his computer, a magnificent AT&T array that covered his desk and two nearby stands.

"Damn, there it comes again," he muttered, peering at the changing divination patterns on the computer screen. "Ibi Gobuo is right, we really have a problem." He sat back, chin in hand, studying the screen. "From what I can make of it, somebody's really messing around."

The *babalawo*'s office was in a small stucco building not far from the *iyalocha*'s apartment. Even through the double plate-glass windows Gaby could hear the thready sound of downtown traffic.

The last thing she had expected to find was a yuppie practitioner of Cuban voodoo, dressed in a natty continental-style black silk business suit, white shirt, and Countess Mara tie with a tasteful diamond stick pin. But then she understood Jorge Castaneda was no ordinary high priest of *Santería*. He was a graduate of Florida State University in Tallahassee—his diploma was on the wall behind his desk—had a large clientele, and was very successful. He was the only *babalawo* in Miami, probably anywhere, he'd assured her, who used a personal computer to interpret the messages of the *Santería* gods. In his late thirties, swarthily attractive with his black hair perfectly styled in a razor cut and slightly-darker-than-gold skin, he was a little concerned about Gaby's bad experience at the *iyalocha*'s.

"It was the heat," she said, and finished the cold 7-Up the *babalawo* had brought her from the drink machine in the hall. She was embarrassed that she'd nearly fainted in the old priestess's apartment. It was just another mysterious symptom, she supposed, of her body's inability to adjust to Miami's climate.

"The *iyalocha* thinks you're *muy sensitiva*," the *babalawo* said, typing in another line. "She thinks you caught a lot of heavy vibrations, that you nearly fainted because you made a . . . ah, psychic connection." He squinted at the screen. "I didn't want to argue with her, but frankly, I don't think you had anything going with the *orishas*, I think it was a real *mundele* anxiety attack. Fainting is a white lady's thing," he went on with barely concealed irony. "It's very restrained. My people, when they're scared, throw up all over the place."

"I wasn't having an anxiety attack," Gaby said stiffly. "It was just the heat." She didn't want to admit how close she'd come to doing that very thing.

"No?" The *babalawo* hit another key and the patterns rolled over again, rather like the combinations in a slot machine. "I think an anxiety attack is valid. You impress me," he said, absorbed in the screen, "as a lady who's a lot more scared than you want to let on. It's the pits to be scared of everything." Before Gaby could protest, he added, "Most *iyalochas* hate referring their clients to a higher authority. Like me. But Ibi got kinda blown away. Your cocos kept coming up *oyekun*. She couldn't believe it."

Gaby clamped her lips shut on a retort. Whatever had come over her at the *iyalocha*'s was a false alarm, a moment's unpleasant dizziness, and she'd tried to tell them so. But David had clucked over her like a mother hen so much that he'd been sent to wait downstairs on Eighth Street. Interviews with the *babalawo* were conducted in strictest privacy anyhow. Even the *iyalocha* wasn't allowed to stay.

Her second blunder, Gaby now realized, was blurting out everything to Jorge Castaneda. She'd been so rattled by nearly fainting, the *iyalocha*, the whole bizarre afternoon, that she'd told the so-called high priest all about the drug deal at the fashion show, the death of Jupiter, the strange sounds in her house, even how many times she had been followed by the black Cadillac limousine. And finally and most regretfully, she'd spilled something she hadn't wanted to reveal to anyone—James Santo Marin's visit to her house during the storm.

The *babalawo* had listened in attentive silence, almost as though he had expected all her secrets to come tumbling out like that.

"Jimmy Santo Marin and I went to Coral Gables High together," he had told her when she was through. At her dumbfounded look, he had grinned. "Oh, yeah, Jimmy went on to the rich boy's school, the U of Miami. I got my diploma up at Florida State." He'd leaned back in his chair, his clever black eyes watching her stunned reaction. "Even back then he was into championship tennis, competitive swimming, broke his leg trying to make first string quarterback, all the usual glory stuff. Of course, if you knew the women in the family. . ." he'd added cryptically. "Jimmy was committed to the classic pattern—firstborn, only son, head of the family, workaholic high-achiever, drives himself and everybody else around him nuts. Jimmy's always been a tiger."

Gaby's mind had reeled. This yuppie voodoo practitioner and James Santo Marin knew, or at least had known, each other? She had been suddenly glad she'd left out the more intimate details of what had taken place on the living room couch. That, she'd decided, was no one's business. Not even a *Santería* high priest's.

"I don't understand what this is all about," she now said a little angrily. "Don't tell me I'm having an anxiety attack, either. I want some explanations."

"Okay." The *babalawo* sat forward in his chair and

recited in careful, academic Spanish, *"'He visto vivir un hombre con el punal al castado.'"*

Gaby stared blankly at him. "I'm sorry. My Spanish is not very good."

"It was written by a very fine poet, José Martí, who also happens to be the great liberator of Cuba. Translated, it refers to someone who is living very dangerously." He added, quite offhandedly, "So Jimmy likes you, huh? Well, he's a great-looking guy, but actually I don't think he's been all that involved with women. Most of it's just publicity."

"I—I'm not," Gaby began with a return of the curious breathlessness that attacked her when she talked, or even thought, about James Santo Marin, "at all involved with—"

"What I'm doing right now," the *babalawo* interrupted, "is setting up on the computer a general consultation for you using the Table of Ifa. Are you familiar with the Chinese I Ching?" He shot her an inquiring glance. "No? Okay, then think of what I do as like casting horoscopes. Actually the Table of Ifa of the Yorubas is based on a system of divination just as ancient and complicated as the zodiac, only it happens to be African and not ancient Babylonian. Incidentally, the Babylonians believed we are descended from the gods, just like the Yoruba. We're not dealing with trash here."

"Oh," Gaby said. "I didn't think we were."

"Honey, you're so polite." He turned to look at her. "But then this whole visit is fascinating," he murmured, openly admiring her. "After all, how many times am I going to get a gorgeous young Anglo society lady in here with a *Santería* problem?"

Gaby's lips tightened. "If you don't mind, can we get down to why I came here? I'd like to know why someone put the *Santería* at my house."

The *babalawo* put his elbows on the computer stand and rested his chin on his fingertips. "Killing the old dog was an afterthought," he said to the lighted screen. "That's not kosher. The chicken was more straightforward. But I agree, nobody went to all that trouble for the *latino* family in the garage. They wanted you to get the message."

"What message?" Gaby cried. "So far nobody's told me what anything means!"

He peered at the display, where a series of patterns were rolling up in long columns. "How's the tummy? The soda pop taking care of it? You sure you feel up to all this?"

"You didn't answer my question."

He sighed. "Miss Collier, because you're a nice Anglo doll and don't practice *Santería*, I'm going to limit some of the invocations, cut out a lot of the deep stuff. You see, in my culture the *babalawo* is witch doctor, diviner, father confessor, and psychologist all rolled into one. It gives me a lot of leeway." He ducked his head, consulting the keyboard. "Has somebody already explained to you that in the islands you could go to mass in the village church, and then practice an African religion like *Santería*, and have the best of both worlds?"

When Gaby nodded, the *babalawo* lifted his well-manicured hands from the keyboard and held them out to her. "See the color of my skin, Miss Collier?" he asked softly. "I'm like most people from the Caribbean. I'm a mix of three races, Indian, African, and white, and I've got the heritage of all three. *Santería* speaks to me just as it speaks to my people, you understand?"

Gaby nodded. She supposed she did.

"Now what I'm doing here," he went on, typing in a command, "is trying to find out why someone is putting a *bilongo* against you. That was the stuff you found at your back door."

She said, hesitantly, "The police seemed to think it was a priestess."

"Don't tell me what the police think. I know all the practitioners. None of them are nuts enough to do something like this." He shrugged. "But I could be wrong. When you get a bad *santero*, when some of them are into Congo *palo*, you get into really heavy stuff."

The *babalawo*, too, had his cabinet of the *orishas*, a piece of plain gray-green office equipment. It also included "heads" made of coconuts covered with clay, and decorated with symbols dedicated to Orunla, the special god of divination. One sat on his desk.

The comparison with casting a horoscope was a good one, Gaby thought uneasily. From time to time the *babalawo* muttered an incantation over his *okuele*, a chain linking eight round medallions of tortoise shell engraved with symbols. The *babalawo* threw it down on the *estera*, a grass mat spread over a table beside his desk, and the medallions formed themselves into simple patterns. Or, as he explained, one and zero, the system of binary numbers. Then he loaded the data into the computer.

"I gather you didn't tell Ibi," he said, "about Jimmy Santo Marin."

"No." The idea that the *babalawo* knew James Santo Marin still unnerved her. "Mostly she talked about a goddess Oshun. And Chango, or something."

"She *what*?" He lifted his hands from the keyboard in surprise. "She did what?"

"There was a jar of honey," Gaby explained a little nervously. She wasn't sure what they were talking about. "She gave me some before I could stop her."

To her surprise the *babalawo* laughed.

"Chango? And Oshun?" He turned around in his chair to face her, his dark face intent. "Did she tell you about Chango's fire and the lightning and the thunder?"

Gaby stared at him, open-mouthed.

"Oshun is the Yoruba goddess of love," the *babalawo* went on. "Honey is her symbol. It's a charm for— Oh, never mind," he said quickly, seeing the expression on her face.

Gaby was thinking that the incomprehensible words and spells of the wizened old black woman in her bizarre temple, and now the high-tech psycho-jargon of this high priest with his computer, were weaving a curious web about her. There was no other explanation for the way she felt.

She gave herself a little shake. Her imagination was running wild, but she could almost sense the invisible strands as they were laid around her, one by one. The *babalawo* knew James Santo Marin. And hadn't Crissette's boyfriend, David, unerringly picked the right *iyalocha* to visit? The real question, though, was not just why the web was being spun about her, but who the spider was at the center of it, waiting for her.

"Come here," the *babalawo* said. "All the way around the desk. I want you to look at something."

Gaby did as he said. When she looked over his shoulder at the lighted computer screen, he pointed to long columns of words rolling up it.

"I'm going to line up the gods of some other ancient religions with the *orishas*. I got this out of a book. Look, here's the Hebrew cabalistic tree of life reading down from Kether, Chochmah, et cetera. Now here are the Yoruba gods. I'm going to line them up with the cabal and on the other side we put the Greek pantheon, then the Roman. Kronos matches Orunla, Zeus matches Obatala, they're both sky gods, and they match the Roman Jupiter." He punched up another line of names. "Here's Oshun-Netzach-Aphrodite-Venus. You see how they're all alike? Here's Yemaya-Yesod-Artemis-Moon Goddess. And here's Chango-Tiphereth-Apollo-Sun God. No matter what you call it, it's an umbilical cord straight to the cosmos and the universal mystery. And it's all just as subjective as Hawking's astrophysical collapsing of time and space."

Gaby wasn't listening. Wasn't there a pattern to everything, she wondered, that had been happening to her from the very moment she'd seen James Santo Marin in the woods of his Coral Gables estate? What if all this voodoo was a wild plot to make her doubt her own sanity? Who, for instance, she mused, looking around the *babalawo*'s office, even knew she was in Little Havana this afternoon?

The *babalawo* pressed a key. The columns of gods faded from the screen and a pattern of black and white circles came up.

"Now when I cast the *okuele* there are only five ways they can lie: all white, three white one black, two white two black, three black one white, and all black. Sometimes it used to take days for a *babalawo* to read the patterns, the combinations are endless. It's a binary system, yes no, go no-go. That's why the computer can process it. But when you get the pattern *oyekun* which is all black, over and over like I did when I was casting your *okuele,* it means something very bad. That's why Ibi Gobuo was so shook."

Gaby backed up a few steps. She had to get out of here, she thought a little desperately. But where was David? If she ran out of the office and down the stairs, would he be below, waiting for her? Or was he a part of this, too?

"Okay, that's the bad news," the *babalawo* said cheerfully. "The good news is there are other patterns called *diloggun* that modify it. Each divination set has a proverb. The one that keeps coming up with yours nonstop is called *Obbara.* Interestingly, it's the only one where Chango and Oshun speak together. It's very ancient. Do you want to know what it says?"

He looked up to see her staring at him. "The *Obbara* says, 'A noble king does not tell lies.'"

Gaby shook her head. "I don't understand any of this," she said. "It hasn't answered any of my questions. I think I'd better go."

He turned back to the computer screen. "I can't tell you anything about James Santo Marin, Miss Collier," he said in a different voice. "You'll have to figure that problem out for yourself. But I don't deny there's plenty of drug dealing going on in Miami."

Gaby suddenly realized the *babalawo*'s long dissertation on the African voodoo religion hadn't gone anywhere because he didn't intend it to.

"You've been stringing me along!" she accused him.

"Now, now, don't get upset." He wasn't smiling. "Remember, I'm not charging you anything for this. And my usual fee is pretty steep."

"I don't care how steep it is." Gaby looked around for her purse. "The *iyalocha* was giving me the runaround, too, wasn't she?"

"Look, I answered the question about what happened at your house." He sounded defensive. "Yes, it was somebody's idea of *Santería*. The *bilongo* on the back door was vicious. I can't relate to it." The *babalawo* turned his back to her, hunching over the keyboard. "But if you have to have a clear-cut message, Miss Collier, okay. I would say that somebody wants very badly to kill you."

The door to the *babalawo*'s office burst open with a bang. The *babalawo* did not lift his gaze from the computer display. He merely said, "Hey, what took you so long?"

Gaby whirled, knocking over the empty 7-Up can. It rolled across the desk and dropped to the floor. She hardly noticed.

The tall figure in blue jeans and a tight black T-shirt filling the doorway was out of breath, almost bursting with fury. The brilliant dark eyes blazed at Gaby.

"Just tell me," James Santo Marin said angrily, "what the hell you think you're doing."

Chapter 11

"*They* telephoned you!" Gaby grabbed for the railing and held onto it, refusing to let James Santo Marin pull her down the stairs from the *babalawo*'s office.

"Damn right," he snarled, breaking her grip with an angry jerk. "I'd break their necks if they didn't!"

At street level Gaby balked, bracing one arm against the door. "You bastard, let go of me. I'm not going anywhere with you! You killed my dog!"

"I didn't kill anybody's dog." He managed to pry the street door open enough to push her through. "Walk nice. I don't want to start a damned riot on *Calle Ocho*."

"You jerk!" She was almost sobbing. "I have a friend waiting for me. Believe me, he'll—he'll take you apart!"

"Who, the Jamaican? I told him to get lost."

"He's not a Jamaican, he's from Trinidad!" She broke away, her hair flailing wildly, the jacket of her new coral suit twisted down over one shoulder. The hot sunshine hit her like a blow and she suddenly sagged. "You're lying," she said weakly. "David wouldn't go off and leave me with—with somebody like you!"

"Get in the car and out of this heat." He steered her to the curb. "What the hell have you been doing, anyway? I ought to cream that son of a bitch Castaneda."

A magnificent low-slung midnight black Lamborghini sports car was parked in the no parking zone. Gaby felt an irrational surge of relief when she saw it. At least James

122

Santo Marin's car wasn't a stretch Cadillac limousine with tinted windows.

She pulled her arm out of his grip. "I'm not going anywhere with you. Keep your hands off me!"

He opened the door of the Lamborghini. "The sooner you get in, the sooner I can turn on the air-conditioning. I'm taking you home."

"You can't." She was undecided now. "My car's parked down here."

"I'll have somebody pick it up." He towered over her, mouth tight with irritation. The rough clothes he wore, the tight-fitting black shirt and threadbare jeans, outlined the muscular lines of his body sexily. "Right now I'm going to take you home," he told her. "You can show me exactly what happened out there."

In spite of the blazing heat a small crowd of loungers had gathered to watch. "I want you to leave me alone!" Gaby cringed under the stares, wanting to be anywhere but there, in a shouting match with James Santo Marin in the middle of *Calle Ocho*. "I'm not going with you. I have to go back to the newspaper and file my story!"

"I'll have somebody call them."

"You'll *what*?" She knew she was screaming like a harridan but she couldn't stop. "You tell my friends to get lost? You'll have somebody pick up my car? You'll have somebody call the newspaper about work I have to do? Who do you think you are, some sort of *king*?"

He gave her a furious look, black brows drawn together like check marks. "Get in the car. *Please*." He emphasized the last word. "I'll turn on the air-conditioning. We can talk."

The "please" made a difference, Gaby told herself. The street was like a blast furnace, and she didn't know how much longer she could endure it. "Remember, I'm not going anywhere with you," she warned, and slowly lowered herself into the sumptuous black car.

He shut the door and walked around to the other side of the Lamborghini. He slid behind the wheel, started the powerful engine, and pulled away from the curb, tires squealing.

Gaby reached for the door handle but it had locked automatically. Gasping, she leaned back against the soft black leather and watched the shabby buildings of Little Havana flash by. Now what? she wondered. She'd been absolutely stupid to trust him. She didn't even know if he was really taking her home.

In the close confines of the Lamborghini, James Santo Marin's physical presence was disturbing. He was big enough, in spite of a lean, rangy frame, to crowd the front seats. The biceps of a bare tanned arm bunched impressively as he shifted gears. His faded denim jeans hugged his long, muscular legs, and on his feet were battered work boots.

Gaby couldn't stop staring. It was the same man, yet a totally different version in jeans and T-shirt, hair tousled, face grim. He looked tough. Low-down, she thought with a sinking feeling.

"There's nothing to see at the house," she muttered. "Everything's been cleaned up."

He shot her a quick look. "Did you get my flowers?" When she looked at him in confusion, he said impatiently, "Roses. Four dozen red roses. I sent them to the newspaper."

It took her a moment to understand. The bouquet that had arrived at the newsroom. The one she thought had been sent for some shopping mall promotion. "You sent *those*?" She couldn't believe it. "But there was no card!"

He turned his head, surprised. "Who else would be sending you flowers? I sent them after I—" He stopped. "After," he said, his jaw clenched, "that night."

That, too, took a minute. *After that night.*

Gaby turned her face to the window. That stormy night and the way it had ended there on the couch in her living room. Until now she had managed to bury the more painful parts of it deep in the back of her mind.

She inched away from the touch of his leg and arm as far as she could. *Who else would be sending you flowers?* He was crazy if he thought he had some sort of claim on her.

When they stopped at a red light on the causeway, she kept the back of her head to him, pretending to be absorbed in the cruise ships in the port of Miami.

"I was out of town for a few days." His voice was expressionless. "Otherwise I would have called you."

If he'd gone out of town Gaby could guess why. No, she hadn't changed her mind about him. He was too flashy, too good-looking, undoubtedly dangerous. Dodd had told her as much. Even the *babalawo* had more or less agreed. He might be responsible for the *Santería* at her house, she thought with a shiver. After all, he had tried to threaten her, hadn't he?

The Lamborghini purred up the driveway and stopped at the Colliers' front door. James Santo Marin got out of the car and walked around to the passenger side to open her door.

"Start from the beginning," he said. "When your friends brought you home and you found the dog."

Gaby stepped from the car and pulled her arm out of his grip. "It's really none of your business. And this wasn't funny, practically kidnapping me. I want you just to leave me here and go back to"—her gaze raked his clothes meaningfully—"to whatever it was you were doing."

"I was working on my boat. I can do that anytime. Now, where did you find the dog?"

"What's the matter?" she asked, her anger flaring. "Are you checking everything out to see if it worked? Well, it did! Beautifully! This *Santería* mess put my mother in the hospital. The police came." He strode ahead of her on the path. She stalked after him, yelling like a harridan again, amazed at herself behaving that way. But she found him, and especially the way he acted, unendurable. "We got the whole neighborhood up in the middle of the night," she went on. "And it scared *me* half to death!"

He ducked under foliage, scraping a hibiscus branch from the back of his neck. "Where did you find the dog?"

"Over there," she said reluctantly, pointing.

She really didn't want to talk about it. To James Santo Marin, or anyone. Jupiter had been such a good-hearted dog, expecting nothing but kindness in this world. But somebody had wrapped a cord around his neck, probably while he was wanting to be petted, and strangled him.

Santo Marin dropped to one knee, his hand brushing the ground. "The dog hadn't been cut open or anything?"

Cut open? The idea was horrifying. She turned away, feeling ill. "What's your interest in all this? Are you just satisfying your curiosity?"

He got to his feet. "My interest is just what you said. That somebody came out here and frightened you half to death with this crap."

She stared at him. "This *crap*?"

"Yes, this crap, this stupid junk." He glowered at her, his eyes hard. "I don't care what George Castaneda's been telling you, it's garbage. And the lunatic who did this ought to be locked up. Take me around the back of the house," he ordered. "That's where they put the rest of the *bilongo*, isn't it?"

"There's nothing to see." He started down the side path and she followed him. "You're not telling me everything!" she cried, frustrated. "I'll bet you know who did it, don't you?"

"No." He didn't turn to look at her. "But I'm sure as hell going to find out."

He pushed through the untrimmed bushes to the back of the house, then stood there, staring at the porch door. "They told me you think you're being followed."

The back terrace was blisteringly hot, even though a breeze blew across the turquoise waters of Biscayne Bay and ruffled her hair. When he turned to her, squinting against the light, the intensity of his darkly handsome face seemed as vivid as the burning sun. But his eyes were angry, dangerous.

"A—a stretch black Cadillac limousine." She knew he wasn't going to believe her. "It's followed me home from work."

Amazingly, he considered it. "There are a million stretch black Cadillac limousines in Miami. Who's in it, can you tell? Man or woman?" He paused a fraction of a second. "Two men?"

She gasped. "Oh, my God, your Colombian drug dealers are following me!"

"Jesus, don't say that!" He was genuinely alarmed.

"You're jumping to crazy conclusions. Besides, I don't know any Colombian drug dealers."

But when he started for the sun porch door, she yelled, "Don't just walk away from me. There were Colombians there at your house, I saw them. That's what this whole thing is about, isn't it? That I saw something I wasn't supposed to!"

He hesitated, then started forward again. "Let's go inside. I want you to tell me about the things you hear inside the house at night."

He even knew about that. It made her furious. "Who told you that? Your friend with the computer?" How she regretted, now, letting the whole story spill out in the *babalawo*'s office. "Did you know the *babalawo* said somebody was trying to *kill me*?"

"With *Santería*?" He looked at her contemptuously. "Are you kidding? You don't believe in that stuff."

"I don't know what I believe in anymore," she wailed. "It was all pretty convincing today—the little African *iyalocha*, your school chum with the computer. Was that all for my benefit? To warn me off again? Oh, God." She moaned, turning away. "I'm so sick of you people!"

"*You people?*" He grabbed her arm and whirled her around. "What do you mean, Miss Collier?" he asked softly. "Are you referring to us uncouth, greasy *latinos*?"

She flinched. "No, no. I'm sorry I said that. I didn't mean it that way."

"The hell you didn't. I know what Anglos think of us, Miss Collier, you don't have to spell it out." He let her go so suddenly, she staggered. "Did you think I was any different? Did Castaneda tell you how *altaclasse* I am? About my mother's pure Castilian blood? And did he brag on his own nice brown skin? Well, I hate to disillusion you, but I'm Cuban, too. My father's Cuban. He's still there, in Cuba." He spat out the words. "He's one of Fidel Castro's long-term political prisoners, an old man in a wheelchair who's had a stroke, under twenty years' house arrest. He'll probably die there."

He turned away from her, his shoulders stiff with anger. "The reason I'm here is that I don't want you defiled with our ignorant superstitious practices. When I find out who did this to your genteel Anglo household here on Palm Island, I'm going to gouge his eyes out. Barbarically. Disgustingly. Does that satisfy you?"

She was horrified. "That's unfair! I don't feel that way, I don't know why I said that. It's just that this whole thing, going to the *iyalocha* today, the high priest with the computer..." Her voice trailed away. "I didn't ask you to come here," she reminded him. "Why don't you just go back to your boat?"

"Forget it." For a long moment they stood glaring at each other, irresistibly drawn by their conflict, neither willing to give an inch.

Finally he turned away. "I want to check the inside of your house."

Gaby followed him slowly. Watching him stalk toward her house, captivated by the tightly-wound grace of his narrow-hipped, long-legged body, she remembered the *babalawo*'s words. *Tiger. Fireball*. He had talked about gouging someone's eyes out. He'd told her his father was still being held prisoner in Cuba. Twenty years. The cruelty of it made her wince. But he still hadn't answered any of her questions. Neither had the others.

He was waiting for her at the door to the sun porch. "You said you heard noises at night," he said tautly. "And something about a tape recorder."

She got her key out and unlocked the door. "I don't know what I heard anymore," she admitted. "There isn't a tape recorder in the walls. I just said that."

The house was tightly closed against the heat and smelled mildewed, like all old waterfront places. Their footsteps were loud on the tile floors. Gaby couldn't help thinking nervously of the night of the storm, when James Santo Marin had come into her house. In the *sala* she avoided looking at the old slipcovered couch. She still remembered too vividly how she had lain there in the darkness, half naked, practically panting for him to make love to her. And his passionate mouth, his long body lying heavily on hers, his trembling hands caressing her bare, aching breasts.

"I need a drink of water," she said loudly. She started for the hallway and the front of the house. "I can't describe the sound, anyway. It's probably all in my imagination."

"Wait," he said.

She didn't stop in the kitchen for the water. The memory of his hard, sexy body followed her like a heated ghost. She rushed through the hall, threw open the front door, and stepped out into the drive, gulping the steamy air. Just the way he looked affected her, she thought wildly, and she couldn't let herself be that stupid. He was bad, evil, dangerous. He was mixed up with drugs! *Stop thinking about him!*

"What about the family that lives here?" he asked from behind her. "Have you been up to check out the apartment since they left?"

"No." If she walked out to the driveway and the Lamborghini, she thought frantically, maybe he would take the hint and leave. "The police looked at it, but I've been busy. And there have been so many other things."

He started toward the garage. "Do you even know if they've been back? Have they removed any of their stuff?"

"No." She had to run to keep up with him. Get rid of him, she told herself. He threw her off balance, raised this strange sexual panic that she couldn't cope with. He had to go, if only for the sake of her sanity. Besides, she had to get back to the paper that afternoon. That was no lie. "I don't know if I've got the key to the garage apartment with me," she said. Ordering James Santo Marin off the property would do no good. She had to outmaneuver him. "The key may be in the house. We probably can't get in."

He had reached the downstairs door. When he turned the knob the door swung open into darkness.

"You won't need it," he said. "Somebody's already been here."

If the sea was an ink pot
And the sky made of paper,
The evil in women
Could not all be written.

If the sea was an ink pot
And paper the sky,
There would be no room for telling
How deeply men lie.

SPANISH FOLK SONG

Chapter 12

Gaby wandered through the apartment in a daze. The bedroom was even more of a shambles than the living room. The larger pieces of furniture were still there, but the Escuderos had taken the curtains, the braided rugs, wiped the kitchen clean of cooking utensils. Even the mattress cover was gone from the stripped bed. Someone had been in such a hurry to pull down the bedroom curtains that the metal rod was bent almost in a bow.

Gaby unhooked the damaged rod and laid it on the windowsill. The box fan was still in place. She turned the switch to see if it had been left because it didn't work, but it hummed into life, pulling a strong, much-needed breeze into the room.

James Santo Marin stood in the doorway, thumbs hooked into his jeans, watching her. "I'm sorry," he said softly.

She shrugged. "Don't be. You didn't do it."

She ran a finger over the top of the battered dresser, through a layer of spilled talcum powder. There'd always been a collection of photographs proudly displayed there: Angel in his First Communion clothes, Elena's dead husband, Rafael, a number of snapshots of all the relatives still living in Cuba. Now there were only tracks in the talcum where pictures had been hastily scooped off the dresser.

"Elena was always so neat, so terribly clean and tidy.

133

I can't believe she'd come back and take everything and leave the place like this." Gaby blamed herself for not checking the apartment sooner. Now, she remembered, there was no one left to help with the cleaning and the yard work. She was going to have to spend the weekend cleaning up the apartment alone. The thought dismayed her. She sat down on the edge of the bed and stared at the mess.

"They didn't do this," he told her. "Somebody came back and cleaned the place out for them."

She lifted her head. "Why do you say that?"

"Whoever it was didn't know what to take. So they took everything that wasn't nailed down."

She threaded her fingers through her sweat-damp hair in a gesture of weariness. "It could have been burglars," she said without conviction. "They rob places for money for drugs."

His black gaze followed the movement of her arm as she pulled her hair up from the back of her neck and held it there, briefly, for a little coolness. "They'd have hit the big house for that," he said. "There's nothing in servants' quarters to steal."

He ought to know, she thought with sudden bitterness. Restlessly, she shrugged out of her jacket and laid it on the mattress. Her blouse was damp with perspiration. "Miami certainly wasn't like this when I was growing up."

He leaned against the doorjamb, his expression enigmatic. "There wouldn't be any drug trade, Miss Collier, if the citizens of the United States didn't fall all over themselves to shove the stuff up their noses. You can't supply a market unless the demand exists."

"Drug dealers are just giving people what they want?" Her voice was tinged with sarcasm. It seemed a century since she had had lunch with Dodd in the Brickell Tower restaurant and she was tired. The trip to *Calle Ocho* in search of answers had come to nothing. Except that she'd made a fool of herself, and been badgered first by the yuppie voodoo high priest and now by this arrogant Latin hunk who thought himself above the law.

His face tightened. "Are we back to that? Because I'm

a *latino,* I'm automatically guilty of undermining upright American society?"

"You said it," she snapped. "I didn't."

He pushed away from the doorway. "All right, Miss Collier. Should I tell you how many times I've been approached in boardrooms, in the men's rooms in expensive restaurants, on the damned country club *tennis courts* by total strangers, by your hotshot Anglo social register types, Miami's leading citizens, because their subtle prejudice says that as a *latino* I *look* like I ought to be able to fix them up with a couple of keys of their favorite recreational drug?"

Gaby's lip curled. "I haven't accused you of anything."

"Or that I ought to do your friends a chummy favor," he went on in the same ominously soft voice, "and pop them a few lines of cocaine if, uncouth grease-ball that I am, I want to be really accepted in sacred WASP inner circles? Do you know what that does to my tender *latino* ego? How goddamned flattered I am by it all?"

"I don't want to discuss it." He was standing over her, and she wished she hadn't taken her jacket off. Her silk blouse was sticking to her, outlining her breasts.

"But *I* want to discuss it. I want to tell you how I feel when I'm trying to close a business deal with some arrogant Anglo asshole who's sniffed so much snow into his brain that he can't see the paper he's signing, can't understand the terms his lawyers and mine have carefully delineated—but who is going to accuse me, two or three days later, of being a dirty conniving spick who screwed him out of his money. And"—his voice hardened—"who tells me on the telephone after he's thought it over that I could make things right if I just let him in on a little dealing occasionally?"

She looked away from him. "I don't have anything to do with your problems!"

"Oh, but Miss Collier, you do." He sat down on the bed beside her. Very close beside her. "Because I see it in your eyes, that same speculation about my Latin viability. Only it's not," he murmured huskily, "whether I can pass you a little cocaine, is it? It's something even more interesting."

"Don't start that." She tried to get up, but he held her by the arm. "Let me go."

"What's the matter?" His hot black eyes were inches from hers. "Worried about the stereotype of the indestructible, screw-anything-anytime Latin sex drive?" he asked softly. "Or even about your own uninhibited Anglo willingness?"

She managed to free her arm. "I don't know what you're talking about."

He raised his eyebrows mockingly. He was so close she could feel his body heat through her clothes. "You don't? Hey, every time I see those beautiful silvery eyes of yours run up and down my body, I know you want to sample the goodies. But you're not sure if I will live up to your expectations, right?"

She tried to inch away from him. "I wasn't 'uninhibited,'" she croaked. "That's a lie! I'm not like that at all!"

"Beautiful Miss Collier, you could have fooled me." He lifted his hand and touched the tumbled strands of her damp hair, frowning when he saw her flinch. "The flowers I sent you were supposed to say that I, at least, remembered all of it—very clearly."

Gaby's heart was pounding. She eyed the doorway desperately. "I've never done anything like that in my life. Usually I'm not, I mean I never have been..." She saw his eyebrows raise again. "I don't mean I'm a virgin or anything like that."

The words had burst out in spite of herself, and she blushed. It was rank insanity to be in the same room with him. He always did this to her. "It was the storm," she said breathlessly. "You took advantage of me."

"I took advantage of *you*?" For a moment he was genuinely startled. "Lady, you're the one who grabbed me and pulled me down on top of you, and then felt me up."

Her mouth fell open. "Is that what you thought? That I—that I *grabbed* you?"

"Well, I couldn't say no, could I?" He was so close his

breath brushed her lips. "God, you tempt me," he muttered to himself. "And I thought this would all go away."

She knew he was going to kiss her. She was trembling from the closeness of that chiseled face with its incredible eyes. Yet she felt compelled to say something to stop him. "You have your own hang-ups," she said breathlessly, "about p-promiscuous Anglos."

"I specialized in Anglo girls in college." He lowered his dark head. "I know what I'm talking about."

She shuddered as he pulled back her damp hair, turning her face up to him. She still couldn't move. "I'm not going to be one of your experiments," she whispered.

"Believe me, you're no experiment."

He ran his warm, firm mouth lightly along her cheek, toward the shivery sensitiveness of her ear. Gaby quivered helplessly. His sensuous mouth hovered over hers, stirring an almost violent rush of need in her body. It was like electricity, the erotic spark that leaped between them. She'd almost forgotten its devastating magic. Totally captive to it, she lifted her arms and wound them around his neck, pressing her body into his.

A soft groaning sound broke from him. His arms tightened around her almost painfully. He smelled of male sweat with an underlay of soap, his body hard and warm, and her mouth opened to him. She felt him tremble, suddenly blazing with desire. Ah, how she remembered that passionate trembling, she thought dizzily, his sexy body and its steely strength!

She was aware that what she was doing was reckless, eminently dangerous. James Santo Marin was almost certainly a criminal, even if he was nearly too handsome to look the part. How could she be doing this, she wondered, wanting everything? When she was sure the attraction was only physical?

She deliberately put the questions out of her head. Everything had passed her by. Love, happiness, even sex, nothing had ever touched cowardly little Mouse. Right now she didn't want to think about anything but this.

She pressed her body against his and slid her hands

down his back, fingernails scraping the ridged muscles, the indent of his spine.

"My God." His hands quickly slid up under her skirt, trembling to find only the thin scrap of nylon panties. "Do you know what you're doing?"

"Yes." She was on fire. A wild woman. That was not even her own voice.

His hand touched her bare skin, parted her tightly clasped thighs, and pressed against the shallow cleft. He stroked the little hooded button of flesh gently, insistently. "Easy, easy," he told her as she jerked up against him, biting her lip against a wild, shivery scream. The sensation was more than she could bear.

He gazed down at her face, her half-closed eyes, lips swollen with naked desire. "*Gabriela . . .*" The Spanish version of her name was incredibly seductive. "Don't do this," he murmured, "unless you want to."

Smiling dreamily, Gaby showed him nothing but total, sensual surrender. He pressed her down onto the bed. She lay passively as he stood up and yanked off his shirt. The muscles of his naked chest and shoulders rippled as he kicked off his boots, then unzipped his jeans and peeled them down his legs. Then he pushed off his clinging black briefs.

For a moment he was outlined against the window in a blaze of hot summer light, his body spectacularly golden, yet vulnerable in its beauty. He looked young, unguarded, incomparably vital. As he turned, the florid shaft of his sex jutted out from him, almost brutishly heavy against his groin's mat of dark hair.

The nearly sinister reality of the naked male body washed over Gaby in a chilling wave. And she was embarrassingly aware that she was still fully dressed, that she still wore her linen skirt, flowered silk shirt, even her shoes. The man who moved to the edge of the bed was completely naked.

She sat up, fighting panic. "I can't do this!"

"What?"

"You heard me." She scrambled to her knees on the bare mattress. Had she completely lost her mind? All he had to do was touch her and she went crazy. "I don't fall into bed with a—with a man in the middle of the afternoon!"

He went very still. He stared at her for a long moment, then he said, his voice expressionless, "Do you want me to come back after dark?"

"No! No! I can't. I don't want you."

He didn't move, handsome features frozen, eyes slitted in dawning anger. Gaby sat back on her heels. She knew she couldn't have said anything worse.

"What are you trying to do to me?" he asked harshly.

She couldn't drag her gaze away from his icy hard eyes. He thought she was playing cruel games. But he was a gangster. An underworld character. She had no business going to bed with him! "You don't want *me*," she blurted out. Her teeth were actually chattering. "I'm not your type."

She saw his hands slowly clench, the long muscles in his arms sliding and bunching under smooth, tanned skin.

"My *type*? Jesus, what kind of a rotten tease are you?" He got the words out with an effort. "Is this some new kind of Anglo fun? To get my pants off and then cut off my balls?"

She was horrified. "Don't say that. It's disgusting!"

"And I thought you were different!" he shouted. "What a damned fool I've made of myself!"

"Let me out of the bed." She tried to scramble around him.

"Are you kidding?" He grabbed her, yanking her to him roughly. His face was contorted with rage. "You tell me you want me, then that you don't, and now you're going to *leave*?"

"No—wait!" she cried.

His hands were already working at the buttons of her blouse. She struggled against him as he yanked it down one shoulder, exposing her brassiere. "We'll see," he growled. "We'll damned well see if you want me."

It was her fault, she admitted that. "You're not going to rape me," she sobbed as he dragged her shirt down her arms and flung it away. "You're not!"

"Isn't that what you expect?" He knelt over her and

grabbed her skirt. She felt the button pop as he jerked it down over her legs. He grabbed her flailing ankle and pressed it down into the bed, furious, implacable. "It comes with the grease-ball approach." He tore her panties off her and flung them away. "Lots of hot Latin action, real animal stuff," he ground out savagely. "Want me to sing 'Guantanamera' while I do it?"

"Don't." She closed her eyes tightly as he nearly ripped her bra off her. He was matching her in cruelty. "I'm sorry," she whispered, her voice full of tears. "I'm sorry—sorry—*sorry!*"

He crouched over her, his hands covering her breasts. "Gabriela," he said hoarsely.

There was a burgeoning ferocity in the way his hands swept down the curves of her hips and legs, stroking her soft, yielding skin with fierce hunger. "You're so damned beautiful," he muttered. "Why the hell do you have to drive me so damned crazy?"

She whimpered as he lowered his dark head to touch his mouth to her hardening pink nipples. Digging her fingers into his hair, she writhed beneath him as he caressed each breast in turn, pulling, teasing, his teeth scraping her skin.

"I couldn't forget this, how beautiful you are," he murmured against her silky flesh. "Your lovely white skin, that fantastic red-gold hair." He lifted his head, eyes blazing into hers. "Oh, damn, Gabriela, you've got me drunk on you, I want you so much."

"I don't want to do this," she said weakly.

"Yes, you do."

His mouth covered hers, claiming her completely. As he shifted his big body over her, she felt a rod of hot silky flesh move against the inside of her thighs.

She tried to pull away, but he lifted his mouth and buried his face in her throat. She could smell the scent of his hair. "Gabriela." The words were muffled. "I'm not going to be rough with you. I can't, even if you like it that way. It's not my style. Just let me love you a little, will you?"

Her heart leaped. That incredible sweetness in the

midst of all the burning virility spoke to her as it had the first time. How could she resist him? James Santo Marin was her own particular madness. As her body melted against him, she knew as clearly as she knew anything in this world that she'd pay for her sins later.

He felt her surrender, and sighed. "Damn, I actually dream of this." He lavished eager kisses on her throat, her breasts, her face. "I can't get you out of my head, Gabriela, you're there all the time." He hesitated. "For me, that's so damned dangerous, it's almost suicidal."

His hands slid under her, clutching her soft bottom and lifting her to him. She could feel him growing harder, bigger against her. Excitement swept over them in a wild flood. He pressed against her, powerfully, and her thighs, warm, damp, opened to receive him. Irresistibly strong, he arched his body and thrust himself into her.

Gaby's cry froze on her lips. Wild-eyed with the sudden, tearing pressure, she dug her fingernails into him as he thrust again. Pain jolted through her. She knew that he'd only partly entered her and couldn't go farther. She felt his body shaking as he pulled back, struggling to maintain control.

"You're not a virgin." He could hardly speak.

Her mind was focused only on the stretching, incredible ache where he sought to enter her. "A-almost."

"*Almost?*" It was nearly a shout.

"Only one time!" She tried to ease around the pressure tearing at her, spurred by a vague but hotly burning need of her own. For some reason her body wouldn't stay still. Beneath her hands his silky-wet shoulders trembled as he strained to hold himself motionless. He was only partially lodged in her, yet she had never imagined anything so intimate, so frighteningly erotic. This beautiful, dangerous man was having sex with her, making love to her. It was really happening. She gasped again. "Only once before."

"Oh, my God." He closed his eyes and took a long, shuddering breath. "Why am I doing this?" His voice was despairing. "It's madness. I should be shot. I even forgot the condom."

They were both drenched with perspiration, trembling with desire. Gaby moved her hips tentatively. He groaned. "Jesus, don't do that. Aren't you listening to me?"

She looked up into his face, dazed with her own incredible feelings. "Darling," he said, "you're too little and tight." Sweat beaded his upper lip. "I didn't take enough time. I didn't mean to hurt you."

He started to pull away but she grabbed at him frantically. She wanted him in spite of the pain. This was all new, but she was aching with wanting him. She couldn't stop now if she tried! "It's all right," she told him. "It's fine."

"It isn't fine." He kissed her mouth, her eyes, her forehead feverishly. "I shouldn't—"

"No!" she cried. She clung to his powerful, straining body, felt him big and rigid in her, and she experienced a burst of fiery tenderness that rose in her like a sob. She wanted him! He had stolen her heart somehow, this burning, difficult, beautiful man. The whole world was centered in him, nothing else existed. "Love me," she urged him. "Just love me!"

She moved her hips, her legs, drawing him into her. He sucked in his breath almost violently. She moved again, startled to hear herself make a little purring sound in the back of her throat. She was all flesh, all burning feeling. She writhed with insatiable need.

He couldn't hold back any longer. With a choked sound he pressed into her, a long, invading, relentless thrust that stormed her senses. Low words spilled out of him passionately, that she was so sweet, so soft, so beautiful. That he didn't want to hurt her.

Maddened and uncaring, they came together, seeking each other in a storm of possessing, drowning in each other. He lifted her hips in his hands and thrust into her again and again, going deeper with each long heavy push. Then with a hoarse cry he lost all control.

Somewhere in the flame-shot darkness of desire Gaby knew there couldn't be a more passionate, potent lover in the world than James Santo Marin. He loved her wildly, caught in the grip of a powerful desire that whirled them into soul-destroying abandon. When she reached the peak, driven to it by the pounding of his frenzy, she cried out and heard his hoarse cry of release answering her, his mouth quickly covering hers as he poured himself into her.

The shocks of his body jolted on and on as he lowered himself to his elbows, his breathing ragged. "Never, never, never like this." His lips caressed her hair, her face, her throat. "Gabriela," he said in hoarse wonder, "it's never been like this for me."

The world came back very slowly: the sound of the humming fan in the window, the stripes of sunshine on the bed where they lay, the simmering summertime heat. Gaby drifted back, too, her body ringing with the last echoes of their desire. James lay on top of her heavily. The feel of him now, and the memory of his rampaging need, left her weak. She tenderly stroked his wet hair back from his brow. *Tiger,* she couldn't help thinking. The *babalawo* was right.

He stirred and looked down at her, fierce, proud, and beautiful. Then he smiled, showing white teeth. "You make me so happy," he murmured.

Her heart contracted painfully. It was totally unexpected, this thing that had happened in the old apartment over the garage on a hot summer afternoon. It was pure and wonderful. It couldn't be bad. *I'm in love with him,* she realized, unsurprised.

"The hell of it is," he went on, gently touching his mouth to her forehead. "I can't do this. I really can't commit myself to anything." He kissed the tip of her nose. "Not a damned thing. Hell, I can't even explain anything. And I want you so much."

She watched those curving, graceful lips move as she fought against the fading of the blissful glow. She'd forgotten everything this beautiful afternoon, making love. But there was one thing she couldn't forget.

Slowly, he stopped kissing her, knowing from her expression something was wrong.

"I'm engaged." It was a hoarse, desperate croak, full

of horror. Gaby couldn't have prevented those words from tumbling out if her life depended on it. She stared up at him helplessly. "I'm engaged to be married!"

The shock was absolute. *"What?"*

She pushed him away. It took all her strength, he was so heavy. She rolled away from him and sat up in the bed. "I just got engaged to be married. *Today.*"

He sat up too, uncoiling his long, naked body. "Married," he repeated, staring at her.

"I'm engaged to be married to Dodd Brickell." It was as though she couldn't stop saying it.

His face registering nothing, he rose from the bed. She watched numbly as he pulled on his jeans. He bent and picked up his boots, but didn't put them on.

"Congratulations," he said stiffly. "I'm glad you remembered. Particularly after we made love and not before."

"Don't say that," she whispered.

He gave her a brief, piercing look. "On the contrary, I mean it. I didn't have much on my schedule for today. So this was a great way to pass the time."

Gaby got to her knees on the bed, still naked. He looked away. "I forgot it," she said, but she didn't believe it herself.

"Then you'd better forget this too." His control was icy. So was his anger. "Am I supposed to say I wish you every happiness? Frankly, to hell with it."

Gaby wanted to go some place and hide. But there was nowhere. She wrapped her arms around her body, shivering, enveloped in despair. She wished the world would collapse. She couldn't face tomorrow. Next week. Next year, the rest of her life. She loved James Santo Marin. Why hadn't she been able to do something before this became such a mess?

"What is it?" he demanded, staring at her.

She couldn't meet his eyes, she was so full of confusion and pain. How could she be in love with a man like this? Subconsciously she must have been sure she was going to marry Dodd. Was this just some dishonest, crazy compulsion she'd given in to, simply because there was something so physical, so strong between them that she couldn't resist him? She was horrified with the realization of the terrible things she could do. Dear God, she hardly knew herself!

Shrugging, he turned away and picked up his T-shirt from the chair.

But at the door he stopped. "One good turn deserves another," he said, his back to her. "To show you how much I appreciate what you—what I got here today, I'll give you a piece of advice straight off the hot-tip line. Whatever you do, don't let your Anglo jock boyfriend scare you into selling this place."

She heard his footsteps receding down the stairs, then a minute later the engine of the Lamborghini starting up. Then the crunch of gravel as it pulled out of the drive.

Chapter 13

Crissette lay stretched out on her stomach on a rustic bench in the shade of a banyan tree, the untied strings of her bright yellow bikini top dangling over the wooden slats. The public park on Miami Beach's Eighty-first Street was almost empty at noon, most of the sunbathers and swimmers having taken refuge in their hotels from the relentless fireball of the midday sun. Beyond the wide stretch of sand the Gulf Stream glimmered like a field of solid aquamarine gemstone, breathtakingly crystal-clear.

Crissette stifled a yawn. "This is some way to take a lunch break, Gabrielle," she drawled. "You gotta admit Miami is no hardship territory, not when you can spend your lunch hour like this."

"Mmm," Gaby agreed absently. She was reading the draft of her engagement announcement.

Gaby was sitting with her feet propped against a railing, below which she could see a beach jungle of sea grape and banyans. She and Crissette had spent all that Thursday morning shooting winter formal wear, a collection of beaded and sequined evening gowns at St. Laurent's Rive Gauche shop in Bal Harbour. The contrast between a hectic three hours of adjusting lights, soothing a nervous shop manager, and encouraging a gaggle of particularly awkward socialite models, and what they were doing now—catching a lunch break and a swim at one of Miami Beach's most beautiful seaside parks—was the better part of Miami's sometimes frenetic lifestyle. As a native, Gaby supposed she'd always taken living like this for granted. Now she was learning to appreciate the exotic environment.

Crissette rolled over on her back, holding the bikini top to her breasts to keep it from falling. Gaby thought that Crissette, with her graceful dusky body, looked more like a professional model than the amateur volunteers she'd been shooting the past few hours. While they'd been at the St. Laurent shop Crissette had bought two summer outfits that, even though on sale, had been dazzlingly expensive, worth several weeks of her salary. The day before, Crissette had bought lunch at an expensive waterside restaurant, picking up the check for both of them because Gaby didn't have the money to spend. But in spite of the bursts of extravagance, Crissette was noticeably restless and edgy, and certainly not very happy. She never mentioned David Fothergill.

"Hey, Gabrielle, is your announcement okay?" she asked lazily. "How does it look?"

"It looks all right." Gaby studied the photograph that had been taken when she'd been working in Florence. She hadn't realized how much she'd changed. The young woman whose photo would appear in the *Times-Journal* wedding announcements column looked like a stranger with her prim smile and pale hair scraped back from her face. She had to admit she certainly wasn't the same person she'd been a little over two months ago. She now had an entirely new wardrobe and a new hairstyle. She even had a considerable tan. Her gaze dropped to the words below her photograph. "Mrs. Paul Aston Collier of Miami announces the engagement of her daughter, Victoria Gabrielle, to Dodson Flagler Brickell III, also of Miami."

Well, she thought, sighing, it was done. The announcement of her engagement would be read by the *Times-Journal's* several hundred thousand readers in the Greater Miami area on Sunday, including all of Paul and Jeannette Collier's friends and Old Miami acquaintances, as well as Dodd's and his family's.

"The bride-elect is the daughter of the late Paul Aston Collier, sportsman and founder of the Marathon Ocean

Racing Cup event, granddaughter of Aston George Collier, a pioneer South Florida developer, and a grandniece of General Robert R. Pierce of St. Augustine. Miss Collier attended Ransom Country Day School in Coconut Grove and graduated from Miami Beach High School. She has a degree in art history from the University of Florida and until recently worked as research assistant for the Ohio State Fine Arts project in Florence, Italy. She is currently employed as fashion writer for the Miami *Times-Journal* newspaper."

Gaby had shown her typed engagement copy to her mother several days ago, taking pains to describe how and where Dodd had proposed to her, there in the Brickell Tower restaurant. Her mother had paid no attention at all. She was absorbed in a story in the Sunday paper about Frank Sinatra's recent visit to Miami Beach hotels, the scenes of his former glory. "He's such an old man," Jeannette had lamented, "in his seventies now. I just can't believe it!"

Gaby had left her mother with the paper. Outside the room a sympathetic nurse had told her not to worry. This indifference, the self-absorbed distraction, was fairly normal for addiction withdrawal. But it hadn't made Gaby feel any happier.

"The bridegroom-elect," she read on, "is the son of Mr. and Mrs. Dodson Flagler Brickell Jr., of Miami and St. Croix. He attended St. Paul's Academy and the University of Miami, and has a law degree from the University of Virginia. He is currently a junior partner in the Miami firm of Brickell, Masterson and Brickell, serves on the board of directors of the South Florida Coastal Bank and Trust Company, and is finance officer for Palm-Mar Development Corporation. Mr. Brickell is a member of the Biscayne Yacht Club, the Eldorado Cotillion, and Polo Bath and Tennis Club. Wedding plans to be announced.

Before she'd left the hospital Gaby had gone to see the cashier about her mother's monthly bill. She had been stunned when she was told it had been taken care of. Dodd Brickell had paid for everything. And was continu-

ing to do so, because her mother's health insurance had
run out.

She put the paper in her lap and closed her eyes,
feeling the sunshine hot on her face. Dodd was a rock, a
tower of strength. The past two weeks he had accepted all
her excuses about the pressures of her job, her mother's
hospitalization, her tiredness, with sweet understanding.
Now that they were engaged she knew Dodd wanted
intimacy. After all, hadn't he been her first lover? Hadn't
she always made it clear she was in love with him? But
Gaby couldn't bring herself to go beyond a few hurried
good-night kisses. Her own deceit, her terrible guilt, were
making her miserable. Still, she knew that no one, not
even someone as patient as Dodd, would believe her lame
excuses forever.

She had told herself over and over there was no
earthly reason why she shouldn't love Dodd now as she
had for most of her life and be ecstatically happy that he
loved her too. Except that reason was named James Santo
Marin.

She felt sick about it. She'd never thought of herself
as an immoral person. Could she ever forget or forgive
herself for what she had done? Sunday's paper would
announce to the world that she was going to marry Dodd
Brickell, but she'd gone to bed with someone else, a
well-known man from Miami's upper-crust Latin society
with reputedly shady connections. A trigger-tempered,
tempestuous playboy, a man any woman would have sense
enough to stay away from! But from the time she'd lain in
James Santo Marin's arms and he'd made love to her,
everything else had ceased to exist. Even now, she thought,
shuddering, he haunted her dreams, disturbed her sleep
with the ghostly memories of his passionate fire.

Crissette had been watching her. "Gabrielle, you look
like you're proofreading an obit. What's the problem?"

"Nothing." Gaby stuffed the proof page back in her
purse. "I guess getting engaged is just more complicated
than I thought."

Dodd had called her several times about plans for
their engagement party, and each time Gaby had told him

that whatever his mother wanted to do about a dinner dance in Palm Beach was just fine. She cringed from the realization that marrying Dodd wasn't going to be quick or simple. It would take months, and she was surprised by her own sudden urgency. Frankly, she longed to get it over with.

Crissette came over to sit down beside her. "You can't fool me, honey, your head's in some other place these days." She looked puzzled. "That Cuban family come back to the apartment? Hey, your mother's okay, isn't she?"

Gaby couldn't meet her eyes. "No, the Escuderos haven't come back. I suppose Angel and Elena are gone for good. As for my mother, she decided all by herself to sign up for the Mount Sinai addiction rehab program. So that's one problem out of the way for a while." She managed a smile. "We don't even have to worry about the bill. Dodd—my fiancé—is lending us the money."

Crissette was still frowning. "Then what is it? Prenuptial jitters? Gabrielle, I never saw somebody who should be happy look so down in the mouth. Kid, you need to ventilate." Crissette was fond of psycho-jargon. "Relate to what's traumatizing you. You can trust me, honey."

Gaby laughed shakily. The one time she'd "ventilated" her problems she'd been in the *babalawo*'s office and the results had been disastrous. The *Santería* high priest had called James Santo Marin. And *that* had ended with a catastrophic afternoon in the garage apartment.

"Crissette," Gaby said abruptly, "are you in love with David Fothergill?"

The other woman looked startled. "What's that got to do with anything?"

"Because he's in love with you. No, David didn't say anything to me," she added quickly. "I just wondered if you knew."

Crissette's face had gone stiff. "I've got no future with David Fothergill. In spite of what you might think, I'm not ready for the old cliché of the black woman supporting a no-good black man in return for a lot of lovin'. Just like"—her voice was cool—"I've never been into tap dancing or eating watermelon."

"Oh, Crissette. I didn't say—"

"No, *I* did," the other woman said sharply. "Look, Gabrielle, like it or not, I'm a middle-class, professional black. My family wants the best for me. David Fothergill is an illegal alien who's got no job, no money, and is probably sleeping in the streets right now." She looked away toward the brilliant vista of sun and water beyond them. "If I love him that doesn't make a damned bit of difference. I'm not going to change my mind."

She got up abruptly and gathered her discarded clothes and shoes.

"Crissette, is David a poet?" Gaby asked. "Has he ever said anything to you about it?"

The photographer snorted. "Baby, all those calypso cats are poets. That is, when they're not being the one genius musician the world's been waiting for, or the new Michelangelo. I've heard that line, too. But all they're looking for is some loving woman to pay the bills."

Gaby had no business asking, but with what had happened to her the past few weeks, she felt she had to know. There was no one else to turn to. "Crissette, was—was the attraction between you and David mostly . . . ah, *sex*?"

"*What?*" Crissette turned to her. "Gabrielle, what's bothering you? Hey, you're not just marrying this Brickell dude because you can't stay out of the sack with him, are you? Jeez, honey, he doesn't look the type, if you'll pardon my saying so."

"Oh, no, not Dodd." Gaby had turned bright pink. "I'm serious. I want to know," she went on desperately, "if you can put aside a—a powerful attraction, forget someone you don't want outside of . . . wonderful sex. Someone who wouldn't make you happy anyway. Like David," she blundered on. "A relationship that couldn't possibly have a future. You know, make yourself forget the whole thing, walk away from it and"—her voice cracked—"be happy."

Crissette stood with both hands on her hips. "I'm not following any of this. Okay, Gabrielle, you want to tell me about it?"

Gaby shook her head, too overcome with misery to

speak. Her story on the Coral Gables fashion show had appeared, complete with the sidebar on James Santo Marin. Looking over the Modern Living section, someone in State News had commented idly that the good-looking Prince of Coral Cables was the same guy who'd had a Miami Crime Commission investigation of his business affairs last year, looking for possible drug connections. The remark had sent a cold chill down Gaby's spine.

It's all wrong, she told herself. You've got to stop thinking about him!

Crissette sat down beside her on the bench, still holding her shoes in her hand. After a long silence she said, "Yeah, I guess it's possible to forget somebody you love."

They sat for a while staring at the sea.

"But not too damned probable," Crissette added.

Jack Carty had noticed the announcement in the Modern Living section. "If I had known you were going to get engaged," he said, his face buried in letters to the editor, "I would have asked you out to lunch sooner."

Gaby, going over the story on the Rive Gauche evening wear, noticed Crissette's photographs hadn't turned out at all well. That was strange. Crissette was tops on the fashion beat. Then she realized what Jack had said. "You were going to ask *me* out to lunch?"

He put down the Sunday sheets and handed her a stack of brightly colored brochures on the Greater Miami Annual Summer Festival. On the top packet he had written: "Cover the fashion angle. Interview who's wearing what. Check with society page."

"Yeah," he muttered, ducking his head again, "it looks like I missed my chance."

Gaby went back to her desk and sat down. Jack Carty's talk about taking her out to lunch was probably a quirk of her imagination. She pulled off his note and stuck it on her calendar. As she thumbed through the festival press material, she remembered her terror just a few short weeks ago at her first press releases, wondering what, exactly, she was supposed to do with them. Now she knew at least half of all press releases were merely sales pushes for fashionwear or accessories and had nothing of interest for a feature story. They were filed in the wastepaper basket.

The Miami Summer Festival, however, was different. The event, sponsored the last week in August by the Tourist Bureau, the Chamber of Commerce, and leading civic organizations, had been invented several years ago to counteract Miami's growing reputation as a crime capital, and to attract tourism during the "dead season," when most of south Florida's attractions came to a sunbaked standstill.

This year the week-long celebration featured a Miami Dolphins preseason game in the Orange Bowl, a world-class pro tennis tourney in Miami Shores, a Goombay-calypso festival on the downtown Miami bayfront, and a street dance and arts bazaar in Coconut Grove. The crowning event was Saturday night's Hospital Foundation Costume Masked Ball at the Deering estate, Vizcaya, the world-famed Italian Renaissance-style mansion and gardens that were now a historical park.

Vizcaya was expected to be jammed with not only Miami, Fort Lauderdale, and Palm Beach socialites, but a sizable jet-set representation from New York, Newport, Southampton, London, Rome, and Paris.

Gaby opened the brochure with interest. All this had started while she was in Europe, but Vizcaya was the perfect place to have a spectacular festival ball. This year two dance bands, one for Latin music, and a star-studded concert with singer-television star Don Johnson of *Miami Vice*, Linda Ronstadt, Julio Iglesias, and opera star Placido Domingo, would be followed by a gigantic fireworks display over Biscayne Bay with Miami Beach and Key Biscayne as a backdrop.

The press release listed the prominent names of the Costume Ball Organizing Committee, most of whom Gaby recognized. Her elbows on the desk, she cradled her head in her hands as she read the list. With the announcement of her engagement in the newspaper Sunday, the costume ball assignment meant she'd be renewing old acquaintances, trying to avoid the subject of her mother, explaining how she'd become the fashion writer for the *Times-Journal*— and dealing with surprise, felicitations, and a flood of questions.

When the telephone rang she jumped. For a moment her heart fluttered fearfully up in her throat. She felt as though she couldn't bring herself to talk to Dodd, to listen to his happy plans for their engagement party one more time.

It was only Crissette down in photographic. "Have you got the memo on the Costume Ball?" The photographer's voice was incredulous. "Can you believe this? Everybody that covers festival night in Vizcaya has to go in costume. It's the pits! The city desk says we go to Robarts Rentals to order them."

The memo about staff being in costume was somewhere on her desk. Gaby was looking under papers for it when Crissette added, "I've got the assignment that night with you, Gabrielle. Jack just sent down the order. Man, don't they know it's bad enough carrying camera equipment without being Cleopatra or a pirate or something?"

"A Night in Venice," Gaby said, finding the gala costume ball brochure. A color picture of Vizcaya's magnificent lawn and Renaissance mansion was on the front. "No pirates. I think more like farthingales and powdered wigs."

Crissette groaned. "You know how big Vizcaya is? Ten acres! And listen—how're we gonna take anybody's picture if they come *masked*?"

Jack's instructions hadn't been clear on that, Gaby realized. Photographic coverage, as Crissette was pointing out, did present problems. "Why don't I go as a gondola," she teased, "and you be a gondolier?"

"Cute, very cute. You pick weird times to be funny, Gabrielle. At two hundred and fifty dollars a head I'm betting nobody'll come."

"*We're* coming."

"Really, I can't talk to you when you're like this. I like you better when you're depressed."

After hanging up, Gaby returned to the committee list. Jack had told her to call the socialite members to ask what costumes they were going to wear. When her telephone rang again she lifted it absently and said, "Fashion desk."

Perhaps it was the second of dead air on the other end of the line that warned her. Whatever it was, Gaby was suddenly tense, her heart pounding, frozen to her chair.

A husky voice said rapidly, "I'm calling you on the advice of my lawyers. Actually, I'll be out of town for some time. It's better that you know—"

Gaby was having trouble breathing, the same problem as always, compounded now by the unrelieved iciness of that wildly familiar voice. She couldn't even follow what he was saying. His voice faded in and out of her consciousness like a badly tuned radio. Harsh words. Something about lawyers.

Oh, God.

"—take responsibility for it . . . because I didn't use any protection . . ." Gaby realized her irrational terror was blocking full understanding of what he was saying, but she couldn't seem to do anything about it. She was shaking so, she could hardly hold the telephone receiver to her ear. "In fact," he went on guardedly, "I've been advised to discuss this with you, because you . . . ah, you might be pregnant."

Gaby couldn't move. She saw the newsroom tilt, go out of focus for a split second. It was as though everything stopped, suspended by her fright.

He seemed to be struggling with conflicting emotions as he added, "Gabrielle? I—we did something crazy. God, how can I say this? I want you to know that I won't duck any responsibil—"

She slammed the receiver down violently. The noise carried. Heads on the rewrite desk looked up.

The words rang in her head. She stared at the telephone as though it would emit the sounds of James Santo Marin's voice again at any moment. Just the idea sent a rush of panic through her whole body. The mere sound of his voice unnerved her. What had he said? He was worried she might be *pregnant*?

Gaby grabbed the edge of the desk with both hands.

Oh, God, she thought wildly, what was she going to do? How could she make this go away?

She realized Jack Carty was standing by her desk. "How about a cup of coffee?" he asked. His tone was too casual.

"I'm all right," Gaby said. She got her purse out of the desk drawer and stood up. He'd said coffee, hadn't he? She was still shaking.

On the way up to the snack bar Jack didn't ask her what was the matter and Gaby was grateful. He brought her hot coffee in a Styrofoam cup and sat down beside her.

"I meant what I said, about lunch."

He was treating her like a shock victim, she thought. She looked around the room numbly, knowing she probably looked like one. She was in the newspaper canteen. Having coffee with Jack Carty, her boss. Close up, he was really much younger than one expected. Freckles. Blue eyes. She knew she was staring, and looked down at her cup.

"The fashion expense account looks very good," he told her.

Gaby was wearing a new sleeveless denim sundress, the swimsuit she'd worn during lunch still underneath. She hadn't pulled her hair back after her swim and it floated around her face in disorder. She felt disheveled, off balance with shock, not as attractive as his eyes were telling her.

She knew he had overheard her telephone call in the newsroom. She was carrying around such a burden of emotion since that afternoon with James, she sometimes felt as though she would burst. But not Jack Carty, she decided unhappily. He was her boss. She'd sworn off confidences. Besides, he'd think she was totally crazy.

She opened her mouth, then closed it. There was nothing she could say. Not even about James Santo Marin calling her at work, now, to threaten her.

There must be something they could talk about. Something safe. Casting about, she thought of one thing that had been bothering her for some time. She asked him about it.

He spooned powdered creamer into his coffee, taking his time before answering. "Is that what's been bothering you? You've been looking as though somebody was on your case, Gabrielle. It had me worried."

"I've—I've had a better grip on the fashion job lately." She glanced uncertainly at him. "Haven't I?"

"Yes, you've been doing okay, stop worrying about it." He didn't look up. "Are you trying to do investigative reporting? Everybody, when they start out, wants to latch onto a big story. But fashion, believe me, is no place—"

"No, not a story," she interrupted quickly. "This is personal."

He fastened his bright blue gaze on her. "You're really going to get married?"

Good heavens, not Jack Carty, Gaby thought with a start. He really hadn't been joking about lunch. She didn't know what to do. The realization that he truly was interested in her took her off guard. Now she was the one who mumbled something inaudible in reply.

His gaze lingered on her face. After a while he said, "The state of Florida has a commission on corporations, a sort of overseer committee. But the easiest way is to go to the Dade County Courthouse and start looking in the land books. All owners are listed in alphabetical order, and by tract number and name, as city and county building licensees."

Gaby's eyes widened. "So if you were buying up some Palm Island property..."

He nodded. "Your corporation would be there."

Chapter 14

The engagement party for Gaby and Dodd at the exclusive Everglades Club in Palm Beach had to be canceled when Dodd's mother fell into a sand trap on the golf course at the Bal Harbour links and broke her leg.

"I've never seen anything like it," Dodd fumed. They were having dinner at Regine's, the chic international club at the top of the Grand Bay Hotel in Coconut Grove, one of Dodd's favorite spots. It was the first time Gaby had ever seen him so out of sorts. He'd sent back two bottles of wine and the maître d' had finally brought a vintage bottle of Moët & Chandon as a peace offering. "It's just incredible to have so many damned things screw up at one time," he went on. "First the engagement announcement, then the jeweler gets that damned yellowish diamond on your engagement ring by mistake, and now mother's accident."

Gaby couldn't understand it, either. "I saw the proofs on the announcement. I checked them myself on Thursday and everything was all right then. I don't know what could have happened."

"What happened," he said grimly, "is that the population of greater Miami has been informed that you're engaged to marry someone named *shrdlu qwertyiuop*. On every goddamned line where my name was supposed to be."

Gaby's lips quivered, but she held back her laughter.

158

Dodd had found it anything but funny. "It's a printer's error," she said soothingly. "They tell me it's not supposed to happen in electronic typesetting, but every once in a while it does. I'm really sorry about your mother, Dodd," she added. "I called her at the hospital today, and she seemed to be in good spirits."

He signaled for the waiter to refill his glass with the Moët. "That's the goddamndest thing too," he grumbled. "Mother's not clumsy, but the thing took her by surprise. Damned dog came bolting out of a clump of palm trees on the sixth tee by the sand trap and nearly bowled her over. Mother lost her balance and went right down into the hole."

Gaby put down her fork and stared at him. "You didn't say it was a dog. You just said she fell into a sand trap."

"Didn't I?" he said absently. "Big black one. Mother said it looked like a Labrador. Now, Mouse," he said, seeing the look on her face, "we've been having some crazy run of bad luck, that's all. Don't start making any sort of connection."

"I wasn't making any sort of connection. I haven't said a word!"

"Well, I knew if I mentioned a Labrador, it would dredge up all that business at the house and upset you." He reached across the table and took her hand in his. "C'mon, honey, you can't grieve forever for an old dog that was, after all, in pretty bad shape. In another year or so you would have had to put Jupiter to sleep."

Gaby managed to smile. Actually, the postponement of the engagement party until Dodd's mother could walk again was a relief. For some perverse reason she was glad for the delay, when before she couldn't move things fast enough. And it was one less thing she had to do in the next few weeks. Jack had assigned her to cover all the top retail stores in the greater metropolitan area as shops and boutiques began featuring fall fashions. She had been traveling from one end of Miami to the other in late summer thundershowers and killing heat, trying to do it all. Jack's reasoning was that in the past the *Times-Journal* hadn't adequately covered what were, after all, lucrative advertisers with fashion features. Now that Gaby was getting better at what she was doing, he wanted her to hit each one.

To add to it, just as she had grown to depend on the help and friendship of Crissette Washington, Crissette had been transferred to the paper's metropolitan news desk. The photographer assigned to fashion now was Harry Holstead, a veteran of the police beat. His fashion shots, unfortunately, showed that Harry hadn't quite mastered the switch. Jack's scathing observation after seeing some of Harry's shots of Burdine's was that Harry had an unhappy talent for making a fashion show look a lot like a police lineup.

Gaby studied Dodd as he cut into his veal marengo with a dissatisfied air. How times have changed, she couldn't help thinking. These days Dodd never asked her about her job, just when she was getting much better at it. He seemed to have forgotten about it with the upsets of the past week, especially the mix-up with a flawed stone for her engagement diamond. He was convinced fate was conspiring against them.

"Mother's compound fracture is pretty painful," he said. "I think she'd appreciate a visit, Mouse. She's at Palm Beach-Mount Sinai." He paused, then added as an afterthought, "Where your mother is."

"Of course." Inwardly, she groaned. Both her mother and Dodd's were in the hospital at the same time. The past week had been bizarre.

Dinner was strained, and Gaby was tired. Dodd took her home early. Then, at the front door, she clung to him impulsively, overcome with a need for his comfort and reassurance. Dodd Brickell was the only man she'd ever loved, *needed* to love. She suddenly wanted to hear that everything was going to be all right. She needed to hear that he loved her, too.

He seemed relieved at her unexpected display of affection. "Of course I love you, Mouse." He put his arms around her and lowered his head to kiss her. But at the last moment Gaby turned her head away.

As though nothing had happened, Dodd took the key from her hand and unlocked the door for her. "Things will be better in a few weeks, honey," he said evenly. "Just hang in there. God knows I'm looking forward to getting you out of this damned house." As he held the door open he said almost pleadingly, "Gaby, darling . . ."

She knew what was on his mind. "I'm tired, Dodd," she murmured, "but it's been a wonderful evening."

Gaby knew she was acting badly, but she didn't want to be alone with Dodd, even for a few minutes' sexy kissing. At dinner he'd again brought up the matter of her staying in the house, and she didn't want to argue any more about it. Nor the other subject, getting Jeannette's power of attorney so the house could be sold.

"Have I told you," she said brightly, "I think I've got somebody to live in the garage apartment?"

He looked glum. "Not a long-term arrangement, I hope."

"No, only temporary." Dodd followed her into the hall while she turned on the lights. A steamy sprinkling of rain had been falling all evening and the shoulders of his yacht club blazer were damp, his thick fair hair beaded with moisture. He had never, she thought, looked more ruggedly handsome. And she couldn't miss the silent appeal in his eyes.

"Darling," he murmured. He tried to nuzzle her hair. "We're engaged, remember?"

Gaby was certain Dodd would never pressure her. He was too conservative to come right out and say they were alone in the house, and that he wanted to make love to her. "Dodd, I love you," she said gently. "But it's late."

"Yes, I know, darling." His hand brushed her cheek. "Have I told you how beautiful you are?" His voice deepened with desire. "Oh, Mouse, I want you so much."

"Dodd, with my mother in the hospital, your mother in the hospital . . ."

He stepped back, his face in shadows. "And your job. Yes, I know."

"Well, it is a lot to cope with." *Just give me time*, she

pleaded silently. *Give me time to forget someone else! God knows I'm trying*.

He turned his head away, his shoulders hunching slightly. "This house has a damned musty smell," he said abruptly. "The roof still leaks, doesn't it?"

"Everything leaks. Including the plumbing. What does it smell like?"

"I can't tell." He looked back at her. "It's not important. Who did you say is renting the garage apartment?"

"Just somebody." She took his arm and steered him toward the door. "In return for the rent he's going to keep the place tidy, do all the yard work."

Dodd stopped at the open door. "*He?*"

"A friend of a friend who works on the newspaper."

He was frowning now. "Gaby, I told you I'd be willing to pay for someone to—"

To silence him, Gaby threw her arms around him and lifted her face to be kissed. With a groan Dodd crushed her to him, his mouth covering hers hungrily.

It was one of the few times they'd kissed in the past week, and Dodd's mouth was warm and fervent, the kiss everything it should have been. Gaby felt a sudden pang of regret for the lovemaking he so obviously wanted to give her. She started to tell him to close the door and come back inside.

"It's not a smell," he said, lifting his head. "It's something else." He sniffed the air, puzzled. "Like the night you had the prowlers." He let her go and stepped back. "Damn, I need to check this house every time I bring you home. Stupid of me to forget that."

He walked away, leaving her standing there, his footsteps echoing in the silent house as he crossed the sun room. She heard the back door slam, then the crackling sounds of underbrush being pushed out of the way as Dodd made a circuit of the outside pathway. When he returned to the front door, he said he'd found nothing.

"I thought it might have been a dead rat smelling up the place," he said as he gave her a brief, warm kiss good-bye. "Put it down on the list of things to do. Get this place fumigated before you sell it."

"Am I going to sell it?" she asked softly.

He groaned. "Mouse, darling, try to give it some thought, will you? There's no other way out for you. Or your mother. Selling this old place will just manage to bail you out as it is."

He gave her a final peck on the cheek before he turned and went back to his car.

A few days later, as they were trying on their Vizcaya ball costumes at Robarts Rentals, Crissette told Gaby that David Fothergill had a job. He was working for a commercial garbage collection company in the city of Hallandale, north of Miami.

"Another job off the books," Crissette said sarcastically. "He called me and told me and wanted to take me someplace to celebrate getting a job, some Jamaican cheap food dump over in Hialeah. I told him to get lost."

Crissette had selected an eighteenth-century Venetian *cisisbeo*'s outfit of satin coat, bicorne hat, and tight scarlet satin breeches. As a long-legged Venetian gigolo she looked exotically unisex.

"In drag yet," she muttered, turning to view her back. "The things I do for the *Times-Journal*." She adjusted the tails of the satin coat. "I wish somebody'd take *me* to Regine's. I understand it's drop-dead terminal chic."

Gaby shrugged. "It's okay. We were celebrating being engaged. And Dodd's a member."

The fitting room was filled to overflowing with discarded costumes. Gaby pushed a pile of gondoliers' striped shirts out of the way and tried to sit down on the one chair. The large hoop she was wearing under her skirts wouldn't fold properly. She stood back up. "Crissette, you look sort of decadent," she said.

"Believe me, honey, I'm straight. But if I wear those flats with the pom-poms on the toes I'll walk like you can't tell. How'm I supposed to wear all this fancy Italian drag and manage a lot of camera equipment too?" she complained. She abruptly pulled Gaby around to the mirror. "Okay, kid, now it's your turn."

They stood side by side, regarding themselves in the

three-way glass. Gaby's elaborate gown had originally been made for a principal player in a Coconut Grove Playhouse production of *Twelfth Night*. The actress had had unimpressive bust measurements, but an unusually tiny waist. The eighteenth-century court dress was made of blue watered silk with gold bead-crusted panniers in yellow moiré. The bodice was cut low and square so that Gaby's breasts, pressed together, looked seductively full. The sleeves were tight and ended at the elbows, and the skirt was ankle-length—a blessing since she was going to have to do a lot of walking through the museum grounds.

Gaby stared at her reflection, her lower lip caught between her teeth. She looked amazingly doll-like, she thought, fragile—and sexy, even with her tawny hair an untidy mess from trying on costumes. For the first time, viewing the beautiful gown, she could understand why the eighteenth century was considered such a libidinous era.

Crissette was staring, too. "Hey, you're one foxy lady, Gabrielle. You sure have changed from the scared-looking chick who came into the newsroom that first day."

Gaby was startled. The words struck a strange chord somewhere in the back of her mind that she wanted to forget. "I haven't changed that much."

"I dunno. I think getting engaged has done a lot for you, girl." The other woman's luminous eyes surveyed her critically. "Before, you looked like somebody who'd never been loved up, if you know what I mean." When she saw Gaby turning pink she said, "Aw, stop that, Gabrielle, nobody blushes anymore, it's like, *très gauche*. You've really got it for this guy, haven't you?"

Gaby stared in the mirror, disconcerted. It wasn't her, she thought. She wasn't this sexy, ravishing creature. It was the costume, nothing more than that.

"I'm not bugging you, sugar," Crissette went on quickly. "Don't get me wrong, I'm happy for you. If you like Dodd Brickell the Third, that's fine with me."

Gaby frowned. "It's going to be hot wearing all this," she said, changing the subject. "This is no great creative assignment. There's no fashion news in a costume ball, except who spent the most money on some ridiculous outfit."

Crissette shrugged. "A wig goes with that. A big white one with flowers and beads in it."

"Forget it," Gaby said, turning away. "I'd die of heatstroke in a wig."

Crissette took off her bicorne hat and ran her fingers through her hair. "I hope you know what you're doing," she said abruptly, "giving David that apartment at your place."

Gaby didn't look at her. "I need someone there at night. Really."

It was Crissette's turn to frown. "Gabrielle, David's not going to keep this job either. The feds know where all the unskilled jobs are in south Florida. They'll make a sweep up in Hallandale and drag him right off that garbage truck, you wait and see."

Gaby had stepped out of her costume and was slipping her street dress over her head. "I hope not. David deserves a break. Tell me, why on earth do people from the islands keep coming to Miami if it's so hard to get a job here?"

"Because it isn't," Crissette said shortly. "You know why we got so many Haitians in south Florida? It isn't just because they love the climate, honey. If Haitian illegals can just make it out to Belle Glade, they can get a job cutting sugar cane. You can't get Americans to do a backbreaker job like that, but the Haitians are trained cane cutters. They know if they can just get some kind of boat into south Florida they can find work around Lake Okeechobee. There's practically a whole town of Haitians living out there around the big sugar mills." Crissette turned in front of the mirror, adjusting her jeans and expensive silk tank top from Rive Gauche. "Immigration doesn't do anything to the sugar companies, only to the illegals when they find them. Same way with Mexican migrant workers."

"You don't think David's in any danger at my place, do you?" Gaby asked, alarmed.

"Danger? The feds might pick up David at your

place. They might charge *you* with harboring an illegal alien. You ever think of that?"

Gaby had always thought David was in the greatest danger on the job. She considered it for a long moment. "I'll just have to take that chance," she said quietly. "I really need him, Crissette. The grass is getting so high I have to fight my way to the front door."

The other woman didn't smile. "That house is spooky, Gabrielle."

"Crissette, I've always lived there. It's my home."

"Have it your way," Crissette said. "Just don't forget I warned you. I don't know what it was like in the old days, but it's spooky now."

Gaby remembered Crissette's words as she parked her mother's car in the driveway. "Spooky" was not a term she associated with her home, but she saw for the first time how it must look to outsiders—the Spanish-Moorish tower, the straggling bougainvillea that climbed the stucco facade, the overgrown hibiscus jungle that almost hid the front door. It had always been home, a safe place. It was strange to think of it any other way.

An oncoming thunderstorm had laid siege to the out-lying parts of Miami just before Gaby had left the news-paper offices. She was not surprised to find the lights were out all over Palm Island. The house was echoingly quiet as she let herself in. She opened a few windows, then went to the kitchen to make a sandwich from a package of bologna she managed to find in the darkened depths of the already-warm refrigerator. After eating by candlelight, she went upstairs to her bedroom.

Thunderstorms and power failures were always expected in south Florida; Gaby's bedside radio was equipped with batteries. The only way to live, she thought as she settled herself comfortably among the bed pillows, was to be able to afford a battery-operated TV as well. That was luxury. She turned the radio on and the sound of Julio Iglesias singing "Moonlight Lady" in Spanish filled the room.

With a strangled sound Gaby grabbed the radio and switched it off.

For a long time she lay in the dark, erasing thoughts of Julio Iglesias, anything Latin, problems with working in a hoopskirt at the upcoming extravaganza at Vizcaya, even David Fothergill, from her head. She ended up wondering about Dodd's remark about fumigating the house. If the house had any odor at all it was mildew and an accumulation of dust. She'd long since stopped waiting for a return of those strange odors that had seemed to cling after the night of the *Santería* when David and Crissette had slept there.

Eventually, in the darkness and with the soothing sound of beating rain against the window, she dozed off.

Why, now, did the dream return?

All this time, of all times?

Even sleeping, some part of her consciousness told her that the heavy, beating thrumming, like drums or the pulsing of the human heart, signaled that her nightmare had begun. She moaned and turned restlessly from side to side to escape it, but she couldn't. Then, with a loud roaring, a tearing of the dream fabric, the dark opened up in a bellow of flame.

Above the shrieking noise a voice called her name.

Tied to the bed, helplessly bound in the nightmare, Gaby struggled, unable to answer. Terror was there, but also great danger. Someone needed help.

She saw a trough of water in a night-black sea, parted by a roaring, blasting wave of sound that tore the air to shreds. At the edges of the trough the ocean curled whitely and fell back upon itself. The roaring was enough to deafen, spearing the mind with pain, an inhuman roar that penetrated the flesh and lodged in the bones, howling, inescapable.

No, no! she tried to tell it, filled with fear of that dark, brooding terror. Nothing listened.

The maw of flames opened up. She was looking into a metal throat of fire filled with blue and yellow flames. Something familiar, something she had seen over and over in everyday life, but failed to recognize.

Then she knew there were men in a dark, cramped

place, bent over flickering lights. The sense of violent speed was there. The inescapable roar of jet engines.

Gaby came awake, on her feet by the side of the bed, screaming.

Around her the darkened bedroom still reverberated with a throbbing, pulsing, roaring assault on the senses. She lifted her violently trembling hands to her face, remembering. Men were there in the twilight cockpit of blinking lights. Oh God, she knew now what that was! Their words, repeated over and over, hoarsely. Someone needed help. One husky voice was heartrendingly familiar.

In her dreams James Santo Marin called to her. Only a fragment, like a bad, interrupted radio transmission. The black trough of the sea opened, formed by the screaming expulsion of heated gases from a jet engine as it skimmed the surface.

Christ, we're too damned close to the water!

Chapter 15

$\mathcal{G}$aby woke in the morning to find the bed a battle-
ground of twisted, tangled sheets, feeling more tired than
she had when she'd gone to sleep. With a groan, she
turned on her stomach and buried her head in the sweat-
damp pillow.

This was no way to forget James Santo Marin, when
her very dreams were haunted by him! She was certain
that something had gone wrong, that he'd been in danger
somewhere. Oh, God, she didn't even know if he was
alive! But the terrible bond that held them captive to each
other had been the conduit for a message.

*I want you. I need you. Now—when I fear I may
never see you again.*

How could she say that she was going to put him out
of her mind and marry Dodd when he wouldn't let her be?
What was he doing? What sort of danger was he in?

The alarm clock went off and Gaby reached across the
bed to silence it. She prayed for just a few minutes more
before she had to get up and go to work. After a night like
the one just past, she deserved it. The clock kept on
ringing. She picked it up and shook it savagely, but still it
kept on.

She forced her eyes open and saw to her drowsy
surprise that she really had shut it off.

The doorbell, she realized slowly. Somebody was
ringing the front doorbell downstairs.

Gaby threw her arm over her eyes and tried not to groan. It was only seven A.M. The paper boy had been paid, the power company meter reader never rang the front doorbell, and neighbors never called at that hour. There was no reason for anyone to be downstairs. Then it occurred to her that it was probably David Fothergill come to move his things into the garage apartment. She jumped out of bed.

Hurrying to the top of the stairs in bare feet and in her old sleeveless nightgown, she paused long enough to call, "Who is it?"

There was no answer.

The cloudless early morning was hot and sultry, and the tile floor of the *sala* was warm to the bottoms of her feet as she crossed it. She unlocked the front door and flung it open. "David, what do—"

She never finished.

The broad, coppery face was almost on a level with her own, since the man stood two steps below in the drive. Straight black hair framed somber black eyes, and a wide prominent nose rose above a full, forbidding mouth. He was heavyset, with huge sloping shoulders like a wrestler. All he needed, Gaby thought, horror-struck, was the pastel suit and mirror sunglasses. But he wore denim work clothes.

She was so stunned she didn't even have enough presence of mind to step back and slam the door, leaving him outside.

"Miss Collier?" the Colombian drug dealer said, looking at her curiously. "Miss Gabrielle Collier?"

Some part of Gaby's brain was still functioning. She tried to shove the door shut, but a huge copper-colored hand seized it and held it open.

"I'm Harrison Tigertail, Miss Collier." He was watching her with unblinking, obsidian eyes. "We're here to fix the roof."

Strange noises were coming from directly above them. Over the Colombian's shoulder she saw an aluminum ladder propped to one side of the front door and a metallic-blue van parked in the driveway.

"Roof?" There was no possible way, she thought wildly, the roof on the Collier house could have anything to do with drug dealers. But then she wasn't sure about anything anymore. "You can't do it," she cried, "whatever it is!" She pulled on the door, trying to hide behind it. "I—I haven't got any money!"

The giant looked her over with careful interest, taking in her bare feet, the sheer cotton nightgown, her disheveled hair. "It's all paid for, including the materials." He produced a business card from his shirt pocket and held it out to her. "We specialize in roofing. Twenty years in the business."

Roof. Paid for. The words finally penetrated. The wrestler-giant's voice was flat, very southern with the distinctive Florida twang. He didn't sound like a Colombian drug dealer. Gaby held the card with shaking hands so she could read it. "Miccosukee Contractors," and under that, "Harrison Tigertail, President." On the bottom was a small metallic-blue logo, a drawing of a *chickee*, a Seminole Indian thatched dwelling, and: "General Construction. Remodeling. Free estimates. All work guaranteed."

She stared wide-eyed at him. "You're Indian?" Her voice was a horrified croak. "A Seminole—a *Florida* Indian?"

"All my life," he assured her solemnly.

Every child in the Miami public school system visited the Seminole Indian tourist villages along the Old Tamiami Trail at the fringe of the everglades. The Miccosukee Seminoles were famous. Fifty families had been driven into the everglades in the middle of the last century by United States troops, only to emerge over five hundred strong in the second half of the twentieth century, claiming federal funds and status as a native American tribal nation, and demanding that a huge administration center be built for them on the highway from Miami to the Florida west coast. They were known around Miami as tough, trustworthy in business, but not particularly friendly.

Indian, Gaby told herself, not Colombian. She raked one hand through her tangled hair, pulling it back from her face in a gesture of utter confusion. Nothing was very real anymore. Her dreams seemed to have melded with life. A Miccosukee contractor named Harrison Tigertail had come to fix the roof. And it was paid for.

She started to open her mouth and then shut it quickly. Dodd, she realized. First her mother's bills at the hospital. Now the roof.

"Wait," she said to Harrison Tigertail. "Don't start anything yet. I have to call somebody."

She left him standing on the doorstep while she hurried to the living room telephone. Dodd was still at home, but ready to leave for the office.

"I really don't think you should do this," Gaby told him, tired and out of sorts, more annoyed than grateful. "I can't let you go on paying for things, especially when I don't know how we're going to pay you back."

"Pay me back for what?" he asked.

"The roofers. The contractor is here to fix the roof. He says it's paid for."

There was a pause. "Tell him to check the address, Mouse." Dodd sounded impatient. "He's got the wrong house."

Gaby leaned against the wall. The heat, the almost sleepless night, the turbulent dreaming, had left a murky lid on her consciousness. It was hard to think. "He has the *wrong house?*"

"I don't know anything about any roofers, Gaby." He was irritable now. "Call me back. Give me a ring at the office when you get it straightened out."

Gaby walked back to the front door slowly. Harrison Tigertail and another stocky, powerfully built Seminole in a coverall, his long straight black hair held with a head-band, were getting more ladders out of the truck. The younger Indian eyed Gaby, and she realized for the first time she was standing barefoot in the bright sunshine, wearing only an almost transparent old cotton nightdress.

"Mr. Tigertail." She crossed her arms over her chest and gave the younger Indian a hard look. "You have the wrong house. Nobody here has paid for any roofing repairs."

The huge Seminole sent the younger man off with the ladder and climbed into the cab of the truck. He returned to her with what looked like an order book. "Collier house at this address." He took out the invoice and handed it to her. "Fix roof."

Gaby looked at the work order, telling herself she should no longer be taken by surprise by any of the bizarre events that dogged her. The paper in her hand described in matter-of-fact words the repairs needed for an extensively damaged roof at this address. The bill was charged to Santo Marin Hermanos, Incorporated, Miami, and stamped *Paid*.

Harrison Tigertail waited until she'd finished reading it.

"Jimmy's out of town," he said with rocklike impassivity. "He won't be back for a couple of days. But you can check it out with him when he gets back."

Gaby told herself it was very hard not to feel that dreams, illusions, even nightmares were taking over her life. Why did she have the feeling that an ominous circle was closing about her?

Take, for instance, she thought numbly, Crissette Washington. Whose boyfriend was David Fothergill. And David had just happened to be able to find a *santera* priestess who knew Jorge Castaneda, the *babalawo*. Who in turn knew James Santo Marin well enough to have someone telephone him to come and get her. Who seemed to tie all this together in some mysterious way with a roofing contractor who knew him well enough to call him "Jimmy."

Harrison Tigertail picked up a bucket of roofing cement in each hand and started for the side of the house.

"Don't start work!" Gaby hurried after him through the overgrown, crimson-flowered oleander bushes, wincing in her bare feet. "James Santo Marin is paying for this, isn't he? And not what it said on the invoice. Not his company."

The contractor put down the buckets of cement and squatted on his heels to open one of them with a pocket knife. "I got my people on top of your house," he said blandly. "You might as well let us go ahead and find out the extent of the damage."

Standing over him, Gaby saw Harrison Tigertail's hair was inky black, so fine and straight the morning breeze ruffled it like silk. "Old clay barrel tiles, aren't they?" he asked. "Made in Cuba long time ago?"

"Yes, my grandfather had them handmade when he built this house."

Her back was growing warm in the sun. A steamy night mist still drifted at ground level under the palm trees. All around them Florida's tropical woodland birds sang loudly, musically. The world seemed peaceful, normal, reassuring. Gaby knew better.

"I don't want you to do anything to this house," she said. The big Indian looked up. "I want you to tell me how you know James Santo Marin."

He sat back on his heels. "In 'Nam," he said shortly. He removed the lid from the bucket and laid it on the ground. "Jimmy flew A-Sixes, and I was his electronic surveillance systems officer."

Gaby sat down abruptly on the unopened bucket of cement and stared at Harrison Tigertail.

"Jimmy was the best damned pilot I ever saw." He thought that over for a long moment, then added laconically, "Still is."

Pilot. James Santo Marin didn't deal in drugs. If he was the "world's best pilot," if he'd flown military jets in Vietnam, it was plain what he was doing now! Miami's most eligible bachelor, the sought-after "Prince of Coral Gables," the incomparably dashing owner of an expensive sports car, a leading-edge-technology yacht, and his own Lear jet, was no doubt one of that great army of smugglers who flew the planes that brought drugs into Florida from South America. Not actually a drug dealer, then, she thought bitterly. That was the job of others, like the Colombians.

"He's always pushing for something, that Jimmy," the contractor was saying, "but it's hard to keep a good perspective here in Miami where *latino* means anything." Harrison Tigertail paused and looked down at the cement he was stirring. "Vietnam sort of pulled everything together for Jimmy. 'Course, we came in late the last year of the war, he was just a kid, but 'Nam was tough, even then. When we got back to the States Jimmy knew what he wanted to do." He carefully put the stirrer on the ground and wiped his hands. "Runs in the family, all that being idealistic and political. Castro's still got his daddy under house arrest down in Cuba. From what I hear, the old man will die before Castro will let him go."

Gaby had followed his words with growing dread. She didn't really want to know anything more about James Santo Marin. He haunted her dreams. She managed to find something of him nearly everywhere.

"What's he doing now?" she blurted. "While he's out of town?"

He didn't look at her. "Didn't he tell you?"

"He—" She stopped short. The telephone call in the newsroom, threatening her with lawyers, that had put her into a tailspin and sent Jack Carty to her desk. Yes, he had said he would be out of town for a while. "You'll just have to pack up your stuff, Mr. Tigertail." The calmness of her voice surprised her. "I can't let you fix my roof. I certainly wouldn't let Mr. Santo Marin pay for it."

He fixed his black eyes on her. "Well, honey, that's between you'n him. But just offhand, why don't you let Jimmy do what he wants to do?"

She stared at him. "*Wants to do?*"

"Well, it's true, Jimmy's been with a lot of pretty girls, really beautiful women, but it's never been anything serious, not even getting to first base, if you know what I mean. I told my wife it just seemed like Jimmy couldn't go beyond being agreeable as all hell, and let it go at that." He shrugged. "Course the last few years he's just been a bunch of wires, hasn't had much social life. I never see him relaxed no more."

Gaby jumped up from the bucket. "I don't know what you're talking about. Actually, I don't even know this man. Look, I'll write you a check," she said, knowing her checking account was empty, "to reimburse you for your trip."

The big man didn't move. "You know," he said, squinting up at her, "Jimmy's gone around with Anglo girls before." He paused. "But he never once got around to offering to fix their roof."

Gaby drew herself up, indifferent to the sun shining through her nightgown. "I'm engaged to be married, Mr. Tigertail. I want you to understand that. Believe me," she added bitterly, "Mr. Santo Marin understands it too. His message is that he doesn't want to have anything to do with me."

Harrison Tigertail stood up, wiping his hands on his coveralls. He said in a low voice, with an intensity that surprised her, "Please listen to me, Miss Collier. This man's just burning himself up, running on raw nerve, and he knows it, but he won't quit. Not even when he sees the end of it coming." He held out a big hand beseechingly. "If Jimmy ain't told you what he does, I can't tell you, either."

Gaby backed away. "I don't want to hear about what he does. And I don't want you to tell me!" She stopped, struck by a sudden thought. "He's not an undercover drug agent." She knew she was grasping at straws. "He's not an undercover cop, or a drug enforcement agent, is he?"

Harrison Tigertail's small obsidian eyes opened wide enough to expose a rim of white. "Lord, no," he breathed. "Not Jimmy. He can't—" He stopped abruptly.

"Can't *what*?" Gaby cried.

The big man looked at her with a strange expression. "Jimmy's no DEA agent, you can forget that. That's the last thing he is. But that hasn't got anything to do with you, noways."

"Nothing has anything to do with me. I can't get a coherent explanation from anybody! But I can do one thing," Gaby cried angrily. "I can tell you to get off my property!"

The corners of his mouth turned up. "If I was to picture somebody who could save something out of this," he said, never taking his inky gaze from her face, "I don't know that it would exactly be like you, soft and pretty and looking like you ain't got no more spunk than a little bunny rabbit. But I think, Miss Collier," he went on so softly Gaby almost couldn't hear, "there's more to you than that. You might be just what we need. Yes, ma'am, I think you come along just in time."

Gaby glared at him, unable to think of anything to say. How could she say anything, when no one spoke sense these days?

"Good-bye," she said with dignity. She turned on her heel and walked away.

At seven-thirty that evening Gaby typed the last of her description of Mrs. F. Schmidt Bonney's masked ball costume, exclusively designed for her by Jean-Louis Sherrer of Paris, and directed it through the newsroom word processor to Jack Carty's attention. Then, in the *Times-Journal's* fourth floor restroom, she repaired some of the damage working in the rain all day had done to her hair, put on new lipstick and eyeshadow, and stood back for a last look at herself.

The jade-green cotton gauze dress she was wearing was dressy enough for dinner with Dodd. Beneath the jacket, thin spaghetti straps held up a tight bodice with plenty of décolletage, and the tightly cinched waist and flared skirt flattered her legs. There was something about the way she looked that kept her staring at her reflection in glass office doors all the way to the elevator.

She noticed that even in the way she moved, there was a subtle, indefinable something that hadn't been there before. She watched her own willowy reflection, bemused. She'd never been sexy, if that was the word. It wasn't sexy. But something softened, glowing, was there.

Her mother's ancient Cadillac was still giving her trouble in spite of its recent, horrendously expensive session in the repair shop. Worse, as she left the building and started toward the parking lot, it began to sprinkle. Gaby prayed for a quick start on the first few tries as she looked in her pocketbook for her keys. A shadow loomed up beside her in the semidarkness. She lifted her head.

She wasn't frightened, but a warning struck somewhere in her consciousness. "Elena?" she said doubtfully.

The shadow almost fell into Gaby's arms. "Oh, Mees Gabriela," Elena Escudero cried. "I have to leave you because bad t'ing happen to your house—*tenemos mucho miedo,* Angel and me! But the *iyalocha* she fix him, is better now, no?"

It was raining in earnest now, a warm summer shower. Gaby peered at her former tenant. "You're right something happened to my house." She was still angry. "You and Angel took all the things out of the apartment without even telling me. A lot of that stuff wasn't yours."

"But is going to make much better, *promeso!*" Elena took Gaby's arm, pulling her away from the car. "Thees *bilongo* put on your house by thees crazy *bruja.*" She began dragging Gaby purposefully toward the street. "Thees crazy girl who is doing these things to you, she don't know what she making. But is all fixed up now. You come with me, we tell you all about it."

Gaby pulled her arm out of Elena's grip. This was all so typically *latino,* she thought, the half excuses, the promises to explain when nothing was ever really explained, the effusive, affectionate appeal to one's patience and good nature. "*Who?*" she demanded. "Who's going to tell me all about *what?*"

"Pleese, Mees Gabriela, Angel and me no can stay in that house!" Elena was actually wringing her hands. "I bring your things back right away. Was a mistake when my cousins came to your place, they didn't know my things, your things, they only mixed up, you know? They carry everything away, those *idiotos,* make me unhappy so I cry." She grabbed Gaby's wrist and again pulled her toward the street. "There somebody want to talk to you. Explain everything."

"No, wait a minute." Gaby was exasperated that Elena had ambushed her in the newspaper parking lot. What was wrong with calling her at home? "Listen, Elena, the police want to talk to you about that *Santería* mess at the house."

The small woman took Gaby's other hand. "Mees Gabriela, pleese, all t'ing fix up right away, you see. You no get married so soon. The *iyalocha* tell you."

"The *iyalocha?*" Gaby drew back. "My God, what has she got to do with this?"

"There, there," Elena said, pointing.

A dark car was parked under the streetlight. For a moment Gaby's heart leaped into her mouth. Then she saw it was not the Cadillac limousine she dreaded but a late model Buick. Uncertainly, she allowed Elena to propel her toward it.

The rear door of the car opened as they approached. The next thing Gaby knew Elena was pushing her from behind. A hand reached out and grabbed her by the shoulder. Gaby half fell, was half dragged into the back seat.

The door slammed behind her.

And all again was in darkness: Such a dream
As this, in which I may be walking now.

PEDRO CALDERÓN DE LA BARCA

Chapter 16

*L*ike most illusions, it was very real.

The marina, with its floodlit rows of sleek power cruisers and luxury sailing yachts against the velvet backdrop of the night, was a maze of pontooned walkways, masts, and softly blinking lights. To anyone who didn't know it was merely a fantastical dream, they might have been somewhere in Miami, or even Fort Lauderdale.

Gaby stumbled along in the wake of the *iyalocha*. If she hadn't known that this wasn't real, she would have been worried about wandering around like this late at night, especially with unreliable people like a *Santería* priestess and her chauffeur-bodyguard. But a hazy excitement, a suspenseful feeling of something about to happen, pulled her along in spite of herself. From the very beginning, Gaby had been told to be patient, that all would be revealed.

It had taken hours. And she was still waiting.

At first, she hadn't intended to cooperate, especially after having been dragged into the *iyalocha*'s car, and she told them so. But Elena Escudero's tearful pleadings and several potent rum drinks made Gaby see that there was no harm in joining—for a few minutes—a rather mysterious, if enjoyable, party at the *iyalocha*'s temple in *Calle Ocho*, complete with a live salsa band and a crowd of elegantly dressed people.

Things after that were slightly confused. Gaby tried

not to worry about it. After all, what difference did it make, being swathed in azure-and-yellow silk gauze that was probably as transparent as it looked, instead of her own somewhat sticky, hot clothes?

Had she been foolish? She remembered something about a dinner date with Dodd. The loud, strangely euphoric party had left her wondering what day it was. She wasn't even certain when she'd changed clothes.

The genuinely warm, supportive people had made it difficult to complain. Everyone was so happy. They'd made it very clear they wanted Gaby to be just as happy, too.

"Nothing bad, all good," the little priestess had promised her as the silk *Santería* robe had been settled on Gaby's shoulders. "Love, be happy, all good t'ings come to you. Bad t'ings over now. Everything be fixed up, you see." Ibi Gobuo's small hands had patted Gaby's breasts and arms, settling the silk, adding strings of beads and shells around her neck. "Chango, he wait for his beautiful Oshun," the old woman told her fervently. "You make him better. Happy, too."

A wet sea breeze jingled the rigging of the big sailing yachts. Over the chatter of hundreds of ratlines the *iyalocha* walking ahead of her invoked her African gods: *O Oshun, illa mi ille oro Illa mi ile oro vira ye yeye oyo ya . . .*

Gaby slowed, uncertainty returning, but the *iyalocha's* driver gave her a discreet shove from behind to keep her moving.

The priestess carried a paper bag with an open bottle of rum in it. From time to time she interrupted her incantations to put the bottle to her lips, then spray the liquid between her teeth and into the air. The sea wind occasionally flung a good part of the rum back at Gaby and the man behind her, but Ibi Gobuo never paused.

Mala ye icu oche oche oye ogua ita locum ocha deguallo oro mama kena oro . . .

"Are we going to another party?" Gaby asked, hopefully.

The one they'd just left had been filled with wonderful-looking people, whose skin color ranged from creamy beige and cocoa-colored to ebony black, magnificently dressed, and so friendly Gaby had somehow had the confused impression the party was for *her*. She stumbled slightly at the step up to the last dimly lit walkway. The hulls of giant luxury power cruisers, like sleeping whales, rose above them.

The chauffeur, trailing behind, seemed to melt into the darkness in his black windbreaker and dark clothes. But Gaby and the wizened *Santería* priestess were as bright as carnival figures. Ibi Gobuo wore tissue of gold and a blue velvet turban with a long white egret feather. Gaby's caftan of hazy blue and gold did not conceal the fact that she had nothing on underneath. Her long shapely legs were perfectly outlined when she moved, and the silk gauze clung to her hips and breasts, revealing pink, thrusting nipples.

The *iyalocha* stopped, spraying the last of the rum into the air. The wind caught it and settled it over the three of them in a pungent mist. "How about a boat ride?" Gaby suggested, seeing where they were.

"*Ella es muy borracho*," the man behind them said, disapprovingly.

The *iyalocha* turned to face Gaby. "You be very beautiful *mundele*." Her wizened face was ecstatic. "You make Chango very happy."

The priestess patted and smoothed Gaby's hair. Blue and metallic gold ribbons had been twisted into tiny plaits to which were attached strings of sea shells, fake pearls, and slightly wilted marigolds. The *iyalocha* gave the braids a final push with cupped hands, and the seashells and pearls rattled.

"Goddess of the rainbow." So much emotion suddenly pouring out of the mummylike priestess was alarming. Her eyes glistened. "Like beautiful Oshun, *orisha* of love."

Embarrassingly enough, Gaby was in no condition to remember what came next. The sea breeze wafting across the open water penetrated the thin silk and made her shiver. She'd been told that in order to experience fully the good things that were coming, she had to hold an image of Oshun in her mind. That didn't seem unreasonable. She'd immediately thought of someone like Crissette Washington.

The *iyalocha* waved her hand. *"Da la candelaria a ella,"* she ordered.

The man behind them produced a small votive candle from his windbreaker, lit it with his cigarette lighter, and handed it to Gaby. The old woman quickly took Gaby's arm, steering her toward a short wooden gangplank.

"He is here now!" The glint in the old woman's black eyes seemed to be ecstatic, unshed tears. "Your lord waits, beautiful lady of the rainbows." The egret feather nodded vigorously. "Go to Chango!"

"I don't think—" Gaby began, but the other woman gave her a push.

"And don't fall on the steps."

Reluctantly, Gaby started down the gangplank. Midway, she turned around to say good-bye, but the *iyalocha* gave such a hoarse, anguished cry that she quickly turned back.

There was suddenly a deck under her feet. The smell of sea water and the sound of waves lapping the hull were all around her. She cupped her hand over the candle flame to keep it from going out, beginning to feel tired. In the middle of the deck was an opening that yawned downward. She crept down steep narrow steps and found herself in a cramped hallway chilly with air-conditioning. She carefully closed the door to the stairs behind her.

The big cruiser suddenly rocked on a swell and she fell against the wall, nearly extinguishing the candle. She was, she thought a little worriedly, wandering around in somebody's boat in the middle of the night, not exactly sober. If someone found her she supposed they might call the police.

Chango, she thought. Ghosts in the attic. Minotaur waiting in the middle of the maze. It would take her longer to turn around and find her way back to Palm Island than it would to go straight ahead and see what lay at the end of the hall.

Sliding her free hand along the wall, she followed it until it became an open door. She turned into it.

The room, too, was candlelit, and large enough to be called a stateroom, with wood paneling and thick, springy carpeting underfoot. It had a bed—the real bed of a luxury yacht, and not a cramped bunk—and the bed was hung with red silk panels that drifted like flame-colored smoke, curling and falling back as the cruiser rocked gently on the swells. Everywhere was the scent of perfume and flowers, gardenias and sandalwood. Tuberoses, musk. Under the floating scarlet silk, Gaby knew, was Chango.

...imbe imbe lorde imbe ma yeye imbe imbe lorde imbe imbe layeye imbe imbe loro via ye oyo...

Echoes of the priestess's chant drifted like the flower scent in the air. Gaby put down the candle on a table and leaned over the silk-draped bed.

She no longer wondered why she was there. Or why someone had told her, "Go to him, *mundele*, and make him happy." It was the very thing she longed, in her heart of hearts, most to do. Was this dream, then, the only way it could be done? For certainly, in reality, she would never have come to James Santo Marin alone.

She rocked on her heels as the huge boat moved, and the light of the candle wavered with her. She supposed she could see how they would think he was one of the *Santería* gods. Chango, they'd told her, was beautiful, mysterious, all-powerful. She had only to look at him, even sleeping, to know he was all of that. He looked as if he truly gathered thunder and lightning around him as he dreamed.

It was madness even to think about loving a man like this, she decided as she sat down on the edge of the bed, but she couldn't help worshiping him with her eyes. He was tenderness and fire. He lay sprawled on his back, his bare feet with their finely sculpted bones and long toes nearest her, then long, strong legs lightly covered with a fine brush of dark hair.

The yacht rolled, and Gaby steadied herself against the bed with one hand. Muscular thighs joined narrow hips, leading to the soft black hair where the thick shaft of his sex lay ruddy, semierect. The eroticism of his body amazed her. Not all of it was breathtakingly graceful; he was sexually put together like a bull.

The flat planes of his belly stretched up to the rib cage, and her gaze roamed over his chest with its strong patterns of muscle under golden skin. A gold small chain with a Saint Christopher medal encircled his neck. She bent over him and braced one hand on the pillow by his head. His face was a mask of stark cheekbones, long arrogant nose, lidded eyes with their thick black lashes. She leaned closer. The fierce mouth that could open to snarl, shout, argue—or smile—was still, tense lines softened, indents at the corners relaxed. There was also what she'd noticed before, the strained skin under his eyes, thumbprints of exhaustion, dark as bruises.

Gaby sighed. He was a sleeping god. He was the man, incomprehensibly, she loved.

She had to kiss him. She had to touch her lips to that cruelly enticing mouth. She had to hold him in her arms because he was a dream that she knew with inexpressible sadness could never come true.

She leaned down, the shells and pearls in her hair rattling softly.

Like a bolt of lightning, something shot into Gaby's line of vision and closed, hard, around her throat. The next instant she stared into cold black eyes.

"Don't move," he murmured, "or I'll fracture your windpipe."

There wasn't any danger of her moving. She couldn't draw enough breath to move or utter a sound. James pulled himself up, still holding her by the throat, muscles bunching and coiling in his bare arms. He propped his body on one elbow, jerking her to him so that he could look into her face.

She saw his eyes widen disbelievingly, taking in her beribboned hair, the gold chains and beads around her throat, her naked pouting breasts under transparent gauze.

"Gabrielle?" She knew from the stunned sound of his voice he thought he was dreaming.

He let go of her and sat up, red floating silk tangling in his arm and shoulder. He jerked at it, cursing. A crimson panel came loose and fell on his head. "Jesus!" He tore at the streamer furiously. "What is this stuff? What the hell's going on?"

Gaby rubbed her throat gingerly. "I'm here because you want me." She paused, trying to remember what she'd been told. But she hiccupped. "I'm supposed to be Oshun."

"*What?*" His snarl ripped into the red-tinted darkness. She smiled at him tenderly. "And you're Chango."

He pulled the fallen silk from his shoulder and tossed it away, still staring at her. "My God."

"God*dess*," she corrected him. "I'm the—"

"Shit!" He tried to swing his long legs out of the bed but she sat blocking him. "Gabriela, tell me, is anyone with you?"

She thought for a long moment, trying not to hiccup again. "No, I think they went away."

He allowed her to push him back against the pillows. The scent of his hair, she found, breathing it in, was warm and musky, like his skin.

He was still scowling. "Are you sure?"

"Yes." She lowered her mouth to the tight line of his lips and rubbed them, her mouth opening to let her tongue trace a warm, wet line of desire. She felt a tremor run through his powerful, naked body. "I am Oshun," she repeated, liking the sound of it.

The carved nostrils flared, suspiciously. "Gabriela, what do you think you're doing?" He tried to sit up again. "Christ, you smell like a distillery! You must have taken a bath in it."

She giggled softly, remembering the *iyalocha* spraying the night with whole mouthfuls of the stuff and the wind blowing it back. "Actually, it was a shower."

She let the tips of her breasts, the tight hard points of her nipples, brush his chest. Her long legs slid sinuously between his and brought his flesh into intimate contact with hers. She heard him gasp, and smiled with her new-found power as she felt him grow and stiffen against her.

Reluctantly, he wrapped his arms around her. His

dark eyes blazed into hers. "Look, Gabriela, I want you to start from the beginning and explain how you—"

"Yummm," she interrupted, boldly loving him. She pressed her soft, warm mouth to his, stroking his lips tantalizingly with her tongue.

He pulled back, holding her slightly away from him. "Will you listen to me? I've just had a damned tough flight tonight. I'm beat. I don't need—"

A choked sound breathed from him as she lowered her face to his throat and nuzzled his damp skin. Her hands slithered down his sides, fingers spread, molding his ribs, his hips, his whole powerful body as far as she could reach.

With all the rum she'd drunk, Gaby thought happily, with the *iyalocha*'s commands and incantations, reality was altered, at least for a time. She was free to do what she'd never dreamed of doing. And what she would never do, she was sure, for any man. It was glorious.

He cocked an eyebrow at her. "You're going to hate yourself when you sober up." He grasped her arms and tried to lift her away, at least that part of her that was pressing so insistently against his crotch, but she only clung more tightly.

"Gabriela, will you stop?" Fine beads of perspiration stood out on his upper lip. "Dammit, this is not the time to do this. You're bombed—and I'm tired of playing games. You hang up on me when I try to talk to you, you tell me you're engaged to marry somebody else, now you show up in my bed. What the hell's going on?"

When she laughed softly, he gave her a shake that set her beaded hair clicking. "You don't take any of this seriously, do you? But then playing around is always a big damned game for Anglo girls, isn't it? Do you know what it means to me to—"

He stopped abruptly. "That things's transparent," he said hoarsely. He caught her exploring hand. "Who got you up like this? In this damned masquerade?"

Gaby wasn't listening. His skin was hot to her touch, the muscles of his taut belly hard and tense. Her fingertip tenderly explored the tight vertical slit of his navel. He jumped. Violently.

"Jesus!" He caught his breath. "Did you expect me to just—lie here, while you do this?"

She saw his body was lightly defined from belly button to groin by a fine line of silky black hairs. She bent and touched them with her tongue, a gentle cat lick, then moved lower.

He clenched his hands, his body jolting as her eager fingers closed around him. She stroked him, tentatively, absorbed, hearing his shuddering sighs in response.

They could never love each other, Gaby was certain, the world held them apart. But they could have each other now. She moved to straddle him a little clumsily.

"Wait," he murmured, "let me get you out of this."

As she lifted her arms over her head he slid away the diaphanous gown and dropped it on the floor beside the bed. Then he held her away from him, drinking in the sight of her as she knelt over him wearing only the strings of shells and pearls, her tiny waist, gently rounded hips, breasts thrusting proudly.

"Ah God, you're so enchanting." His trembling fingers cupped her breasts with exquisite care, his thumbs stroking the tight nipples. When she moaned, he whispered, "What is it you do to me, Gabriela? Why did I find you now, when I can do nothing about it? Why is it that when I'm with you the world turns into a place I can almost live in?"

"I love you," she whispered. She saw his skeptical glance. It didn't matter. She wanted to please him, this beautiful man. She wanted to lavish him with her love.

She pressed the length of her smooth body against him, but he abruptly rolled over on top of her, making her cry out in surprise. Then his mouth took hers roughly, ravishing her with a long, devouring kiss that left her whimpering.

"I swore I'd never do this." He kissed the warm wet hollows of her throat, her ear, her shoulder, hungrily. "I thought I'd never hold you like this again. Gabriela, I don't know what this is about, waking up and finding you in my bed, but I don't want to know."

She pulled his head up by his black hair, the softest thick silk to her fingers, so that she could look into his eyes. She couldn't know that he warred with himself at that moment, that he couldn't resist her. She saw only his vulnerable scowl and thought she'd made him angry.

"I do want to love you," she told him sincerely.

"Then show me." He brought himself between her legs with tense, shaking care, his fingers gently opening her thighs, remembering she'd had difficulty taking him before. "Love me now, Gabriela. I need you to love me." He buried his face in her fragrant hair. "Oh, darling, there's never been anyone else for me."

He possessed her in one driving stroke. Poised between the stunning pressure of his body and her own mindless ecstasy, she nearly fainted with pleasure. He was the lightning and the storm in passion's dazzling fury, and she was the sky and the sea, surging, retreating only to return again, the center of her body in flames.

He filled her powerfully, whispering love words in a rough-soft murmur. "Gabriela, darling." Shivering with desire, his control was tenuous.

She wrapped her legs around his hips, hearing his inarticulate cry as she slid her fingers between their bodies and touched him.

There was a desperate sweetness in their lovemaking. She clung to him, one hand curled in his hair, dragging his mouth to hers, as wild as he. Streamers of silk came down around them and they tangled in them, pleasure building unbearably until the earthquake waves began. He held her, watching her face as she peaked. Then his body clenched, and he joined her violence with a loud, tearing groan as he poured himself into her.

They drifted back to earth, gasping, breathless, tangled in silk. After a moment he lifted himself on one elbow, still gasping, to look down at her. "Are you all right?"

She buried her face against him, tasting his smooth

wet skin, the salty tang of his sweat. "I made love to you," she murmured.

Breathless, he managed a husky laugh. "You're smashed."

He rolled over, holding her so that she lay in the curve of his arm. He took a long unsteady breath. "You've got to tell me," he said softly, "how did you get in this mess? Do you have any idea what you're doing here?"

She smiled, her eyes closed. "I'm Oshun and you're Chango. You sent for me."

"Sweetheart, don't give me that garbage." He absently stroked her wet hair back from her forehead. "Are you going to tell me?"

"Mmmm." She snuggled closer.

"Gabriela? Will you listen to me?" He turned to her, frowning. "There's something I have to tell you and there's so little time. I tried to tell you before, that Harrison Tigertail and I flew A-sixes together in Vietnam. He was my electronic surveillance systems officer. Do you remember what he told you at the house? He didn't come there just to fix the roof."

He shifted his body to look down at her. "You're not listening to me."

She was curled against him, the palm of her hand under one cheek, as close to him as she could get. For several long minutes he didn't move, studying her. His face, unguarded now, expressed more than he would ever tell. Then he carefully slid his arm out from under her and got out of the bed, naked body glistening in the candlelight.

Without bothering to pick up a robe he strode into the hall, then up the ladder onto the deck, footsteps pounding.

Gaby was sleeping. She never heard James Santo Marin shout furiously into the night, "All right, Castaneda, you son of a bitch. Where are you?"

Chapter 17

*D*odd's voice on the telephone was savage. "Dammit, I was sitting here waiting for you last night! You don't think I'd accept a message at the last minute from some idiot who wouldn't identify herself saying that you had to work and couldn't keep our date, did you? I didn't believe a word of it. I thought our date was still on."

Gaby put her hand over the earpiece of the telephone. The newsroom was quiet and Dodd's voice carried. Through the pounding black fog of her hangover she said tonelessly, "Dodd, something did come up."

"Of course the damned police wouldn't do anything," he went on angrily. "All I got was that MPD regulations require a wait of twenty-four hours before filing a report on a missing person. Hell, I couldn't let it rest there, I was worried sick. Mouse, are you listening? I got the damned mayor of Miami out of bed last night!"

Gaby didn't answer. There was undoubtedly a moral lesson in all this, she thought. She'd been persuaded to go to a strange party at the *iyalocha*'s temple, she could hardly remember who'd brought her home, and now she had a splitting headache. Worse, the clothes she'd come home in were so strange, like something out of a carnival sideshow, that she had bundled them up and stuck them in the kitchen garbage. She had no idea where her good green dress was.

She would never again, she vowed, listening to Dodd's

furious flow of words, stand in judgment on her mother, or any other person with alcohol problems. She had some idea, now, of how awful it would be to face lost days—nights—that you couldn't remember, dogged by the terrible guilt and fear of something you might have done without knowing it.

She looked down at the morning's accumulation of messages on her blotter. She was due at a newsroom staff meeting on the coverage of the Vizcaya masked ball in ten minutes. She didn't know how she was going to survive that, either.

Dodd's voice stopped. Gaby realized she hadn't been listening. "It was . . . ah, sudden," she said, hoping that was the right answer. "I knew you'd understand."

"Is that all you're going to say? You're not even going to tell me where you were?"

She rested her head in one hand. She wished she knew so she could tell him. She might have been anywhere last night. "Dodd, I can't talk right now. I've only been at my desk a few minutes, and they want me in a meeting."

Dodd had told her that a Miami police car patrolling Palm and Bougainvillea islands had reported to police headquarters that she'd returned home in the early hours of the morning. When he received the report, Dodd had called her at once, both angry and concerned. He'd sat up all night in his Brickell Tower condominium, he'd told her, not daring to move from the telephone. He was even more furious when Gaby told him not to come over. That she would talk to him later in the morning.

There was no way she could have faced Dodd at four A.M., straight from an experience with a *Santería* priestess in a marina somewhere. And after what had seemed like a dream of meeting James Santo Marin that turned out, when she found the undeniable evidence of their lovemaking, to have been not a dream, but *real*. All she had wanted to do was crawl into bed for a week.

Unfortunately, at seven o'clock Harrison Tigertail had arrived with his roofing crew. She'd only had a bare two hours sleep, and was certain her life was turning into the proverbial nightmare. Her head was killing her and nothing made much sense. "Am I in the middle of a drug war or something?" she'd screamed at the Seminole contractor. "You're here to keep an eye on me, aren't you?"

He had stalked off without speaking to her, to work with his roofing crew.

"Well, Mouse, what *were* you doing," Dodd demanded, "staying out all night? Where the hell, in Miami, would someone like you *go*?"

Gaby stared down at her pile of unopened mail. Dodd would never connect Gabrielle Collier, the woman he'd known for most of his life, with a drunken wanton in a wild transparent dress in the company of a voodoo priestess and other strange characters. And who had ended up again, in spite of being engaged, in another man's arms!

"Dodd," she said, "is Mar-Belle Development Company a part of Brickell Corporation?" When there was only startled silence on the other end of the line, she went on, "Mar-Belle is listed in the building license file as currently renovating four houses on Palm Island, and that you and your father are the Mar-Belle corporation officers."

She could have stopped there, but some guilty hangover demon drove her on. "I think I know what you were trying to do, especially the way my parents have always mismanaged their property and finances. That is, if you were involved with a company like Mar-Belle that's buying up old houses on the island to make showplace estates, it would probably be sensible to try to get my mother's power of attorney. So you could handle the sale of our place yourself and see that it was done right."

Gaby had an almost cruel sense of detachment as she listened to absolute silence on Dodd's end. "I know you weren't going to cheat us or anything like that," she said. She didn't know that, but she owed him the benefit of the doubt. "I still don't see why you didn't tell me."

It had occurred to her that Dodd might just hang up. With something like relief she heard him clear his throat. "Mouse, darling, for God's sake," he said hoarsely, "let me explain."

"Was it because you knew Jeannette couldn't handle it, and you thought I couldn't, either?"

"Dammit, I haven't done anything yet!" he roared. "Will you please listen? If I'd had the power of attorney, yes, I would have worked a sale of your property to our company. But a fair and equitable sale. I wasn't going to—"

"You don't have to yell," she said, putting one hand over her eyes. "But if we're going to get married there has to be a certain amount of trust between us. This sort of thing doesn't help."

"I wouldn't cheat you or your mother," he said feelingly, "please don't accuse me of that. Look, Mouse, you're not going to live in that old place after our wedding, and once Jeannette is through with her very expensive rehabilitation program at Mount Sinai, she's going to be looking for a condominium in Bal Harbour or maybe even Lauderdale. Think of your mother, honey. She's *got* to sell!"

"Are old houses on Palm Island bringing a lot of money?" Gaby's tone was innocent. "I've been away in Europe for five years, so I'm not up on these things."

He groaned. "Mouse, waterfront property in downtown Miami is highly speculative. What do you want me to say?"

She knew what she wanted him to say. "I hear it's a good investment if you buy up houses in blocks. Very, very profitable. The building licenses at the courthouse show Mar-Belle has bought up most of our street."

He waited for a long moment. "Dammit, Mouse, we can't discuss this over the telephone, there are too many variables, and it sounds like hell! Look, have dinner with me tonight. I'll do what I should have done in the beginning. I'll bring the Mar-Belle plans for the Palm Island development and show you what's being done."

Gaby lowered her head, the receiver still clasped to her cheek. What had she just done? she asked herself dully. There couldn't have been a worse time or place to bring all this up, but she had. She'd wanted, for some not very charitable reason, to back Dodd into a corner. Did it all boil down to the fact that Dodd had been high-handed, even as he'd thought he was looking after her and her mother?

"I can't meet you, I'm working late," she told him. "Half the newspaper is assigned to Vizcaya tomorrow night, and we've got a meeting right now to go over who's going to cover what." She remembered to ask, "How's your mother?"

"Fine, fine." His voice was tight. "When am I going to see you? We can't leave this dangling. We have to talk about it. Our plans are still on, aren't they? You haven't had any... ah..." He hesitated, but had to make sure. "... second thoughts, have you?"

"Nothing's changed, Dodd." Gaby couldn't help a rush of regret for the mean-spirited way she'd brought up the business of the Palm Island property. "Look, I'll see you tomorrow night."

"Tomorrow night there will be thousands of people milling around at Vizcaya," he reminded her. "And the Bankers' Club is hosting the Festival Committee reception at seven-thirty. Darling, I can't do it. I'll be tied up for most of the evening."

"Afterward." Tomorrow night was in the distant future. First she had to get through this terrible day. "I have to file my story by nine-thirty, but we'll talk then."

"Mouse, I love you."

"I'll see you at Vizcaya," she said, and hung up.

Crissette stopped by her desk a few minutes later.

"Everybody's been looking for you, Gabrielle. Why didn't you call in late?" She peered at her. "You feel all right?"

"I did call in late." Gaby avoided the other woman's eyes. "I just got here."

"Hey, something's happened." Crissette hadn't missed the flush, the hectic look of exhaustion. "Want to talk about it?"

Gaby shook her head. "David moved into the garage apartment last night." She pressed her fingertips to her temples, wondering if the uproar inside her head would go away in time for the newsroom staff meeting. "I just found out before I left this morning. That's part of the reason I'm late. I had to go see if he needed anything."

"Yeah, I brought his things over in my car."

Gaby lifted her head painfully. "You helped David move?"

"Well, he doesn't own much." Crissette looked defensive. "Only a couple of boxes of clothes, his stereo, and some books. He needed a car, and I said yes."

"Oh, Crissette, I hope—" Gaby had been about to blurt out something about taking love when you could get it, but she'd caught herself just in time. "I hope things work out," she said neutrally.

During the *Times-Journal* staff meeting the giant masked ball at Vizcaya generated the usual banter about summer festival week assignments. In all the stories on festival week there had, fortunately, been only a few sour notes. The Dolphins lost the preseason exhibition game at the Orange Bowl and the sports editor, who had predicted a fourteen-point win against the Dallas Cowboys, took considerable ribbing. Wednesday night's Goombay street festival had been devastated halfway through by a violent thunderstorm. The reporter assigned to it had struggled with a write-up that, unfortunately, was criticized by the Miami black community as too downbeat. Staff enthusiasm was running low for the final gala on the grounds of the Deering museum.

"This idea of the press in costumes is unworkable," Jack Carty said bluntly. "Reporters and photographers in fancy dress have to come back here before deadline and file their stuff. The city room is going to look like the last act of *Don Giovanni*."

"It keeps out gate-crashers," the managing editor said. He didn't even look up. "At last year's costume ball, people were coming in the gates passing themselves off as reporters, security guards, waiters, even telephone linemen. The rule this year is that the press and television not only have to show ID's, they have to dress appropriately. This is a museum. With a crowd this size there has to be some way to ensure stuff doesn't walk off the place wholesale."

"How big is the crowd, anyway?" the head of photographic asked.

"At last count, somewhere over three thousand." Someone whistled softly. "Also, we've been notified the governor's bringing his staff and half the legislature from Tallahassee. Upscaling Miami's image is the idea."

He handed Jack the assignments schedule. "Let's see if we can slide those celebrity interviews with the stars to the airport. Do them at Vizcaya only as a last resort. Don Johnson lives here on Star Island in Miami. Why can't we get to him now?"

"He's out of town until Saturday night." Jack pushed the revised schedule down the conference table to the reporters. "Placido Domingo's just canceled. But I'll see what we can do with Julio Iglesias and Linda Ronstadt."

The managing editor leaned back in his chair and put his hands behind his head. "We cover the event tomorrow night with four teams working until deadline. That means everybody but Frank has to be back here by nine-thirty."

The inside sections of the *Times-Journal* Sunday edition were made up by Thursday except for the front and second pages, which were held open for late-breaking news. But this week the front page and the second photo pages were being held, too, for the Vizcaya coverage. Which put all of them, except the reporter covering the stage show, whose story would go in Monday's edition, on tight deadlines.

The managing editor went on. "Frank covers the show, Elizabeth and Pete do features, color, and also any unexpected hard news, like the fireworks blowing up ahead of time." He looked down the table. "The fashion desk covers what every one of the three thousand is wearing." He actually smiled. "You can handle that, Gabrielle?"

"Sure." Gaby could hardly speak. The photographic chief and Jack Carty were smiling at her too. For the first time in a *Times-Journal* staff meeting, Gaby realized through her hangover, someone had actually said something friendly, even encouraging, to her.

*   *   *

When Gaby got home, David was in the driveway to meet her.

"You're in for a pleasant surprise, Miss Gabrielle. Your former tenants brought your things back. The television, the utensils for the kitchen. They even put the curtains back up."

Gaby stared, uncomprehending. "Elena and her son? They don't want the apartment back to live in right now, do they?"

He shook his head, walking with her to the door. "They say relatives in Sweetwater are putting them up. You know the boy was involved with what happened here at your house, don't you?" he added quietly. "I had a chance to talk to him, away from his mother. Angel's story is that strangers came here to the house that night and threatened him, and he had to help. But not killing the dog," he said, seeing her face. "Angel says he doesn't know how that happened."

"Do you believe that?" Gaby stopped and turned to him. Tiredness had her trapped, her nerves screaming. She didn't know if she could stand any more. "I'd like to get my hands on Angel. I'd get a straight story out of him! Who were these strangers, did he say?"

"A man and a woman." When Gaby started, he went on, "Yes, that's what I thought, too. The man could have been a chauffeur, but Angel's not sure. The woman wore sunglasses, even though it was night, and he thinks she had a scarf over her head."

Her thoughts were whirling. She really was too tired to think. "No wonder the Escuderos left. Angel was a part of it! And they left my mother in the front hall . . ."

"I know," David said. "I was here."

"And this is the way those people repaid us for everything my mother and father did for them!" Gaby was almost screaming. "Angel let—let *criminals* onto our property to do unspeakable things, harm my mother, and then they just took off!"

"They were frightened, Miss Gabrielle."

"Angel says someone forced him to help with *Santería* voodoo? They made him put chicken blood and feathers all over my back door, kill my dog, and he doesn't know who they are? I don't believe it!" Her hand was shaking so she couldn't find the lock to the front door. David took the key from her. "I'm going to call the police. That detective, what was his name?"

He stood back and held the door open for her. "Don't do anything rash, Miss Gabrielle. It was not the *iyalocha* that night who came here to do the *bilongo*. It was a man and a woman the boy never saw before."

She stopped short in the hallway on her way to the telephone. "What?"

"Today," David said quickly, "I had a talk with Mrs. Escudero, while she was here, too. She told me a lot of things." His expression changed. "Don't be downhearted," he said gently. "It's hard on you now, but you will see, Miss Gabrielle. Everything is going to turn out very all right." His old smile returned. "I tell you, it's practically guaranteed."

Gaby took back the door key. She was exhausted and aching, very close to weary tears. "David, nothing's going to turn out all right. You just don't know how messed up things are." She took a deep breath, hating the way she sounded. "But I guess I'll survive."

"Oh, you will do more than that." He stepped down the steps into the driveway and into the shadows. "Believe me, Miss Gabrielle, all good things are going to come to you. You see, Angel's mother, she told me where you went last night."

Chapter 18

Vizcaya was spectacular.

Hidden spotlights came on at the moment the red ball of the sun dropped down into Biscayne Bay, illuminating clipped hedges called parterres, terraces, urns, statuary, and a profusion of fountains behind the late James Deering's seventy-two-room replica of a Venetian *palazzo*.

Crissette adjusted the settings on a small Minolta camera and groaned. "Oh, man, why can't I be freelancing this? Why do the best shots always happen when I'm covering a story for the newspaper?"

They were on Vizcaya's main garden level where pools of water flowed down through carved stone waterways to the miniature Palladian folly the Deering heir had called a "casino." The gardens were patterned after those of the Villa d'Este in Europe: branching off from the main paths were the walled Secret Garden where booths were selling champagne and soft drinks, the maze, the Marine Garden, the Theatre Garden, and finally the Fountain Garden, where a Latin orchestra and a rock band alternated in a travertine structure imported from the town square of Italy's Bassano di Sutri.

Crissette switched from the Minolta to her Nikon, training it on two University of Miami students, one dressed as Saint George and the other as a papier-mâché dragon breathing real smoke. "Gabrielle, did you remember to bring all our lists?"

Gaby had them all, including a few she was sure they wouldn't need. During the evening they would be working with the names of publicity-seeking guests who'd notified the *Times-Journal* in advance as to what they'd be wearing, and how they hoped to be photographed. They included the prestigious Palm Beach socialites who came down to Miami's bigger galas, the wealthy young Fort Lauderdale professionals, the chic, influential Jewish community from Miami Beach, wealthy Latin society, and a sprinkling of black politicians.

The *Times-Journal* planned a special eight-page Sunday supplement on summer festival week, and coverage of this last event had been allocated maximum space. In case Gaby ran out of material—or, heaven forbid, Jack Carty wanted another sidebar—she'd been provided with a guidebook that told how the heir to the International Harvester fortune and his sybaritic artist friend, Paul Chalfin, had designed and built Vizcaya in the early 1900's, and how in the 1950's the city of Miami had acquired it from the Deering family for a museum.

The night, the surroundings, were beautiful. Excitement was in the air. Gaby's main problem was navigating Vizcaya's distances in her eighteenth-century costume. She wasn't the only one. Crissette, working with several cameras slung around her neck, had already stashed her bicorne hat in a concrete urn. And at the VIP reception at the main house Dodd Brickell, dazzlingly handsome in an eighteenth-century *condottiero*'s uniform, had given Gaby a hasty kiss behind some potted palms, swearing he'd have heatstroke if he didn't get out of his watered silk jacket and into something cooler in time for the star-studded show.

Crissette climbed up to a stone table to take a shot straight down the stair-step pools that glimmered romantically in the concealed floodlights. "I thought this would look like a TV costume movie," she said. She trained the Nikon on a troupe of masked gondoliers, courtesans of the quattrocento, Venetian doges, and Harlequins and Columbines from some imaginary commedia dell'arte. "But this is ridiculous. It looks *real*. It's spooky!"

Gaby smiled. "I knew you'd say something like that."

The predicted full moon hadn't risen, and the sky was hot and overcast. A soggy veil that was not quite mist lay over the sparkling fountains and merrymakers in a convincingly dreamlike haze. The gardens at Vizcaya looked as though they'd been waiting for years to come alive in just this way.

"Say, Gabrielle," Crissette called to her, "did you know Deering bought all this land from a Mrs. William Brickell? Any relation to the guy you're engaged to?"

"She was Dodd's great-great aunt, I think." At the reception Dodd had murmured something to Gaby about not working too hard that night, and giving up the damned fashion job at the earliest possible moment now that they were going to be married. The remark had bothered her. She knew she was going to have to talk to him about it. Gaby was beginning to like what she was doing very much.

The flow from Vizcaya's main gates grew heavier and the costumes even more interesting, although not always in keeping with the announced theme of a masked ball in eighteenth-century Venice. Looking for interviews, Gaby stopped a tall, good-looking Mark Anthony and a button-nosed Cleopatra while Crissette took their picture. The grinning pair, both actors at a Miami Beach dinner theater, admitted their costumes were "sort of left over from last year's New Orleans Mardi Gras."

Hordes of bodies filled the paths on each side of the reflecting pools. Some of the guests were coming from earlier cocktail parties around Miami and showed it. Gaby had to squeeze through the crowd gripping her heavy skirt with both hands, as it had a tendency to wrap around people's legs.

The last time she'd seen herself in a mirror, at the VIP reception at the main house, she'd wondered all over again at the convincingly doll-like eighteenth-century court lady she appeared to be in yellow-and-blue satin, her swept-up hair adorned with loops of fake pearls, her little breasts pushed up seductively. The trade-off, she was learning, was the trouble one had in stiffened petticoats and hoops in milling crowds.

A publicity assistant from the museum caught up with her just below the steps to the casino. "Gabrielle Collier, it's me, Muffy Schantz!" Gaby recognized the Harlequin in cone-shaped hat as a debutante of some years back. "I didn't even know you were back from Europe," Muffy cried. "But I saw your engagement announcement to Dodd Brickell in the papers."

She turned to two women wearing satin gowns and high, white powdered court wigs, who were about to be interviewed by a WLVE-TV camera team.

"Estancia, I want you to meet an old friend of mine, Gabrielle Collier. Gaby, this is Mrs. Fernando Santo Marin and her daughter, Pilar. Mrs. Santo Marin is on the Mercy Hospital Board, one of our charities."

It was bound to happen sooner or later, even in a city the size of Miami. Still, Gaby was taken by surprise and embarrassingly tongue-tied. Unfortunately, being embarrassed made her blush. She nodded to James Santo Marin's mother and sister awkwardly. The older woman gave Gaby a quick smile of acknowledgment before she turned back to the TV camera. But the young sister fixed Gaby with a particularly venomous glare, not even extending her hand.

"I know you." Pilar Santo Marin's voice was low, the words barely audible.

How could she? Gaby wondered. She'd never met James's family. She noticed she and Pilar Santo Marin were wearing similar gowns in blue-and-yellow silk, although the other's was exquisitely made, obviously not rented from a costumer, like Gaby's. Both Santo Marin women were lovely, even more so than their newspaper picture, with their dark eyes and sculpted features—features that Gaby suddenly found too familiar.

The admiration, Gaby saw, was not mutual. Pilar Santo Marin gave her another pointedly baleful look and deliberately turned her back to watch the television crew.

At Gaby's elbow Muffy Schantz was chortling. "Dodd Brickell, you lucky dog! Remind me to take you to lunch and tell you all about the ex-wife, will you?"

"Yes," Gaby said automatically. A cameraman for the television news team pushed in between them just as Crissette came loping up, reloading her camera. "Hey, Mama Santo Marin's still a foxy piece, isn't she, Gabrielle?" she said sotto voce. "I got some good shots."

Gaby had hardly paid attention to Señora Estancia Santo Marin. The younger woman's words still troubled her. *I know you*. Gaby wracked her brain, fruitlessly. She was sure they'd never met. And equally sure James hadn't said anything about her to his family. But there had to be some reason, she thought, baffled, for the ferocious dislike she'd seen in the woman's eyes.

A sudden surge in the crowd pulled Gaby toward the front of the wooden stage where technicians were trying out the microphones. In the Fountain Garden the Latin dance band was playing "Abracame," a Brazilian song made popular by one of the guest stars, Julio Iglesias, who was still at the reception at the main house. Floodlights bounced off the low-lying clouds, and from time to time there were a few sprinkles of rain.

"Hey, Gabrielle!" Over the heads of the crowd Gaby saw Crissette pointing to a Greek temple-style gazebo above them on the second terrace. "I'm going to get some wide angle shots from the high ground," the photographer yelled. "Meet you behind the stage later."

They had arranged a regular meeting place if for some reason they were separated: around the back of the casino where the television vans were parked and where the gardens ended in an artificial waterway that emptied into Biscayne Bay, hidden by the trees of Mercy Hospital next door.

While Crissette took her wide angle shots from the upper terrace, Gaby got the names and addresses of a Venetian doge and his gray-haired wife who were collectors of the Murano glass of Venice, and wanted to talk about it in detail. After the Murano glass collectors, Gaby spent some time with two interior decorators from Chicago. Finally, dry-mouthed with talking and with slightly aching feet, she approached a muscular young gondolier who turned out to be one of the hired security guards.

"Hey, if you don't want to interview me," the gondolier said from behind his black satin mask, "how about a pizza later? I get off at two o'clock. I can meet you any place you say."

Gaby sighed. "I'm working. But thanks."

"You're gorgeous," he called after her. "I'll be here until two A.M., remember?"

Gaby ran right into the arms of a stocky domino standing in the cross axis of the gardens.

"Do you want to be interviewed?" she asked. The domino was big enough to be interesting, about the shape and size of a small mountain. "I'm a reporter from the *Times-Journal*. I'm doing a story on why people are wearing the costumes they—"

"Honey, you don't want to interview me." The figure in the all-encompassing black gown and hood had a definite baritone Florida drawl. "But I'd appreciate it, Miss Collier, if you'd let me keep you in sight."

Gaby stepped back. For the second time that night she was speechless.

The domino took her by the elbow, moving her out of the way of a group of strolling minstrels carrying mandolins and guitars. "I have to keep looking for the top of that pretty curly head," he said in her ear. "The way you're ducking in and out of this crowd, it ain't easy."

"Harrison?" He was the same size and shape, but with the concealing folds of the black domino Gaby couldn't be sure. "*Harrison Tigertail?*"

He pushed back the mask, his copper features impassive. "Just stay around where I can keep an eye on you, hon," he said in his rumbly voice. "I don't want to have to send the whole Miccosukee nation out into the everglades looking for you."

Gaby could do nothing but stare, open-mouthed. What in the name of God was the roofing contractor doing at Vizcaya at a glitzy fancy dress ball? Telling her not to move around too much? So he could keep an eye on her?

"Harrison?" She couldn't stop repeating it, it was so bizarre. But the big man was already moving away. In seconds, the tentlike black shape of the domino disappeared in the crowds.

Gaby looked around, still shaken. The floodlit gardens, the surreal make-believe revelry reinforced a return of the horrible feeling that she was being followed—and watched! She put a trembling hand to her forehead. She could never be completely sure she wasn't going crazy. That was one possibility she'd never rule out.

A couple headed for the dancing jostled her to get past. Someone spilled champagne down the front of her costume. She didn't even hear the apology. She whirled around, stumbling on her skirts, suddenly filled with a compelling need to see Dodd. As always, she needed his reassurances, his strength; she needed him to take her in his arms and just hold her for a few minutes. She needed him to reassure her about her sanity!

Getting through the crowd to the foot of the terrace stairs was a major undertaking. As Gaby stepped out of the flow of people into the shelter of the clipped-hedge entrance to the maze, the crowd parted for the governor's party. They were coming from the reception with a wake of reporters, press aides, and television cameramen, headed for the stage where there would be opening ceremonies at nine o'clock. Gaby spotted Dodd's blue satin *condottièro* costume on the periphery of the group.

"Dodd!" She knew she didn't have much time. Crissette was probably waiting for her by now behind the casino. She moved along with the governor's party and when Dodd got close enough she grabbed him by the sleeve.

He had had more than a few drinks that evening. Gaby could smell the liquor on his breath. But he looked devastatingly handsome, big and broad-shouldered and rather swashbuckling in the bright blue Venetian soldier's costume.

It was impossible to talk to him now, she saw, disappointed.

"Will you call me at the newsroom?" she yelled.

She lost her grip on his arm as the governor's bodyguards cleared a way toward the show area. Dodd turned, walking backward a few steps. "I'll be late," he said apologetically. "I'll call your house when I get through. Midnight?"

She nodded and waved her hand. She was left just outside the yew arch as the crowd followed the governor's party and the TV cameras. For the first time she saw a tall man in a white ruffled shirt and red satin military coat standing a few feet away, inside the maze. He'd apparently been watching her.

The light was dim. At that moment they were the only ones near the clipped green hedges of the labyrinth. As he walked toward her, Gaby couldn't tear her gaze from his leanly powerful body, magnificent in the tight-fitting breeches and scarlet coat. He stopped in front of her and she looked up, straight into the black gypsy eyes of James Santo Marin.

"Why can't you do what Harrison Tigertail told you to do?" he asked in exasperation. "Stay where he can watch you. Dammit, if anything happens to you I'll..."

He left it dangling, staring at her with an expression of angry frustration. He looked tense and edgy in spite of his brilliant costume; the dark smudges of fatigue under his eyes were more pronounced than she remembered.

That wasn't the only thing Gaby remembered.

For the first time, as she stared at James's handsome face, the full realization of where she'd been with the *iyalocha* and what she'd done on board the luxurious yacht, with *him,* flooded over her.

She'd managed to bury it all in the back of her mind somehow so as not to think about it. Now it popped out. Every detail. Inescapable.

"It was some sort of *trick!*" The words spilled out of her. "The party, the clothes, the weird ceremony and chanting. It was all to get me in bed with you," she cried. "When I didn't even know what I was doing!"

"Gabriela, look, don't let's argue about anything right now, especially not what happened that night. I'll explain it to you later." He seized her wrist, pulling her to the maze's entrance. "You've got to go back where Harrison can watch you. It's important."

"I don't have to do anything!" Her wrist felt as though

it would break, she was twisting so hard to get free. She was close to weeping with rage and humiliation. "What a rotten thing to do to get sex! Did you pay the *iyalocha* to slip me something in all that rum?"

"Will you shut up?" He wrapped strong arms around her, holding her still as she fought him. "Listen to me, Gabriela, this is all my fault. Jesus—you don't know how much I blame myself! I would never have done this to you. It wasn't my idea." His voice cracked. "Say that you believe me, for God's sake!"

She was too amazed by his vehement words to say anything. She tilted her head back and looked up into his anguished face with alarm.

"Please, my darling," he murmured, lowering his head, "do what I tell you."

When he kissed her, his desperation marked her with soul-destroying power. It was as though he was claiming her for all eternity, fiercely branding her with his overpowering need. Gaby, whimpering under his blazing onslaught, was too confused to respond. She felt the skin on her lip part, painfully.

She used both hands to wrench herself away. "What are you trying to do to me?" she cried. She put her fingers to her mouth.

He stepped back, his face drawn. "Forgive me. I didn't mean to do that."

"I don't think you mean to do anything," she hurled at him. She dabbed at her sore lip. "I don't think your friends do, either. But that doesn't mean I'm crazy enough to put up with any of this!"

"Wait a minute." He started for her as she turned away. "Gabriela, go back to Harrison and stay with him," he ordered. "I can't explain. Just do it!"

But she'd had enough. "Get out of my life!" she yelled, flailing at his hands as he sought to grab her. "Stay away from me!"

She broke and ran, holding up her skirts with both hands, racing into the night as though her very life depended on it.

If James followed her, Gaby soon lost him. At the

water pools she paused long enough to look back, and he was nowhere in sight.

At the back of the casino a green lawn swept down to a small waterway, partly choked with water lilies, that led to the outer bay. The lagoon had been designed originally to bring one of James Deering's yachts to the little pleasure house at the end of the gardens to pick up guests after an afternoon's tea and card playing.

Gaby lunged over the grass recklessly, filled with a hurting, thwarted despair. She couldn't stay in Miami knowing that James Santo Marin was there, appearing anytime, anywhere, to haunt her with—oh, God—the memory of what it was like to love him! She couldn't make any sort of life for herself with Dodd Brickell, when the ghost of someone she could never love again was always there to confront her!

She stepped on the edge of her gown, heard it rip, and halted. Several television vans were parked under the trees. Except for one portable floodlight pointed at the threatening sky, the space was dark.

Where was Crissette? she wondered. The back of the casino was so dark there was little chance of finding anyone.

Gaby had just turned to retrace her steps when she saw the familiar satin coat and blue knee breeches of Crissette's *cisisbeo* costume coming around the far side of the casino. The photographer had obviously gone around one side just as Gaby had gone around the other.

"Gabrielle?" the other woman called to her. "What are we doing back here in the dark?"

Gaby opened her mouth to answer, then caught her breath. A shadow was following Crissette. A large, stumbling figure, indistinct, that the other woman couldn't see.

Several things passed through Gaby's mind in that instant with surprising clarity. Whoever was trying to catch up with Crissette was a maintenance worker or other museum employee, and no one to worry about. Then the shadowy figure staggered and nearly fell, and she thought he could be a drunk or a gate-crasher. The figure dropped slowly to his hands and knees and stayed there. At precisely that moment Gaby could see him well enough to know that the man following Crissette was David Fothergill.

Gaby started to run.

Crissette turned, astounded, as Gaby charged past her in the darkness. "What is it?" she yelled after her.

"David?" Gaby was screaming. "Is that really you?"

He was still on his hands and knees, unable to get up, just a few feet beyond the casino's walkway. Shakily, the big Trinidadian lifted his head. Gaby gasped. Blood was pouring from David's nose and his eyes were half closed. Behind her, Gaby heard Crissette scream.

"They came to your house," David managed hoarsely. "There are men looking for you. Bad ones. They beat me up, they wanted me to tell where you go tonight."

Crissette threw herself down on her knees beside David. "Oh, God," she cried, "what the hell happened?"

"Men..." David began again. He slowly lowered himself to his elbows, shaking his head, not able to go on.

But Gaby had heard enough. "Wait right here," she said irrelevantly, as David was in no condition to move. "Don't try to do anything. I'll get somebody to help!"

"Get the security guards," Crissette shouted after her. "Around the front."

Gaby raced across the back lawn of the casino, staggering in the soft, lumpy turf. A motor launch was coming slowly up the dark little lagoon from the bay, a small searchlight playing on the shore.

Vizcaya security guards in a patrol boat, Gaby knew instantly relieved. She veered off and ran down to the water's edge, waving her arms. "Over here!" she called to the boat. "He's hurt. Over here!"

The launch slowed and the bow bumped the muddy shore. A man, indistinct in the darkness, leaned forward, peering into the gloom.

"*Quién es?*" he asked.

Gaby stepped out into the mud at the edge of the grass. "Can you get a doctor? Please hurry, there's a friend of mine who's—"

"*Es ella!*" another voice exclaimed.

Ya es la hora
De empezar a morir. La noche is buena para decir adios.

Now is the time
To begin dying. The night is ready for good-byes.

JOSÉ MARTÍ

Chapter 19

The River of Grass is fifty miles wide but only six inches deep. It begins as a broad, freshwater drainage from Lake Okeechobee that flows down across the everglades for hundreds of miles to the southernmost tip of Florida, where it eventually meets the sea.

Under the blazing subtropical sun the vast, crawling river appears as a giant mirror reflecting the sky, broken by islands of oaks and palm trees called hammocks, its surface covered thinly with the waving marsh grass that gives it its name.

At night, it is an endless black void of faintly glimmering swamp measured in time, not distance. It was also, as the airboat pounded and roared over it, the inescapable tunnel of Gaby's nightmare. She sat slumped in the front seat between the two heavyset men, the airboat driver on his platform behind them. In the hours since they'd left Vizcaya, she'd experienced a slow climb back from stunned, mindless terror to frantic, fruitless plotting to escape, to a resigned attempt to try not to think, not to feel too much in order to survive.

She still couldn't believe that she'd been dragged from the masked ball and into a motor launch without, apparently, anyone knowing what was taking place. Sometime later—it could have been an hour, or more or even less, she didn't have a way to gauge time—she'd been transferred with her mouth taped, her hands tied in front of her, but still very much alert and conscious, to a pickup truck on a bayfront street somewhere in Miami. They'd driven miles along a highway, off onto a dirt road, and finally to a deserted launching ramp where she was half lifted, half dragged into a waiting airboat.

In all that time no one had seen her, sounded an alarm, or called the police, as though dragging a bound, gagged woman in an eighteenth-century Venetian costume through the streets of Miami was nothing unusual.

It was too late, now, for Gaby to realize that she should have screamed at the first sight of the men in the boat at Vizcaya. It might be hours before Crissette thought to call the police. After all, her last words had been that she was going for help!

Gaby choked back a helpless sob under the tape that sealed her lips. If Crissette waited until she got back to the *Times-Journal* newsroom before she reported Gaby's disappearance, it might be morning before anyone notified the police.

Unless Dodd...

Dodd, Gaby thought with a leap of hope. Dodd would know something was wrong right away when he called, tonight, and didn't find her at home.

But would he? she asked herself suddenly. The last time she'd broken a date with him she'd refused to explain anything, told him, in effect, to mind his own business.

The man beside Gaby leaned forward to peer into her face. Talk was impossible, for the roar of the airboat's propeller blades was deafening. The shadowy driver on his high seat behind them wore big metal ear guards. Since they'd gotten into the airboat the Colombians had communicated by sign language.

Gaby felt the touch of his big hand on her cheek as he checked to see if she had stopped crying. She jerked her head away violently.

She'd been sobbing for hours. She knew now it was stupid, useless, but she'd wept helplessly in the first burst of panic when she was sure they were going to kill her. In the pickup truck, as they'd crossed the outlying streets of

South Miami, she'd cried fresh tears of frustration, because by that time the Colombians had told her what they wanted her for. Not to kill. No, they'd assured her, not that. Only, the bigger Colombian had said, grinning at her, as a last resort.

A burst of wind rushed across the swampland. The airboat passengers sat hunched, unprotected, as the downpour began. In the darkness the shadows of shallow islands passed, veiled by the deluge, as they roared deeper into the labyrinth of the everglades.

Even Gaby knew the vast marsh was a natural refuge for drug dealers. There were crude air strips in its depths where planes from South America delivered their cargoes of cocaine. The everglades was so vast, so impenetrable, that even the police, special drug enforcement agencies, the United States military, couldn't patrol it adequately. That was where they were taking her.

The man next to her put his arm around her shoulders and drew her close. In the darkness she remembered a broad, brutal face and hot black eyes, a beer belly already lapping over his belt. He was more friendly than the other man. He was the one who'd told her why they'd kidnapped her. He'd also explained that they knew she was James Santo Marin's sister.

Stiff with cold, Gaby was in a drenched, semiconscious stupor when they stopped. The older Colombian tried to rouse her by shaking her violently. It was daylight, she saw through half-closed eyes, stormy and gray, still raining in bursts. They were somewhere in the depths of the everglades at a large, thickly wooded island big enough to accommodate several wooden sheds roofed with palm fronds to camouflage them from the air. A sleek white seaplane rested under a camouflage net in a tiny lagoon.

When she didn't respond quickly enough, the man impatiently grabbed her under the arms and hauled her out of the boat. He was visibly disgusted when she fell to her knees on the sandy strip of shore, her legs too cramped by spending all night in the boat to hold her up.

The younger Colombian finally picked her up in his arms and carried her to the nearest shed.

"Don't worry," he told her as he pushed open the door with one knee. "*No queremos violarte.* Understand?" He barely spoke English. His hands lingered in a friendly way on her knees as he settled her on an empty wooden box. "No rape—no *violencia.*"

Gaby understood what he was trying to tell her, but he liked touching her too much. She didn't really believe him about the rape.

The *violencia* was something else.

He squatted in front of her, black gaze on the revealing front of the low-cut gown. "Pee pee?" he asked huskily. "I bring bucket."

She shook her head. Her body was still stunned. It had been hours since she'd had any food or water. She didn't need the offered bucket.

After a few minutes of looking at her hungrily, the man went outside.

Gaby sat hunched on the box in the shed, her tied hands in her lap. Her costume was a soaked shroud around her, but she didn't dare ask for a blanket or call attention to what she was wearing. She longed to be able to rub her eyes, burning from so much weeping, but her wrists were bound together too tightly. She could only manage to bring her knuckles up to swipe, ineffectually, at her face. The freezing costume and her aching, bound hands were nothing, Gaby knew, compared with what could actually be in store for her. Anyone who lived in Miami knew about Colombian drug dealers and their speciality, *la violencia.*

In Spanish the phrase meant simply "the violence." But for the savage Colombians, who had made it their own special way of doing business in the already unspeakably brutal drug trade, it was much more. *La violencia* stunned even hardened criminals. It was very direct, and very thorough. In one apartment in north Florida a drug dealer's entire family had been massacred; the police had found the hacked corpse of a week-old baby in the kitchen sink. Cutting off a finger or two as a message to holdouts was considered trivial. The Colombians preferred to gouge out an eye with the promise of the other to be delivered quickly if an agreement couldn't be met.

James Santo Marin, Gaby had been told, was a holdout.

She stared at the dirt floor, too exhausted to hold her head up. The rain drummed on the shed's leaking roof and a drip of water struck her arm. The morning air was noticeably cooler. She shivered uncontrollably, from both nerves and the penetrating chill.

She tried to will herself not to think about James. She'd been led to her destruction by her own stupidity and a beautiful, reckless man who'd made love to her. What a fool she'd been, she told herself, trying not to weep again. When the Colombians found out who she really was they would kill her. After they'd done other things.

She struggled to keep her control, fighting hysteria. The younger man spoke only a few words of English. He'd made it clear, though, that they wouldn't rape James Santo Marin's *sister*. They only wished to persuade him a little. They wanted Santo Marin's cooperation, not a blood vendetta.

Gaby closed her aching eyes to rest them. She had figured out that the drug dealers had gone to her house on Palm Island looking for her. They had found David Fothergill there, and had beat him up when he wouldn't tell them what they wanted to know. Their alternate plan had been, apparently, to go in search of the rest of the Santo Marin family at the masked ball at Vizcaya.

She'd had several hours now to think about what the Colombians would do to her when they found out she wasn't James Santo Marin's sister.

Gaby was on the verge of another bout of tears when the older Colombian came in with the airboat man. They stood and looked at her for a long moment. The older man said something at length in Spanish.

"We no touch you," the airboat driver translated. "When your brother understands we have let you stay pure, he will do what we want. We leaved that message for him in Miami."

Gaby lifted her head. She was deathly afraid of these men, the way they thought, the savage rules they lived by. They were animals. "You've got to take me back," she said thickly.

The airboat man folded his arms over his chest. "Santo Marin must do business with us, that is what we want." When she only stared, uncomprehending, he went on, *"Nuestro tigre* is a hard man to deal with. We persuade him with you."

Nuestro tigre. Our tiger.

It was what the *babalawo* had called James. Yes, he was a hard man to deal with, she'd agree with that. She knew now she'd been caught in some kind of drug dealing between James and the Colombians.

The airboat driver shifted from one foot to the other. "We left message in Miami that we take you. We say Tomas do so-and-so with you, while we wait for answer. And more so-and-so if we wait long."

The older Colombian lifted his hand. *"No violar su hermana,"* he said gutturally. *"Solamente persuadir, no más que eso."*

Not really to rape her. Just to say so.

The door to the shed banged open with a gust of wind and rain. The younger Colombian stood there with a blanket in his hand.

"Your brother," the airboat man said, glancing at the other man, "better hurry up and answer."

There was a shortwave radio close by in one of the other sheds. Gaby could hear it. Between the storm bursts the tinny radio voices penetrated the shed where she was. Listening to them, Gaby supposed the Colombians were waiting for their answer from James.

By now, of course, the Santo Marins knew none of their family were missing. Oh, God, she thought frantically, would James think of her, know she was the one the Colombians were holding? She was too exhausted, now, for panic. She was filled with hollow blankness in which her thoughts ceaselessly chased themselves around in her mind and wouldn't stop.

The *Times-Journal* must have notified the police by now that one of their reporters was missing. The odds for finding her weren't good.

The everglades swallowed drug smugglers. Law enforcement officers searched endlessly in the marshes and swamps for hidden airstrips and receiving sheds just like this one. The newspapers were always full of such stories.

Gaby's tied hands were swelling from lack of circulation; she no longer had much feeling in them. By noontime she was crying again with the pain.

The younger Colombian brought her some beans and rice on a plate. She turned her face away. He stuck a fork in her tied hands. Her fingers were too numb to drop it. "I no untie your hands. You eat." When she didn't answer he shrugged and put the food down on the floor. But this time he didn't go away. He leaned over her, fleshy-faced, grinning, and pulled the adhesive tape from her lips slowly, watching her pain as it ripped the skin away.

"Tu no eres su hermana," he said softly.

You are not his sister.

Gaby looked up at him, eyes wide with fear.

He carefully set the strip of adhesive tape down by the plate of beans and rice. "Yeah, you not his sister." The smile grew. "I know. You don't speak Spanish."

Gaby trembled as she felt his big fingers unfastening the hooks and eyes of the costume's bodice. When she tried to pull away, he jerked her back to him roughly.

"Don't hurt me," she managed to say hoarsely.

"Not hurt, just fool around a little. Maybe," he breathed as he freed the last hook and opened the front of the costume, "Santo Marin no answer. Then maybe we do more. But..." He hesitated, distracted, as his thumb brushed the soft undercurve of her breast. "Not now."

She should have been trembling with fright as he pulled her clothes away to expose the white rise of her breasts, then abruptly jerked the bodice down to reveal

the thrusting pink nipples. But a more primitive need
kept her very still, waiting for his next move.

He sucked in his breath, his stare fixed on her naked
breasts. "You lookin' good," he muttered.

He was such a jerk, she thought. Her mind throbbed
evilly with the knowledge. He'd given her a *fork,* not a
spoon.

His big, rough hands closed over her breasts, cupping
them as he half closed his eyes. He began to stroke them
in molding circles, breathing heavily.

"You're not supposed to touch me," she whispered.

"Not suppose to touch *sister,*" he corrected her. He
kept one hand on her breast, kneading it, as the other
hand seized her knee and shoved up the soggy heavy skirt.
When she jerked her legs away, he grabbed her knee
again, this time not gently.

She moved her bound hands, experimentally. "You're
not supposed to touch me," she repeated.

He stepped back, never moving his gaze from her
exposed breast, and undid his belt. Gaby tried to rise from
the box, but he caught her with one hand and pushed her
back down again. The small black eyes were heavy-lidded
with desire as he watched her struggles. "Open mouth,"
he said huskily.

Stubbornly, Gaby clamped her lips shut.

The front of his clothes were open and the long fleshy
shaft of his sex protruded, dark with engorged blood.
Slowly, deliberately, he leaned toward her, both hands now
toying with her breasts, squeezing them together, forming
a deep, silken valley.

"He'll kill you for this." As the words tumbled out she
knew they were true. Whatever else she knew about
James Santo Marin, she was certain of this. He might be a
drug-dealing criminal, but as surely as she was trapped
now and helpless, forced to submit to what was being
done to her, she knew James would kill this stupid, brutal
animal just for touching her.

She clenched her teeth as the man very deliberately
massaged her face, her tightened, unyielding lips with the
tip of his rigid flesh. He thrust against her, his deep

rasping breaths loud over the roar of the rain, his fingers tangled in her hair at the back of her neck, holding her still as he moved, his big, lumbering body shuddering. He breathed out a noise that was part bellow, part ecstatic groan.

"You want to kiss it," he muttered. "Tell me."

When she remained silent, he scowled. "Open mouth."

Gaby shook her head.

He seemed to shrug. He lifted his big hands and put them at the sides of her face. Then his index fingers bored cruelly at the hinges of her jaw.

For Gaby, the world went black.

She stood the pain for one agonizing second. Then something poured over her like a sudden dousing of liquid fire, and she was unable to hold back from what she knew she was, inevitably, going to do. The fork he had given her was still clasped in her bound hands. Her face twisted with fierce anger and hatred, she thrust both arms up, shoving her weapon between heavy thighs, under pendulous flesh, the whole force of her body behind the attack.

She heard his scream of agony mixed with shock and disbelief. Then she felt a blow at the side of her head that made the room spin wildly. The Colombian lurched against her, nearly knocking her from the box.

Storm noises suddenly burst in upon them like an explosion, making the walls of the shed rattle. In confusion Gaby heard a sharp, staccato banging and the loud *whump*! of something landing outside.

The door flew open.

She was on her feet, hands held out in front of her, body braced, waiting for them to kill her. The Colombian was still screaming, kneeling on the dirt floor and holding his groin, blood seeping between his large brown hands.

In the doorway crouched the *babalawo*, holding an automatic weapon. Behind him was James Santo Marin and, crowding in with them quickly, Harrison Tigertail.

In that blinding moment truth was like the freeze frame of a film, when all action is miraculously stopped, sharp, vividly etched, full of violence.

It was broken abruptly when James pushed past the

Chapter 20

"It's not my full title," the *babalawo* said, looking untypically modest, "but I *am* what you might call your friendly agent-on-station in Little Havana."

He was sitting in the hospital room's one chair, dressed as Gaby had last seen him in the everglades in a dark blue windbreaker, black turtleneck sweater, and muddy slacks, smoking a Havana cigar under a framed sign on the wall that said, "Thank You For Not Smoking." He still looked, with his handsome, slightly jowly face, like a well-fed yuppie, except that one eye was partly swollen shut, and a moderately deep gash on his upper lip was held together by two tiny black surgical stitches.

None of the hospital staff—the nurses, the technicians administering tests, or even the doctors—had asked the *babalawo* to put out his cigar. He seemed to wield authority even inside places like Dade Memorial Hospital.

It was all so strange, Gaby thought as she pushed her dinner tray away, the food on it almost untouched. Her hands were still swollen, wrapped in temporary bandages, which made it awkward to eat, even if she'd had an appetite. She supposed the overnight hospital stay was necessary, but her body was full of adrenaline and manic energy that just wouldn't go away.

"I don't understand what that means," she said, "agent-on-station. Are you some sort of cop?"

The *babalawo* reached into his windbreaker and pulled

out a black leather wallet. He flipped it open with one hand in an easy, practiced movement like the detectives on television, and held his identification up for her to see. "Federal Bureau of Investigation, Miami Area. I've been a public servant, Miss Collier, laboring in the more forgotten levels of drug enforcement, for these fourteen long years."

He didn't fool Gaby one bit.

Coming in from the everglades in the ambulance, she'd heard the attendants talking about the three men who hadn't waited for the weather to clear and for the state police helicopters. They'd taken Miccosukee dugout canoes into the swamp to storm the Colombians' hideout themselves, the way it had been done in Vietnam. Gaby had known who they were talking about. How could she forget that particular moment when Harrison Tigertail, James Santo Marin, and the *babalawo*, Jorge Castaneda, had burst through the door of the drug smugglers' shack to rescue her?

The FBI man, according to the ambulance crew, had quite a reputation. Two years ago he'd been in charge of the sweep in South America that had flushed out the kingpin of cocaine, Carlos Lehder. After that, the rumor had been that Castaneda had retired. Now it looked as if he'd just gone underground, right there in Miami.

Never, Gaby thought, staring at him, would she have imagined the hip, fast-talking *babalawo*, friend and associate of the *iyalocha* and all the followers of the murky world of *Santería*, to be a federal law enforcement agent. But she was convinced now. He'd been called out into the hospital corridor several times by the state patrol guarding her door to confer with various people. Some were obviously very important law enforcement officials from, she gathered, Tallahassee and Washington; a few were hospital public relations people who wanted to know about a television interview; and, a few moments ago, he'd talked with Gaby's own bosses, the managing editor of the *Times-Journal* and the newspaper's publisher, Gardner Hedison. Gaby had heard the *babalawo* tell them she wasn't allowed visitors yet. Which wasn't exactly true.

"An agent-on-station," the *babalawo* was saying, "is an all-purpose operation. He usually holds down some place in the community where he can monitor developments like...ah, well, like our friends the Ochoas you stayed with in the everglades, tracking them when they try to move in on leading citizens and persuade said leading citizens to let them come into their big banking and import-export businesses." He paused, studying her through a cloud of cigar smoke. "So they can, among other things," he said gently, "launder their drug money."

Gaby looked down at her tray. He was talking about James. The leading citizen who wouldn't cooperate with the Colombians.

"We could have gotten killed," she murmured, remembering the guns, the sheer terror of that moment when they'd burst in. "Even you got hurt."

He touched his lip. "Well, I wasn't exactly injured in the action. The eye and lip were...an expression of severe disapproval from our mutual friend in the chopper coming back. Jimmy blames me for a lot of things, but especially for using you as a decoy."

Gaby sank back against the pillows in the bed. She was almost afraid of what the *babalawo* was going to tell her. "Then he never was a holdout."

"No, he's not a drug dealer. But, yes, he was a holdout. When the Ochoas initially approached him, Jimmy contacted us right away, and we asked him to cooperate, to play along. Eventually, the strain really got to him. I don't think Jimmy realized he was going to have to play the part for almost two years until we could get them all into the net. But that's another story. Look," he said, settling in his chair, "consider his position—rich, successful, and with his setup, his companies, he had everything to offer the Ochoas. They needed him. They couldn't understand why he didn't want to get even richer. But the big problem was maintaining the front, keeping the pace going, with all the pressure they put on him. It was tough."

Pressure? Tough? she thought. Did the *babalawo*, Castaneda, the FBI agent, realize what his words really meant, these things she'd seen in James that had baffled and frightened her? And that she knew now he'd had to accept because he couldn't explain them to her? She'd even thought he'd been flying drug planes!

"The other thing Jimmy's pissed at me about," Castaneda went on, "is that some of my people got carried away playing Cupid. I'm really sorry about that. If there's one thing Jimmy hates its *Santería*. It drives him nuts. He's had a few problems with it himself in the past." He frowned, not looking at her. "He's especially burned with me about the *iyalocha*, Ibi Gobuo. You know, that night on his boat."

Startled, Gaby sat up. "His boat?"

"Believe me," Castaneda said quickly, "I had nothing to do with that. I gotta admit Ibi is far out, there's just no way to hold her down. These people are passionate, warmhearted. *Latinos* are very hung up on *amor*. They just wanted Jimmy to be happy, that was all."

He'd left her far behind. "That night on his boat?" she repeated.

He had the grace to look uncomfortable. "Yeah, well, Ibi got it in her head you could be some manifestation of Ochun when you nearly passed out in her temple. It might have been the heat and an upset stomach, but she took it for real. That the *orishas* had chosen you to deal with something that had them worried."

Gaby could only goggle at him.

"Hell, they're all crazy about Jimmy. Dare I say," he added, looking sly, "half of Little Havana worships him like a god, anyway? Jimmy's living on the ragged edge, maxed out. He needed love and someone beautiful like you and . . . that's what they had in mind." He saw the look on Gaby's face. "Hey, look, it wasn't all just giving you some drinks, doing a little mind-adjusting to put you in his bed. This was very serious stuff, between Chango and Ochun. These people don't play around. And in spite of what you might think, Tiger's no womanizer. Like *zero*. Jimmy stays too damned busy."

"James was cooperating with you," she said slowly,

"to help catch the Colombians. What has this got to do with *Santería*?"

"I'm trying to tell you. The Hispanic community's very devoted to Jimmy. Also, they know Jimmy and Harrison Tigertail are into something dangerous, but very straight, even patriotic. That's something they can relate to." He shrugged, eloquently. "They wanted to help."

Gaby lay back against the pillows again, feeling, for the first time, the pull of deep weariness. The story of the everglades rescue and raid had been on local Miami evening television news. She'd already seen the evening papers the nurses had brought in, with banner headlines: "DARING EVERGLADES RESCUE," "DRUG-RELATED KIDNAPPING."

Front-page pictures had featured Gabrielle Collier, Miami fashion reporter, in a dramatically torn and water-soaked eighteenth-century gown, being helped out of an ambulance. There were photographs of the Florida State Patrol manning the roadblocks on the everglades highways, the federal parks service that had been called out to help with search operations in the swamp, even the Dade County Deputy Sheriff's Department. But although Gaby had looked, there'd been no pictures of Harrison Tigertail's tribe. In newspaper accounts the Miccosukee Seminoles were only mentioned briefly as "guides" who'd helped in the search. Even more curiously, conspicuously missing was any reference to the three men who had, with the help of the Miccosukee Indian nation, taken canoes into the everglades in the storm to be the first on the scene to rescue her.

Why did Castaneda pretend everything had been explained? Gaby said, "You're not a real *Santería* high priest, are you?"

"I'm a computer engineer. I believe in everything. Nothing's impossible in binary numbers. I thought I proved that."

He stood up and paced around the room, stopping finally to look out the night-dark window at the rain. With his back to her he said, "Look, don't feel bad about the night on the boat, will you? Ibi Gobuo likes you, and that's saying a lot, considering you're a *mundele*. But the things she believes in say to her and others at times that the *orishas* come down to take over us ordinary people. Like if you got this great beautiful godlike guy... ergo, you got a god."

Gaby closed her eyes. "I thought he was a drug smuggler. I thought he was a pilot who flew in drugs, and all the time he was cooperating with the law." She looked up suddenly. "The police have him? I saw them taking him away at the highway, when I got into the ambulance!"

"The police don't have Jimmy in custody. He did get a little carried away. You know his temper. He was still calling his lawyers, trying to get the Ochoas the electric chair, until about a couple of hours ago. If they'd let him personally throw the switch, he'd do it. He was pretty racked up."

"But they didn't rape me, you know that." She sat up in the bed. "You see, the—the Colombians thought I was his sister. We were wearing practically the same clothes."

"You were the Ochoas' first choice, honey," he said quietly. "Don't minimize the danger. It's a very classic means of persuasion, grabbing the subject's girlfriend. When the Ochoas came to your house and you weren't there, they tried to find out where you were from your tenant. You saw what happened to him."

"But David didn't tell them where I was. He tried to warn me."

Castaneda shrugged. "They were going to snatch either you or Pilar because Jimmy was still stalling them. On our orders."

"Is David all right?" she asked anxiously.

"He's a big strong guy, he'll live. Legally? It's too bad he got caught for doing a good deed."

She was still confused. "But they're not going to arrest James?"

He sighed, patiently. "Miss Collier, the citizens of the United States owe Jimmy a big debt for his part in apprehending the Ochoa drug ring. He's a hero. We asked him to cooperate because every federal agency in Miami wanted the Ochoas' base in the everglades. We'd been tracking it for five long years. We knew our tiger would do anything to help, even if it meant driving himself to the wall. Which," he added, "he was practically doing already."

"Yes, I know, but he really doesn't work for the FBI?"

Castaneda's smile was back. "Good old Jimmy. He never told you, did he?"

"Told me *what*? Look, I've—I was *kidnapped* last night and dragged out into the swamps by—by animals and mauled." She couldn't hold back an involuntary shudder. "Believe me, before all this started I'd been leading a quiet life!"

"You've been a very brave person," he said, clamping the cigar between his teeth. "I was just getting to that."

"Getting to *what*?"

"Actually, we're going to express our appreciation for your part in this by making a few things smoother for you. All you have to do is make a simple deposition about being kidnapped, no testimony in court. We'll keep it to a minimum."

"Make a *what*?"

"You don't think it ends here, do you?" He looked untypically grim. "These drug-dealing bastards hire high-priced defense lawyers and they fight conviction with all the money in the world. The international cocaine cartel supports them. It takes months, sometimes years to put this slime away. I think I can speak for everybody connected with drug enforcement in south Florida when I say what you did is greatly appreciated, Miss Collier. You're a brave lady."

He paced the room again, stopping once more at the window. It was still raining hard. Water poured down the glass of the night-dark window, turning the neon lights of downtown Miami into glittering, multicolored gems.

"It wasn't a deliberate decision on our part to use you to attract the Ochoas, and Jimmy has a right to be mad as hell about that. But when the Ochoa brothers snatched you, you were able to lead us right into federal kidnapping charges against them. And we know we can make *those* stick. Even if," he said, grinning, "the trial will probably have to wait for Tomás Ochoa's physical therapy. They tell me that that fork broke off at the handle when you—ah, speared him." When she looked shocked, he said quickly, "Hey, cheer up, I hear the story's spreading all over the international drug world. You may have invented the American answer to *la violencia*."

Gaby felt sick. The memory of that moment in the shed was still much too vivid. "You don't know what he was doing to me," she whispered.

"It didn't happen, that's what's important. What's probably more important is I kept Jimmy from killing the pig. But only just barely."

Castaneda paused and looked down at the glowing end of the cigar. "Look, he's downstairs. He told me he's going to be out of town again and he wanted to get this straightened out before he goes. He asked me if I thought you were up to it, physically, emotionally, after what you'd been through, and I said I'd see."

Before Gaby could speak he added, "Also, your fiancé Mr. Brickell has been waiting very patiently, although I can't say very happily, in the visitors' lounge here on this floor. Would you like to see him first?"

"Dodd? I don't know."

"Jimmy's got his mother and sister with him." Castaneda hesitated. "If this is what I think it is, maybe I'd better stay with you until it's over."

Gaby shook her head. "If you mean James," she said quietly, "that won't be necessary. I can see him alone."

Castaneda picked up the telephone from the bedside stand. He dialed only one number and hardly waited for the other end to answer before he said curtly, "Send them up."

Gaby had just enough time to slip on a hospital robe over her cotton gown, a task made painfully difficult by her swollen hands, and run a comb through her hair before she heard footsteps coming down the hospital corridor. Then the door opened and Estancia Santo Marin and her daughter Pilar came in, followed by a tall figure in a dark summer-weight silk suit, the shoulders lightly spattered with raindrops.

Gaby hardly noticed the women, her eyes were so filled with the wonderful sight of James Santo Marin, his dark unruly hair slightly wet, the expression on his rigid face set, formal, unfathomable.

There was an awkward silence. Finally he said as though they were strangers, "Miss Collier, I'd like to present my mother, Estancia Santo Marin, and my sister, Pilar."

The women turned their dark eyes on her. They were both dressed in black. James's suit was black. They looked, Gaby thought uneasily, like they were going to a funeral. The air was suddenly thick with tension.

"Yes, I know," she said. "We've met before." She was wondering what would come next. Why were his mother and sister there, at that hour, at the hospital? After all the events of this particularly hectic day?

As if in answer, James took his sister's arm and shoved her forward almost roughly. "Tell her," he said harshly.

The hard grip just above her elbow forced the woman to one knee, her full linen skirt brushing the floor. Her mother stepped forward, protesting, "Jaime, *por Dios*—"

He shook her off. "Tell her," he snarled.

Pilar Santo Marin's mane of beautiful black hair fell forward, hiding her face, but Gaby heard her sob, "I put the *bilongo* at your house."

For a long moment the words didn't register. Gaby was more upset by the sight of the weeping woman kneeling before her, her obviously distraught mother, and James's towering rage. "Oh," she murmured absently, "I mean, that's all right."

When she looked up she felt the full impact of James's black, furious eyes burning into her. "Tell her the rest of it!" he ordered.

The girl's shoulders were shaking. "We didn't mean to kill the dog," she wept. "It was an accident. He tried to bite Luis."

"My dog?" Gaby stared at her. "You mean *Jupiter*?"

James's face contorted with disgust. "She has the damned chauffeur hypnotized too. He'll do anything for her. God, there's no end to it!" He let go of his sister's arm and she sank to both knees, crying loudly. The mother bent over her, wringing her hands. "The maids—ignorant people—teach them this garbage when they're in the damned cradle, when they're children. How do you," he asked bitterly, "fight against something like that?"

Gaby felt numb. The emotional drain of the past twenty-four hours and now this was too much. She looked blankly from one face to another. What did they expect her to do?

"She's obsessed with hate," James said. "She was in love with an Anglo and he dumped her, broke the engagement. What a big deal." He roughly nudged the weeping woman with his knee. "Now she hates Anglos. All Anglos. From the time she heard me ordering flowers for you her little brain has been busy with this crap, hating you too. She's been following you in the car, making the damned idiot chauffeur help her, chewing on her hate, casting spells, doing all this. She thinks she's some kind of god-damned *Santería priestess!*" He stepped forward, towering over her. "I should have strangled her the first damned time I found her doing this stuff!"

"Ah, Jaime, don't!" Señora Santo Marin threw herself in front of him. But it was Gaby she looked to, pleadingly. "Miss Collier, please forgive my daughter. We have caused you so much trouble. My son is so humiliated for this. Can you understand? We are all *destruido*—destroyed!"

Gaby was afraid the beautiful woman would throw herself to her elegant knees too. "Oh, no," she said hurriedly, "I mean, of course I understand . . ."

"I'm going to send her to a psychiatrist," James shouted over his sister's hysterical wails. "I'll commit her myself if I have to."

Gaby winced. All this emotion was horrendous. The young woman had done something stupid and vicious. Gaby supposed she could believe they were all totally destroyed. They were certainly acting like it.

"Is this necessary?" she tried to say over the clamor. "I mean, perhaps he, whoever he was, said something to make her hate people who were—"

James, his voice cutting like a knife, broke in. "Don't tell me you forgive her."

"Well, why not?" Nothing all that bad had happened, after all, she thought. At least nothing she hadn't survived! It was actually a relief to find the *Santería* at her house was due to some vengeful girl who'd been jilted and not something else. "Look, I can understand how she would feel. About me, I mean."

James's sister looked up, her wet, swollen face sullen. "I don't need you to forgive me."

The door to the hospital room opened. One of the state patrol troopers stood there, looking for the source of the noise. And so did Dodd Brickell.

One look at James Santo Marin and Dodd pushed his way into the room. "What the hell are you doing here?" he demanded.

For a moment, both men tensed, projecting their dislike. "James, please," Señora Santo Marin said quickly.

James shot Gaby a quick glance from under black brows before he turned away. But she had seen his gypsy eyes full of pain. And something like hatred.

He inclined his dark head stiffly. "Please excuse us." Gaby had never seen all that fluid, masculine beauty so completely rigid. "We were just leaving."

Señora Santo Marin hesitated as her son and daughter turned to the door. "Thank you," she whispered. Her eyes held Gaby's for a long moment, soft and warm, with a flash of something curious, questioning. Then she, too, was gone.

Dodd took Gaby in his arms as soon as the door shut behind them. "I can't stand those damned people. But at least that crowd spoke English. Want to tell me what that was all about?"

When she didn't answer, he gently patted her back. "Mouse, darling, just remember I'm here. Everything's going to be all right. It's all over."

She took a deep breath. What she had seen on James's face left no hope. It was the end of the world. She was numb, not able to feel anything. She could only partly understand the humiliation, the insult to *latino* honor, the fierce, wounded pride. She supposed as a family they could never forget it.

And she was sure of his opinion of *her*.

"Yes," she said, her words muffled. "Everything's going to be all right."

De carne se puede
Hacer una flor: se puede,
Con el poder del carino,
Hacer un cielo, y un nino.

From flesh
A flower can be made;
From the power of love
A heaven, and a child.

José Martí

Chapter 21

Mid-September was the worst, everyone agreed: hot and miserable, the peak of hurricane season. Even the South Americans had gone home. But the open back terrace of Sunday's on the Bay on the causeway to Key Biscayne was jammed with a fashionable lunchtime crowd in spite of a sky full of brownish-purple clouds and punishing humidity.

"We could always go inside, in the air-conditioning," Gaby said as she reached Crissette.

The other woman stood up at the table to give her a hug. "It wouldn't be Miami if we didn't sit outside in the heat. Jeez, Gabrielle," she murmured, holding Gaby at arm's length, "you look fantastic. Black cotton voile pants? Gold chains and a Valentino jacket?"

Gaby smiled. "I'm glad you think it's a Valentino, because it's really a Jordan Marsh markdown. The buyer called me and told me to come in and take a look at it." She hesitated, sliding into her chair. "You know, I'm getting perks now. Not freebies, that's unethical, but discounts, little extras. Stores call me when they have a sale. It helps, because I'm still not making all that much money."

Crissette was wearing an ultrademure navy blue linen shirtwaist dress with white accessories. When Gaby raised her eyebrows the photographer looked a little sheepish.

"My Trinidad clothes. David's gotta stay in the islands

241

at least six months before he can apply legally to get back into the States, even after we get married."

Gaby hadn't heard the good news. "Oh, Crissette, I'm so happy for you!" She took Crissette's hand and gave it a squeeze. "Are we celebrating? Are you going to invite me to the wedding?"

Crissette managed to look gloomy. "Yeah, I guess so. You can come down and help me with some of my culture shock. I'm still having a major problem with my middle-class attitudes."

Gaby's mouth quirked. They looked as if they'd changed roles, she thought, with Crissette in her somber clothes, her mane of glossy black hair tied back severely.

"The Caribbean is really cosmopolitan," she tried to assure Crissette, "full of exciting people from all over the world. You're going to love it."

Crissette looked even gloomier. "I guess so." She opened her navy kid purse and pulled out several photographs. "Gabrielle," she said, leaning across the table and lowering her voice, "I got some pictures of David's family in Trinidad. His mother wrote me this nice long letter welcoming me to the family. You know what? David's daddy is a British *magistrate*. I mean, take a look at this!"

She handed Gaby a snapshot of a very dignified black man in the white curling wig and black robes of a British judge.

"Good heavens." Gaby couldn't laugh; she'd hurt Crissette's feelings. "He's certainly imposing."

"Yeah, you can say that again." Crissette gazed across the restaurant terrace, her pretty, angular face pensive. "Here all this time I thought David was some bum hanging out on garbage trucks. What I didn't know was that he *wanted* me to think that, since he's into the struggles of the common man and changing social and political structures, and all that stuff he got into when he was getting his degree at the London School of Economics. And before," she added, sighing, "he decided to be a radical poet."

She looked at Gaby uncertainly. "I'm scared, Gabrielle. I'm going to be spending almost a year in an upscale black society in Trinidad that's way outta my experience. David's even got an uncle who was made 'Sir' somebody. You know, knighted by the queen!"

Gaby couldn't hold it in any longer. Crissette looked perplexed for a moment, then joined her in the laughter. "All right, I deserve it. Go ahead and say it."

"You love David," Gaby reminded her.

"Love him? Oh, lordy, Gabrielle, what am I complaining about? David's going to write books," she rushed on, her expression now one of radiant softness, "and I'm going to do the photographs, and if we don't move back to Miami we'll have a whole bunch of little kids in white wigs that talk like a steel band! You should see pictures of the rest of David's family. His mother's a pediatrician, his two sisters are accountants . . . Honey, that's when I went out and bought all my J.C. Penney dress-for-success coordinates!"

They gave their order for drinks. This was their last lunch together before Crissette left for Trinidad to join David.

"Well, hell, I don't have any choice," the photographer said, "since David was deported as an illegal alien. I can't marry him in Miami, the new law won't let me. So I go to Trinidad. And David starts all over, applying for immigration."

"Crissette, I feel so sorry about David." His deportation had bothered Gaby. "If I hadn't dragged him into all of this . . ."

"Put it out of your mind, Gabrielle," Crissette said quickly. "David knew what kind of a risk he was getting into when he came out to Vizcaya that night to warn you, but you know David. He wouldn't have done anything else. That's the way he is. Besides, it was kind of a relief when the cops arrested him. It ended the suspense. For me, anyway."

Gaby shook her head. "I owe David more than I can ever say. That was the bravest thing in the world for him to do, to lay his freedom on the line like that."

"He wasn't the only brave one. You didn't do so bad yourself." Crissette studied her intently. "You know, Gabrielle, that Colombian would have killed you. You didn't put him all the way out of commission when you stabbed him, and your hands were still tied. Did you ever think of that? I mean, that when he got his act back together he was probably going to do something really terrible to you?"

"It's strange, but all I remember is that I just didn't seem to care. I hated what he was doing to me so much, my reactions were totally primitive. Like some other woman, not me." She drew a shuddering breath. The memories came back at times much too vividly. "I'm not really very brave," she murmured. "All my life people have been telling me what a coward I am."

"You? A coward?" The other woman stared at her. "You have a weird image of yourself, Gabrielle. Some women would have had a nervous breakdown. But you put it all behind you, got your act all together on the job. Hey, is it true Jack Carty's going to hire you an assistant because you've upgraded the fashion desk so much?"

"Only part time," Gaby said modestly. "I have to share her. Two days a week she works for the society page."

When she'd left the newspaper that morning Tina Ramirez, the new fashion-society intern, had been sitting at Jack's desk looking eager but baffled as the features editor outlined some of her duties in his usual negative, nearly inaudible monotone. Tina was smart and determined. Jack had been hunched into his shoulders like a turtle, but giving the pretty brunette furtive, even appreciative glances. Gaby couldn't help thinking the situation looked promising.

"I'm going to miss Miami," Crissette said, sighing. Below them on Sunday's pier sailing yachts and streamlined power boats were unloading fabulously dressed, gloriously tanned passengers. "A lot of people don't dig all this glitz-by-the-sea, the *latinos*, the sunburn, the tourist hype, the crazy lifestyles, but I'm a native, honey, this is my territory." She took a large gulp of her tequila sunrise. "Frankly, I think this is the best place on earth. I hate to leave, even for a couple of years."

They watched a sleek Cigarette power cruiser tie up to the dock, driven by an especially good-looking, bare-chested young man in French jeans. The racy boat, the handsome young man made the same thoughts cross their minds.

"I can't believe," Crissette said, watching the figure below jump out of the Cigarette's cockpit to secure a line to the dock, "that it was that Santo Marin guy's sister all the time. That she put all that voodoo stuff at your house that night and scared us half to death. Did you ever find out if the chick was a real nut case? I mean, did they ever have her committed?"

"Oh, she's still around." Gaby found the right neutral tone. "They don't commit people for practicing *Santería*, I suppose."

Actually, Gaby knew Pilar Santo Marin was more than just "around" Miami these days. Last week's *Times-Journal* society pages had reported that the young Coral Gables socialite had returned from an art seminar in Paris and was looking forward to beginning her new position as events coordinator for the Luis Gutman Art Galleries in Bal Harbour. It didn't exactly sound, Gaby had thought wryly, as though James Santo Marin's sister was keeping up her voodoo. But one never could tell.

The society pages had also run a photograph of James in a magnificent Armani tuxedo escorting his sister and the exquisite daughter of the French consul to a chamber music concert. The caption said Miami's unofficial "Prince of Coral Gables" had just won the annual Catalina-San Diego powerboat run in his advanced design yacht, the *Altavida*.

Gaby remembered the yacht. She'd seen a part of it—James's stateroom, draped in red silk *Santería* streamers dedicated to Chango—that few knew about. At least in that way.

"Hey," Crissette said softly, "don't look like that, honey. Nothing's that bad."

Gaby couldn't smile, and was surprised at the depths of her pain. "The strange thing is that right up until the time James—I mean, her family—caught up with her, no one really knew who was doing the *Santería*. The priestess, Ibi Gobuo, kept saying something about a crazy girl, sort of an amateur witch, but she didn't know, either."

Gaby paused as the waiter served their salads. "The *Santería* people didn't take her seriously. But there *was* something there, Crissette, even though I can't really describe it. David felt it. I had these truly awful nightmares. There was even a sort of odor. It used to be in the house at night, late, when it was quiet. It always reminded me of green islands in the sea, flowers and smoke. Even food cooking." Her tight smile returned. "The only one who ever thought it smelled bad was Dodd."

Crissette was still watching her thoughtfully. "You haven't set a wedding date yet, have you? Are you happy, Gabrielle? I mean, are things going to work out for you?"

A chilly gust of storm wind swept across the terrace, the threatening clouds suddenly much darker. Sunday's waiters and busboys began turning chairs against the tables, anticipating a retreat inside.

Gaby couldn't answer questions about her happiness. That subject, too, was painful. "Well, everything's worked out, hasn't it?" she murmured. "Nothing really bad happened to any of us, after all. David got beaten up by the Colombians, but then when you saw him like that you realized how much he meant to you, remember?"

Crissette put down her fork. "Girl, are you kidding? You were hassled by some fruitcake chick with a hate thing against non*latinos* who followed you in a big black limousine and did *Santería* against you—"

"But that put my mother in the hospital." Gaby had thought it all out, determinedly. "Jeannette probably wouldn't have gone for treatment of her alcoholism if not for that incident. I think having all those things happen to me lit a fire under me for the first time in my life. I just tore into my job and look how its turning out."

"Honey, are you trying to make a case for all these disasters?"

"And if I hadn't been kidnapped," Gaby continued, "David wouldn't have been caught by the police and deported. And you probably wouldn't be going to Trinidad to get married."

Crissette stared at her. "Gabrielle, what about your poor dog that got killed? What about practically being raped by a Colombian drug dealer and having to shish-kebab his private parts? Were those fun things, too?"

"Well, of course Jack Carty thinks it's the biggest joke of the year," she admitted, "that I tried to turn Tomás Ochoa into a soprano, but I really wouldn't have cared if I had." She paused, sadly remembering the family's faithful guardian. "As for poor old Jupiter, Dodd was right. He was getting so old we probably would have had to put him to sleep sometime this fall. I'm glad I didn't have to face that."

"I see you got everything figured out," Crissette said with some irony. "I guess that's one way of dealing with it. But Gabrielle, are you going to marry old Dodson Brickell"—she dragged the words out—"the Third, or are you going to get things settled with the guy you're really in love with?"

Gaby didn't look up. "I don't know what you're talking about."

Crissette made a derisive noise. "Listen, girl, when are you going to go after what you want? And stop standing around just waiting for things to happen?"

"Good heavens, I don't do that!" She faltered, unable to meet her friend's eyes. "Besides, it won't work. I—I hardly know him. We're worlds apart."

Gaby looked down at her half-eaten salad. She'd had weeks to think about a relationship based on physical desire—and she was sure it was no more than that between James Santo Marin and herself. She'd told herself over and over again they had nothing in common: a too-beautiful, fiery-tempered playboy virtually worshipped as a god by a large part of the population in Little Havana, with all the entanglements of his Latin background; and she, Gabrielle Collier, a not-very-assertive, financially strapped remnant of a once-prominent Old Miami family who'd had to steel herself to meet the challenge of even a minor newspaper job. If anything, she thought, sighing, James had too much pride. And she didn't have nearly enough.

She just wished she could get over the strange, terrible ache of missing him, because it was ridiculous. All the times they'd been together, they'd hardly had what anyone would call a conversation. They'd made love. They'd argued.

They had nothing going for them, she told herself for the hundredth time. They were totally incompatible. She just had to stop going over it in her mind, and forget it.

"Did you ever *want* to get to know him, Gabrielle?" Crissette asked. "Or did you sort of subconsciously think it was better just knowing him as, you know, a *latino*, something different, a real big turn-on, an experience, but not really a permanent part of your life?"

Gaby hadn't been listening. Now she only blinked. "Crissette, you *know*?"

"What? That he's the guy who tried to throw David down a flight of stairs on *Calle Ocho* because he thought David was getting you into some kind of weird trouble? And that half the women from here to Jacksonville would die just to ride in his Lamborghini? Like *rich*? *Gorgeous*? Lemme see, looks like Lorenzo Lamas and Rob Lowe rolled up into one sexy hunk?"

"Stop." Gaby put her hands over her ears. "It really isn't funny."

"I didn't say it was. Not when his little sister wanted to get you killed. That's not cool. But you can't blame him for that."

"I don't blame him." Her voice was low, desolate. "You don't understand, Crissette. He blames *me*."

The diners were gone from the windy terrace and the busboys were stripping the tables of their linen. The oncoming storm rattled the ratlines of the sailing vessels docked below them on Sunday's pier. Most of their owners were at the bar, settling down for an afternoon's drinking.

"And you're going to accept that?" Crissette was annoyed with her and showed it. "I mean, this guy's been humiliated, his whole ethnic background's just screwed him up, not to mention his kid sister. And this dude is *American*. He was born here! Also, he thinks he put you at risk with the drug dealers, doesn't he?"

Gaby was gazing far away at the storm clouds between Sunday's and the mirrored, glittering skyline of

Miami. "It really doesn't make sense, does it?" she murmured. "I suppose so much happened so quickly I just couldn't get it all straightened out." She hadn't thought of the *iyalocha* for weeks, but for some odd reason now she was remembering Ibi Gobuo's plots about the lightning god, Chango, and the goddess of love, Oshun. "But you're right, Crissette," she said. "I do sort of wait and let things happen. That's not a very good way to live."

"That's one way of putting it." Crissette shook her head. "Gabrielle, I know a lot of what happened to you was classified, the feds were into it and covering their tracks so as not to blow a lot of their drug operation covers, but I picked up some things around the newsroom. It's a great place for gossip. This Santo Marin guy came out into the swamps to get you, didn't he, in a sort of commando raid? Look," she said urgently, "I know you're basically a sort of retiring, non-ego-driven person, but doesn't that suggest something to you? Just a little teeny bit?"

Gaby had been avoiding those particular conclusions. James seemed to be quite satisfied with what he was doing now, she told herself. Racing his boat in California. Taking the French consul's daughter to a concert in Miami.

"Gabrielle, I hate to leave you like this." Crissette took her arm to stop her even though it had begun to rain. "What are you going to do? Honey, you gotta realize—"

Gaby gently freed her arm. "I do, I really do, Crissette. I'm working on a lot of decisions. The best way I can."

She didn't want to say anything to Crissette to take the edge off her joy over her marriage to David. But until that moment, in spite of their friendship, Gaby hadn't known the extent of her envy.

"Actually," she said lightly, "I think it was easier stabbing a drug dealer. Then I didn't have to think about anything. I just did it."

The wind increased as Gaby looped through downtown Miami and took MacArthur Causeway out to Palm Island. She switched on the radio for a weather report, but could only get bulletins about low pressure areas across southern Florida with little chance of hurricane development, so she turned it off.

When she pulled up to the front door, however, the driveway was already thickly littered with wind-torn leaves. A bucket left behind by Harrison Tigertail's roofers had been pushed out onto the grass by the gusts. Gaby stood back for a moment to look at the replaced roof, its barrel tiles glowing brownish pink in the murky light.

Harrison was the key to so much that had happened, she thought. In a very direct way she owed him her life. No one but a Miccosukee Seminole could have guided Castaneda and James into the everglades so skillfully to look for the Colombians' drug base and rescue her.

It was common knowledge in south Florida that the Seminoles knew most of what went on in the everglades. In the sixties, when the Cuban exiles were being trained for the Bay of Pigs at a secret base in the swamps, the Miccosukees not only knew they were there, they tracked the exiles' every movement. But because the Seminoles regarded it as basically the white man's business, they said nothing. This time Harrison's tribe had helped. Otherwise, Gaby knew, she'd never have been rescued.

Gaby walked through the *sala grande*, the terrazzo floors echoing to the click of her heels, and closed and locked the louvered windows on the sun porch and checked the door. The big house had a spare, cool feel to it now that the furniture was gone.

Upstairs, she took one last look at her mother's bedroom, the banks of mirrors, faded coral wallpaper, the vast walk-in closet that had once held hundreds of Jeannette's fabulous gowns.

As she closed the windows and drew the blinds, Gaby was still surprised that Jeannette had accepted the idea of a condominium apartment in Surfside so easily. Only time would tell if it would really stick.

Her own bedroom wasn't quite empty since the movers hadn't taken her bed, a folding chair she intended to leave behind, and her suitcase. She rolled up the sheets tidily, then realizing the laundry hamper was gone, left the linens in the middle of the mattress. A check of the bathroom reminded her that a small box and some equipment from the drugstore were in the bedroom wastebasket. She picked it up to carry it downstairs to the kitchen garbage.

At the top of the stairs, on the gallery that ran around three sides of the *sala*, Gaby stopped, savoring the stillness of the vast room below. Closed up, the air was already growing warm and slightly stuffy.

Did she feel sad? she asked herself. Sentimental? The house was full of memories. She remembered her grandfather sitting in his wing chair by the hooded baronial fireplace, sipping his four o'clock Scotch and water. She'd been allowed to watch Paul and Jeannette's elaborate, exciting parties from the darkened second-floor gallery. Now the framed photographs of Arthur Godfrey, Jackie Gleason, and the Miami Beach celebrities of the past, taken down for storage, left ghostly, empty rectangles on the plaster walls.

Standing there, it was also impossible for Gaby not to remember the strange, haunted nights following the *Santería*, the nightmares and the dreams. But whatever had been there once, it was gone now.

The sound of a car in the driveway broke her reverie. She picked up her handful of trash and ran downstairs, stopping in the kitchen to toss the empty box into the last container of garbage.

She stepped out the front door just as Dodd got out of his Porsche. He watched as she put the key in the front door and locked it for the last time.

"Mouse—" He seemed to remember suddenly she detested the old nickname. "Gaby, you don't have to do this, you know."

She held out the key and, reluctantly, he took it from her. "You haven't thought this over." He followed her down the driveway to her mother's car. "All these weeks, and now you change your mind. A telephone call, for God's sake, this afternoon. Left on my answering machine."

"I didn't want to call you at the office," she said.

"That's crazy. You just didn't want to talk to me. Look, I haven't mentioned this to my family. There's still time—"

"I think you'd better." She opened the trunk of her mother's old Cadillac and put her suitcase inside with the others. "At least we don't have an engagement party to cancel again. And I haven't picked up your ring at the jewelers. You'll have that back."

"This is just nerves," he said, frustrated. "They tell me that's normal with these things. You're just feeling a little—"

"Dodd," she interrupted, turning to face him, "do you think I'm a coward?"

"Coward?" He looked momentarily disconcerted. "On the contrary, I think you have the normal good manners of someone raised in your circumstances. You do need someone to look after you, though, someone to love and provide for you. That doesn't necessarily mean—"

She turned away. 'It would be a mistake," she said shortly. "I'm sorry, but it would."

He followed her around to the driver's side. "Gaby, believe me, it wasn't the house. Is that what's bothering you? This place was just the last property on the island to complete the parcel. I was going to explain it to you later."

She kept her back to him. "Dodd, don't you know you always wait too long to explain things?" She took a deep breath. Although she'd thought this over on her drive home from Sunday's and knew all of it was true, it was still hard to say. "I waited years for you to explain why you never called me, spoke to me after we made love that time. I waited and waited for you to explain to me why you got married. I even waited in Florence for four years for you to tell me you'd gotten divorced. I know it was stupid of me not to realize you weren't going to tell me you were going to make a big profit on my mother's house, either."

"Now, whoa there, I told you it was nothing illegal! For God's sake, we were going to get married!"

"It's my fault." She turned now to face him squarely. "I was waiting all this time for you to do something about loving me. I never stopped to think about doing something about it myself."

"Doing *what*?" he cried, exasperated.

"It just happened again. Something else has been decided for me. It's sort of crazy." She hesitated. "But you don't believe in anything like that, do you?"

"How can I tell what I believe in if I don't understand what you're talking about?"

She wanted to make this easier for him. After all, it was hardly fair to blame Dodd for her own illusions. "You won't miss my loving you, Dodd, you never have. You'll find someone else."

"Dammit, you haven't given me one good reason for any of this. Not yesterday. Not this morning when I tried to talk to you. Not now!"

"Oh, Dodd," she said softly, "you were always someone I wanted to run to. Maybe you were the safe, caring lover I never found." She got in the car and swung the door shut. "But I think I discovered that loving someone is really very, very different. Not safe, not predictable at all."

He looked not only angry but baffled. "Gaby, don't just give me the key to the house and walk away! Dammit, where the hell do you think you're going?"

She started the engine. It really wasn't necessary to answer Dodd anymore. She was going somewhere to keep an appointment that would take all the courage she ever possessed.

She hoped it would work, she thought as she backed the car around Dodd's Porsche and out of the drive. After all, she'd been pretty brave with the Colombians.

Chapter 22

"*I*'ll check you past security at the gate," Harrison Tigertail had said, "and take you down to the spooks' flight area. It might take some time, the debriefing, and I don't know when it started, so I'll wait with you."

No, Gaby had told him. She wanted to do it alone.

They stood in the parking lot of a Class A restricted area of Homestead Air Force Base south of Miami, and Harrison was reluctant to leave her.

He raised his voice to shout over the mind-shattering roar of jets taking off from the runway just beyond. "Just don't stray from the parking lot, hear? You don't have a pass and this is a high security area."

Gaby tried to keep him from seeing the extent of her terror, but her knees were wobbling.

"This was your idea, remember," he said. "Still want to go through with it?"

She nodded again, wordlessly, wrapping her arms around herself, holding down by sheer force some of her body's desperate shivering. She'd chosen to make this effort to bridge that terrible gap between herself and James, and here she was, so riddled with nerves that she was in danger of falling apart! It was almost too much to be thrown right into the middle of all the dreams, the nightmares coming true. It took all of what was left of her control not to grab the big man beside her and start screaming that the engines of the military jets that rose into the stormy sky were the transparent circles of fire she'd seen before, in her dreams.

But how did you talk of nightmares and dreams and voodoo spells to someone as stolidly matter-of-fact as Harrison Tigertail? Who, according to what he'd told her, had been doing impossibly dangerous things for more than a decade since he'd been back from Vietnam? And who talked about perilous top-secret missions as casually as others would talk about a perfectly ordinary part-time job here south of Miami?

He looked down at her, squinting against the storm's fading light. "Are you all right?"

Gaby had steeled herself for this, told herself that perhaps she had known all along that under the layers of deceptions, fantasies, unbelievable illusions, there lay a deeper, final secret.

She'd been right.

The first thing Harrison had told her was that if a mission failed, if anything happened to them on their secret flights, the United States government would deny that any such operation existed. Even the pilot and electronic surveillance systems officer did not exist. There would be no record of their names. The Cuban government, if responsible for any incident like shooting them down, would issue a full denial also.

"If anything goes wrong, nobody knows anything," Harrison had said. "Those are the rules of the game."

Even the military jets they flew, A-6-E's, were painted black, with no registration numbers on their body or wings, no forms of identification anywhere. The runways were top secret, restricted, separate from Homestead Air Force Base's regular military operations. Two or three times a month James Santo Marin and Harrison Tigertail flew out of there with not even their families knowing what they were doing, on their dangerous, supersecret missions. A special operations branch of the CIA had recruited them for this years ago, when they'd been a top air reconnaissance team in Vietnam.

Beside her, Harrison hitched up the groin pad he still wore over his flight coverall and shifted his helmet to his other arm. *Just don't make him more miserable than he already is,* he'd warned her. *He's edgy, maxed-out from a bunch of night flights like this because he's the only Cuban Spanish-speaker we got in the A-sixes to monitor their transmissions, plus all this on top of what Castaneda got him into. He's pure hell to live with.*

"Jimmy's going to kill me for this," Harrison muttered now. He had finished his part of the debriefing for the mission they'd just completed. Now they were waiting in the parking lot outside the building where James was finishing his. "I should never have let you talk me into this. It's a good thing this was the last sortie in this series." He scratched the back of his neck. "But that don't mean Jimmy ain't gonna blow sky high when he sees you."

In the next few minutes, Gaby thought, James would cross the parking lot on his way to the equipment room where he would turn over his pressurized flight coverall, his helmet, and his other gear, and get into civilian clothes. She was shaking. She still hadn't formed the all-important words that she was going to say. She only knew that she had to see James Santo Marin.

Harrison held out his hand, testing for a few drops of rain. "Looks like we're going to get that storm that's coming. You sure this is what you want, honey? It ain't too late to back out."

"This is what I want," she said.

He planted a hasty kiss on her cheek. "Okay, I'm going to get out of here then, because here he comes. All hell's going to break loose."

The door in the low concrete building on the far side of the parking lot opened. A figure, silhouetted against the light, looked up at the darkening sky with its occasional flashes of silent lightning, then stepped outside.

Gaby watched that familiar silhouette with a wild fluttering of her heart. She had almost forgotten that James moved like no other man she'd ever seen. In the oncoming storm's light, the fluid grace of his body in the fighter pilot's coverall of olive-green nylon, swinging his heavy helmet by its strap, revealed him as the man with whom she had somehow fallen in love, never so perfectly realized as in that moment: powerful, quietly confident, solitary, his dark head bent. A beautiful man, brave and strong. By some instinct she'd always known that. Even when she thought the worst of him.

The storm framed him in clouds split with intermittent bright threads of lightning. Fighter jets were taking off on the runway just beyond. Under their fusilages their roaring engines were like wide mouths of transparent fire. The man coming toward her was almost mysteriously enveloped in glimmering dark brilliance. She stepped out of the shadows, his name on her lips.

He saw her and stopped.

His eyes were dark, unreadable shadows. He said, unsurprised, "Harrison told you."

A sudden gust of wind flattened Gaby's skirts against her legs. She lifted a trembling hand to hold back her hair so that she could see. "Yes, that you fly together now, the way you did in Vietnam." As always when she was excited, her words tumbled out in a rush. "Because the government called you back a few years ago to fly secret missions in a—a—"

He didn't supply the word she stumbled over. Instead, he stared at her as though weighing the improbability of finding her there, in the last place he expected her to be. "A-Six-E surveillance jet," he said finally.

"Yes, yes, those." At least he didn't look angry, she thought. Nor hating her, like the last time she'd seen him. "You fly to Cuba, out over the Bahamas sometimes," she rattled on, "and then down along the coast of Cuba, Harrison told me, under the Cuban military radar to monitor—Is that right, monitor?—the sites on their coast where the Cubans could install missiles."

There was another coldly appraising silence. "It's routine electronic surveillance."

It was far from routine. Gaby understood a little, now, about the pressure he had endured being involved in not one, but two, undercover operations that would have destroyed a weaker man. Harrison Tigertail's descriptions of their flights alone were hair-raising, even to someone like herself. The Russian-built SAM missile sites on the coasts of Cuba were ready to fire at any time at an intruder like the black-painted surveillance spy plane James flew. They flew only a few feet above the water, under Cuban coastal defense radar, always in danger of the jets, so close to the surface, sucking up sea water into the intakes and inducing engine failure. Add to that the dark, the subsonic speeds, and the knowledge that at any time they could be discovered and shot down with no more acknowledgment than the deep official silence that both countries observed about such things.

She dreamed it all, Gaby told herself. She saw them one night when they must have been in danger, and she woke up from that nightmare screaming. She wondered if James would believe her if she told him.

"Why are you here?" he asked, his expression bleak. "Do you want to tell me what this is all about?"

Inwardly, Gaby quailed. Was there no way to appeal to him? To break through his icy *latino* pride? "When Harrison told me why I couldn't get in touch with you, that you were on a mission, I told him I'd come here if I had to." Her voice cracked. "All this time you let me think you were a drug dealer!"

"What else was I supposed to do? It was Castaneda's undercover operation." Lightning flared over them and she thought she saw something change in his carefully expressionless eyes. "Where's your fiancé? Or are we going to ignore that?"

"I kept falling in love with you," she cried, "and hating myself for doing it!"

He seemed to start. He had every right to be wary of her, she thought frantically. She'd been foolish, frivolous. Everything she'd done so far had only reinforced his opinion of her.

"There was no need," he said stiffly, "for you to come on base looking for me. If you want me to apologize again for my sister, I'm sorry about the troubles she's caused you. I'll also apologize profusely for Castaneda and the *Santería* crazies he involved you with."

"But I'm not angry with your sister!"

"You should be." He flung her an angry look from

under black brows. "After all the hate for Anglos, she's back with that idiot from Palm Beach again."

"Who? Not the one who—"

"Right." His lips tightened. "The one who backed out at the last minute because he had second thoughts about marrying a *latina*. Even a rich one."

Gaby clapped her hands to her mouth. Didn't he see? she thought wildly. She tried not to burst out laughing. In the midst of the noise, the dark, the oncoming storm, James's words about his sister fell together with alarming significance, another piece in a queer jigsaw puzzle. Ibi Gobuo's *Santería* must have gone berserk in an excess of overkill! *Crissette and David. Pilar Santo Marin and her Palm Beach socialite.*

Chango and Oshun.

She stared at the man before her in his rakish tight-fitting fighter pilot's suit, at a loss to tell him what she so desperately wanted to. At a loss, even, to know how to begin.

The burden of the covert missions he flew with Harrison, on top of the Colombian drug dealers' attempts to force their way into his businesses, was more than most men could have dealt with. The strain had been tremendous, and yet he had kept it all going without once breaking or betraying himself. Or the people around him.

He had superhuman strength and courage, she thought, overwhelmed with admiration. He'd deliberately allowed people to think that he was a flashy playboy, a possible drug dealer, without once revealing what he was really doing for his country. She loved this proud, unbending man so much in that moment, her heart ached.

She took a deep breath. "I think you are the most magnificent man I've ever known. If you don't hate me, if you feel that you could love me . . ."

For a second he looked as though he hadn't understood what she'd said. Then he dropped his helmet on the asphalt and in the next moment she was in his arms.

"Love you? God, you drive me crazy!" His mouth was over hers quickly, tenderly desperate with passion.

When he broke the kiss, Gaby gasped for breath.

"You looked as though you hated me," she managed to say, "that night when you came to the hospital."

"You've had me bewitched, woman. I don't know what in the hell I've been feeling. From the moment I looked up and saw you sitting at a table the afternoon of that fashion show, with a pencil behind one ear and your hair blowing in the wind, just like this." He touched his mouth to a red-gold strand at her temple. "I thought you were the most adorable, wonderful woman I had ever seen. And I wondered why you looked so worried."

She wound her arms tightly around him, her cheek pressed to the slightly damp fabric of his flight suit. "I didn't know how to write." She laughed tremulously. "I was scared stiff."

He tipped her face up to him. "You didn't know how to write?"

"It's a long story." She pressed herself against his hard, lean length, loving him, yet terribly afraid. She was going to ask for his trust, and she was not sure he had any reason to give her that after the capricious way she'd treated him. "I love you," she whispered.

His arms tightened around her. "Ah, Gabriela darling, do you know the chances we took, coming together like a couple of crazy kids, to make love? The whole thing's been crazy! There are things I can never make up to you. These stupidities you've had to endure at the hands of my sister. Those other lunatics with their *Santería* garbage." He held her away from him, frowning. "The worlds we come from are too different."

She lifted her gaze, loving him more than she could ever have thought possible. It was true, some strange magic had brought them together and wouldn't let them part, brought them back to each other time and again.

"I nearly got you killed," he reminded her. "Don't forget that."

She smiled. "Your friend the *babalawo* would say it's all part of something that he can predict on his computer."

He scowled. "It's going to be a long time before I can talk to you about Castaneda. If I had known he was going to—"

She put her fingers over his mouth to shush him. He kissed them, quickly, ardently. "Let me see them," she said. "Put them on, I want to see what you look like."

"God, you know everything." He muttered something about Harrison Tigertail under his breath. Slowly, he reached into the breast pocket of the flight suit and took out his eyeglasses. When he slipped them on he looked down at her, brows drawn together in the familiar proud scowl.

She stifled a bubbling laugh. "Oh, they're very... impressive."

He kept scowling. "They eliminate night flying. I suppose Harrison told you that too. Which means the A-Six-E missions are over. At least for me."

"Yes." She could see this was something he accepted, but not happily. She remembered the tension, the marks of fatigue he always carried, a man stressed, pushed to his limit. Now the gold-rimmed glasses made him almost ludicrously serious, reserved.

She tilted her head to one side. "You look like a banker now," she murmured. "It's much better. It's not as sexy, so I won't have to fight off the women who want you."

"Gabriela..."

"Marry me," she said boldly. She saw the fire leap in his eyes as he reached for her. "You don't mind my proposing, do you?" She laughed shakily. "You're going to have to, anyway."

He froze, black eyes blazing. "My God."

"You said you would, remember? You called me at the newspaper and said—"

"I know what I said." He snatched her to him. "Are you sure?"

She thought of the box she'd thrown away before she'd left the house. "The test showed positive." She looked up at him anxiously. "I almost didn't come here. I didn't think I wanted to tell you. I didn't want to trap you into—"

"Trap me?" He rained hungry, half-ferocious kisses on her mouth, her nose, her chin. "I love you." He breathed a hot, passionate caress into her neck, under her ear, his hands sliding down her waist to her hips, to pull her against him. "I'm glad you're going to have my baby."

"You'll be happy to know I'm no longer engaged to Dodd," she said primly.

"So is he, I hope."

"That's not kind." She quivered, totally distracted by his caresses. "It's strange, but you know, I couldn't let him touch me, even kiss me. Talk about bewitched." She moaned as his teeth nibbled her ear lobe. "After I met you—" She stopped, unable to go on.

Wind gusted out of the dark clouds and a bolt of lightning, silent, flickering close, lit the sky.

"Darling, I love you," he said hoarsely, "but I'm a Latin, and if I stand around necking like this in the parking lot much longer it's going to ruin me."

A sudden spattering of rain drenched them. He picked her up and spun her around, slowly, smiling his pure joy. She stared at him. With the storm light, the beginning downpour, the wind tousling his hair, James Santo Marin was as she remembered him that first night, coming out of the dark tempest lit by lightning. He was a man made for loving, vulnerable and passionate and proud. She felt a thrill that was part apprehension, part love.

Gaby didn't believe in such things, and she knew he hated them. If she mentioned some of the mysterious, bizarre happenings of the past few weeks that involved that even more bizarre belief, *Santería*, she knew how he would react.

But, Gaby was thinking as lightning cracked and the rain began spattering them, pelting his hard, handsome face with crystal droplets, he had never looked more like a god.

NORA ROBERTS

- ☐ 27283   **BRAZEN VIRTUE**   **$3.95**
- ☐ 26462   **HOT ICE**   **$3.95**
- ☐ 26574   **SACRED SINS**   **$3.95**
- ☐ 27859   **SWEET REVENGE**   **$3.95**

DON'T MISS
THESE CURRENT
Bantam Bestsellers

THE LATEST BOOKS
IN THE BANTAM
BESTSELLING TRADITION

BANTAM
SHOP-AT-HOME
C·A·T·A·L·O·G

Special Offer
Buy a Bantam Book
for only 50¢.

Now you can have Bantam's catalog filled with hundreds of titles plus take advantage of our unique and exciting bonus book offer. A special offer which gives you the opportunity to purchase a Bantam book for only 50¢. Here's how!

By ordering any five books at the regular price per order, you can also choose any other single book listed (up to a $5.95 value) for just 50¢. Some restrictions do apply, but for further details why not send for Bantam's catalog of titles today!

Just send us your name and address and we will send you a catalog!